THE LIGHT OF DAY

(a beyond the horizon novel)

By Kristen Kehoe

To anyone who has ever had to battle to see tomorrow. Here's to you, one day at a time.

Chapter One

Jake

When you're twenty-two and watch every dream you've ever had drain down the toilet in just under two minutes, there's not much to do except bend over and take it. People try and cheer you up, try to make you see the glass half full and all of that bullshit that some optimistic prick has made millions writing about, but you know it isn't, and it won't be because one look at the doctor's face when he took out the x-rays confirmed what he hadn't yet: you're done. Find a different dream.

I was twenty-two and six days old when this occurred. Twenty-two and six days old and six months away from my senior season and the truth of the Major League Draft, the one that I had been working toward my entire life.

I'd gotten the call, the green light, the go ahead to begin the future I'd always wanted. It was my second call, second to the one that had already come the previous March, but I'd declined my June draft pick and chosen to finish my career at ASU, to go my senior year and get bigger and stronger, and because, really, all I wanted was a title.

What I got was a busted elbow and a crushed career. Yeah, I shattered that fucking half full glass.

Now, at almost five months past my twenty-second birthday and the day my future was shattered, I've got a hangover on the horizon and my eye on a brunette who walked in an hour ago. She's tall, long and curved, not bony like most girls I've met in the past few years, but healthy looking. No nose candy or other recreational drugs for this one. Nope, her skin's too clear, her curves too toned. *Healthy* is how I'd describe her. And fucking stacked.

I can't see her eyes well from here, but I'm sure they're clear, too. I haven't seen her drink anything but water since she came through the door, and I haven't looked away from her in the hour she's been here. That's also something new.

In the past few months, there's been little to keep my attention for more than a few brief moments, which is why I took medical reprieve from classes with the intent of going somewhere else next semester and starting over. Just the phrase makes me drink from my cup. Starting over. Finding something else. Looking beyond what I was to what I can be, which isn't what I wanted to be. Fuck. Not even Jack can cure that thought, no matter how deeply I gulp him down.

Another look at the brunette has my eyes finally meeting hers. I recognize the golden haired angel she's standing next to, but I can't place her at the moment. I haven't slept with her, that's for sure; too innocent. The brunette looks clean, but there's something darker about her, something mysterious, like a secret that she's wearing on the outside, showing the world without saying a word. The angel next to her looks just that: angelic, sweet, pure. I'm not pure, and I'm not looking for it. I'm looking for hard, rough, mind numbing… something. Anything to finish what the alcohol can't and make me forget for a while.

I keep my eyes on the brunette as I set my drink down. It lost its appeal an hour ago when I saw her, and as a result the drunk I was headed toward has now softened to a buzz. I can't explain the pull that I feel, but I can say I don't want to let it go. It's been too long since I've felt this need, this force to do something besides wallow and I'll be goddamned if I skip over it.

Standing, I wait for the ground to settle beneath my feet and take my first step toward her.

Chapter Two

Cora

When your cousin asks you to be her maid of honor, you accept, even if the thought of it makes you want to vomit, not because you don't love your cousin, but because the idea of happily-ever-fucking-after is a joke you've been sold one too many times. Worse than that, looking at your cousin makes you want to believe in it and that just pisses you off all over again.

Despite how nauseous the whole idea makes me, I watch as Mia stands at the rather large party hosted by her fiancée's teammates at some house on the ASU campus, waiting for the love of her life to arrive home from some baseball trip, and I can't help but be just a little envious of her. She has it, and if ever someone has a chance at happily ever after it's her. And she deserves it. Maybe this is one of those times that justice actually comes to those who deserve it and Mia, the nicest, most giving person I've ever known, is getting hers in the form of finding someone who loves her beyond all bounds. And maybe that's why mine has never worked out; I don't have a nice bone in my body, and rehabilitated or not, I'm no better a person sober and celibate than I was drunk and promiscuous. Drunk just gave me an excuse for being a bitch.

"You okay?" Mia asks me and I nod. No way I'm going to tell her that being at a party a week before her wedding is making me want to find a razor and end it.

"The question is not if I'm okay, cousin, the question is if you're okay. We're closing in on your last days of freedom. Any wild wishes you need to live out before the big day?"

She laughs and shakes her head before sipping from her drink, her first and I'm betting only for the night. Yep, where she's a poster child of self-control, I'm the opposite. Eleven months clean and I still think about taking a quick drink, finding an easy mark who's looking for the same thing and checking out for a few hours because it's nicer in the dark than it is in the world.

But the world always comes back, I remind myself, and when it comes back after a night of overindulgence, it's a lot uglier than it was when you checked out in the first place, and so's the person you wake up with. So, instead of giving in to my urges to drown myself in a bottle and/or a body, I grab some water and sip from it, keeping an eye on Mia as she watches the door for her betrothed while scanning the room and observing those people around me.

As expected, there are more girls than guys, but that's because we travel in packs. Well, most of us. I never have. Mia has been my one and only true friend since we were little and when I was growing up I thought that was okay. Other girls were the enemy, my competition, the person who stood in between me and whoever I wanted and so I rejected them, making sure to stay alone.

Now, at almost a year sober and celibate, I'm realizing that connections and relationships are necessary in order to live. I can't explain why, except that without people I want to find that dark hole and sink.

It's Mia who's pulled me out time and again since our freshman year of college, when I decided I was going to be the person my mom always thought I was, but Mia wouldn't let me sink all of the way. At the end of our sophomore year, she'd had enough and sent me to rehab, a thirty day detox where she visited me every chance she was allowed. Not because she wanted to check on me, but because she wanted me to know that I wasn't alone.

Then I transferred cities, moved to San Diego to work and move in with her. For the past year she's been my backbone, my base, and now it's time that I stood for her. In seven days, she's marrying her first and only love, and I'm going to stand there in the champagne dress she trusted me to choose and smile even if it kills me. For Mia, I can do it, even if I'm still learning how to stand for myself.

When my eyes meet the dark brown ones across the room, I'm surprised to feel the small jolt of electricity. *Interesting*, is my first thought. And *dangerous*. I was in the game long enough to know a train wreck when I see one, and this gorgeous package has CRASH written all over him.

From his seated position I can't tell his entire height, but I've assessed enough men in my life to know it's more than most of the guys here, an easy six-four or six-five. I take in his shaggy brown hair that screams baseball player, with its curling ends and sun lightened spots that my trained eye knows are less calculated than those from a stylist. His skin is olive, darkened to a bronze from what I can see on his arms, arms that are toned and long, strong, only marred by a distinct swirl of black ink on the inside of the left, but its shape I can't tell.

When Brown Eyes sets his drink aside and stands, I wonder if it's smart to be looking at him. When he starts over to where I'm standing, I go from wondering if it's a mistake to knowing it's a mistake to keep my eyes on his, and yet I don't look away.

For the first time since I got out of rehab, I'm tempted by the opposite sex and not just the oblivion he can bring me, and for some reason that's scarier. I'm not thinking of safe and healthy, I'm not even thinking of alcohol, which is usually where my temptation comes from. I'm thinking of his skin, warmed and golden from the sun, and how it would feel against my much paler skin, which suddenly feels cold as I look at him. I want explosions, mind numbing explosions and warmth, touch and feeling, cravings that remind me I'm still alive.

And that line of thinking is what sent me to rehab in the first place. Straightening my shoulders, I bring myself up to my impressive five-nine—which has jumped to almost five-eleven thanks to my new Prada wedges—and meet Brown Eyes head on as he stops in front of me.

"Name," he says in a voice that's low and scratchy, like he hasn't used it in a significant amount of time and he isn't happy about using it now. And still, he commands my attention in a way that makes me sure he's used to getting what he wants.

Shivers break out on my arms and I think, *well done.* And then I remember that the girl I used to be is the one who would have responded to that in under twenty seconds, had his shirt off in double that. I'm different now, because Mia believed I could be and because I want to be; deep down underneath all of this stuff and these feelings, I want to be different, too.

Uh-uh, Cora, I tell myself. *Explosions are only so fun, especially when someone else is lighting the fuse.* Thinking that I need control so this doesn't get out of hand, I quirk my brow.

"You first."

Chapter Three

Jake

I don't know who this girl is, but fuck if I'm not hooked. The whiskey that's swimming through my blood has no effect once I hear her voice, straight sex laced with challenge, but before I can take the bait she's thrown back at me, the angel next to her speaks up.

"Jake?"

I'm not sober, but I'm rapidly getting there, so when that voice says my name a second time, it penetrates my brain enough that I look over and a name pops into my head. Not just a name, rather, a face, a person. A *friend*. A sounding board when I was so drunk I couldn't stop the words that spilled out of me all those weeks ago. Shit.

"Hey, Mia, how's it going?"

My words come out slower than normal from the thick tongue that's stuck in my mouth and, though I know the room's not actually moving, I have to lean on the bar next to her to keep my feet planted. The brunette next to her is no longer looking at me with hooded, I-want-you eyes, but curious ones. I hate curious eyes, even when they're the color of the sea, gray and green swirled into the deepest blue you've ever seen and all wrapped into one stormy package meant to sweep you away from land and into the abyss.

As of late I've wanted that, the floating, the leaving, the darkness over the light, but with Mia next to her, Murph's Angel as I've always thought of her, I know this girl isn't mine for the taking no matter how badly my body wants to take her, even in its slightly fucked up state.

"I didn't know if you were going to be here. Ryan said you were thinking of moving before second semester."

Mia's comments bring me back and I look away from the siren and back at the angel. "I was. Am," I correct myself. "But I can't let my boy walk down the aisle without me." I give her a grin and hope it looks more real than it feels. When her return smile is small, I know I've failed.

"Jake," she says a little quieter and I know what she's about to say before it comes out of her mouth, so I shake my head. No. I won't deal with it, won't hear it, won't talk about it so don't fucking bring it up. She reads my signal loud and clear and nods. "Thanks for staying. It means a lot to Ryan, and to me, that you did."

"Does that mean you'll reward me and introduce me to Blue here?"

I watch my siren raise her brows in curiosity and hope it's not just because I want to meet her, but because she wants to meet me too. Mia's eyes—a clearer blue than those that seem to have bewitched me—widen briefly before she clears her throat and makes introductions.

"Cora Whitley, Jake Ferrari. Cora's my maid of honor," I hear Mia say and I nod. "And my cousin. Jake played... he's a friend of

Ryan's from school. And a groomsman," she finishes as her cousin just keeps eyeing me.

There's a part of me that understands that I shouldn't want to pursue this girl any further. She's Mia's cousin, the one I know Mia doesn't share a lot about, but who is more sister to her than her own; more, she appears to be her friend. Mia and I have been tight for two years now, since her man and I started hanging out more and more, focusing on our prospective futures that were so similar. Now, just Ryan is focusing and I am... not. Because focusing hurts, which is why I'm standing in front of the blue-eyed brunette wondering how the hell I can forget who she's related to and let her take the pain away, just for tonight.

Even as I think it, my body starts revolting. Nope, one night wouldn't be enough. Whoever this girl is, she's made me care more in less than sixty seconds of face-time than anyone has in months.

When neither of us moves to shake the other's hand and instead just stand there, Mia clears her throat and begins to make small talk about the wedding. I push her voice to the back, content to stand and stare at Blue, with her gorgeous skin, long limbs and unabashedly female figure. Goddamn, if I was even a shadow of the man I'd been she would have been mine forever, no question. But now, well, now I want her to be with me because for some reason I'm sure she's the one who can take the pain away.

When Mia gives a small intake of breath, I check back in and glance over, ready to suit up and pummel anyone who's touched her. She might not be mine, but nobody fucks with my boy's girl. But instead of a stranger, it's the man himself, and instead of fear on Mia's face, it's love. Pure love. Jesus.

It almost knocks me back a step, that look. The one that says she sees everything when she looks at him, just as his says he's ready to give her anything as long as she stays his. It's painful to watch, painful to look away from.

I can't remember the last time I felt like that about something or someone.

When I look over at my siren, her face tells me she feels the same but before I can lean down and ask her to take a walk, to get her alone and figure my feelings the fuck out, Ryan sets Mia down and grabs Blue. I watch as her shoulders relax, as her arms go around him and her face shows genuine joy.

Christ, if I think the angel is beautiful, her smile is nothing compared to my siren with her hesitant smile, the one that says she isn't used to feeling this way, that maybe she doesn't quite know how but that she's learning.

I table that as Ryan releases her and leans toward me. I hold up my hands and paste a smile on my face. "You're pretty, but if you kiss me I'll kill you."

He just laughs and grabs my hand, bringing me in to pound on my back the way we always have. I mock shove at him, smoothing my hand through my hair, adjusting my shirt and making a show of checking my clothes out. "What'd they do to you up there, man? You're holding on tighter than usual."

I make the joke because I don't want the real answer. Even

Blue can't touch my pain now, can't get me to forget what I'm missing, what I blew. And it makes me sick.

As if he can tell, Ryan shrugs and settles his arm around Mia's shoulders. "Can't a guy just be happy to see his girl and one of his best friends?"

"As long as that happy keeps his clothes on, we're good to go."

Blue snorts and Mia blushes from the roots of her hair to the tip of her nose when Ryan cusses. "One time, man, and you got me drunk on moonshine. What did you expect?"

"A little decency and self-control."

"Yeah, well, your pretty face proved to be too much temptation. Add in the tattoo and it was a package I couldn't resist."

"You're telling me. I slept zipped in my sleeping bag with one eye open."

The banter with Ryan is easy, and it's working its magic, bringing me into focus, away from the heaviness and the blinding ache that is memories, and the dullness that is alcohol. It's bringing me back to the here and now, with him and his angel and the siren behind me. Alcohol or not, she's gorgeous and she's captivated me. Cousin of the angel, though… that makes her different.

It's one thing to hook up with a girl you know isn't going to mean more than the night, as long as she's on the same page. And I'd be lying if I said I hadn't changed a few girls' minds and put them on my same page in the past few months. But hooking up with a random and looking for a good time is a long way from hooking up with a girl who's connected to you through two of the only people you care about. Especially when said girl appears to be the only thing you might want to care about, even if you can't.

That thought halts me and has me easing back a little. I don't fucking like it—I don't know this girl, don't know why she sparked my Spidey-Sense until I had to look away from the group I was talking to earlier and focus only on her, don't like that she has me thinking about feeling when all I want to do is *not* think.

Why is she my port in the storm when I'm comfortable drowning?

"Keep glaring at me, baseball boy, and I'm going to make a scene and ruin your game with all these pretty females that are fluttering around, trying to get your attention."

That voice sends chills down my arm, not because it's sexy—though there is that—but because it's familiar, like I've heard it before and it was important to me. When her eyes flash to mine, I see that I was right about her cover.

This girl is no angel, and for reasons beyond me I want to know why.

Chapter Four

Cora

I have to give him credit, Brown Eyes — *Jake* — knows what he's about, and if he continues looking at me like he is, I'm going to do one of two things: punch him and cause a scene, or jump him and ruin everything I've worked for.

Currently, I'm making no move because for the life of me I can't decide which is really the road I want to take. In the back of my mind I remember the words from group counseling a couple of months ago: *if something seems too tempting, too hard, or just makes you uncomfortable, walk away. Don't let uncomfortable situations push you to relapse—walk away.*

I'm saved from having to do just that when I hear the unmistakable voice of the Scientist behind me. Disgust, mixed with just enough righteousness and an overall loathing for anything remotely contemporary coats her every word.

"Jesus Christ, who are all of these people and have they ever heard of skin cancer?"

Even Jake shifts his focus over my shoulder as the words slice through the noise of the crowd and bring a wince from Mia. I smile and turn, watching in amusement as Mia's best friend from high school marches her way through the swarm of bodies, breaking up some couples as she plows straight through their mating rituals and ignores the death glares she gets.

Nina Torres (the Scientist, as I've always called her) couldn't give two shits about social graces, as evidenced right now when she throws a snide look at a girl who dares to complain that Nina muscled by her. "Watch it, Blondie, too many words at once will send you into convulsions."

I grin as the girl sputters in Nina's wake, and watch as her boyfriend of four years—Max-- follows behind her with an amused smile on his face, his hands tucked safely in the pockets of his shorts, his green eyes alight with laughter.

"Must you make friends everywhere we go, Torres?" Max asks her.

"What can I say, I'm a real people person," she tells him as they come to a stop in front of us. Her eyes narrow and latch onto me. I lift an eyebrow.

"Barbie?" she asks.

"The one and only."

"Well, what the hell did you do to your hair?"

"Oh you know how I like to change things." I lift a sardonic brow at her and motion to her black cropped shorts and white and black V-neck. It's a standard outfit for the Scientist, one she's been wearing a variation of since I met her years ago, and though I would never admit it, the stark color choices and simple lines look amazing on her. And I know damn well her shorts are tailored to fit her which is a new development and definitely a nod to fashion in her world, but I play along with our little game nonetheless.

"Nice outfit. Looks familiar."

She grins, her white teeth glowing against her beautiful skin, that's simply a luck of genetics. Nina wears no make-up, and this is the one time I would recommend it. Her heritage gifted her almond eyes that are almost black behind her square black frames, a dark sweep of shiny black hair, and brown skin the color of creamed coffee that's twice as smooth. When she catches me studying her, she grins.

"You change teams while I wasn't looking, Barbie? That's quite the stare you're giving me."

I hear Mia groan behind me, but I bark out a laugh and tug the Scientist in for a hug. "Goddamn, Nina Torres, I'm happy to see you."

"Yeah, I guess I'm glad to see you, too." She hugs me back, squeezing me in a way that reminds me of the last time we saw each other, when I was too pulverized by life to care about myself and she was too pissed off to let me give up. When she leans back, her eyes are a little misty and I feel my own tear up.

"Christ, I'm glad to see you here. And not that you weren't pretty before, but I gotta say I prefer this look. It's a little more content. Not so *fuck you* to the world. Or yourself."

I sigh and nod, staring right back. "You look gorgeous. Don't tell me you've actually started using the skin regimen I recommended?"

This does the trick and has her eyes clearing as she scoffs. "Do I look like I have time to pamper my skin? I'm three courses away from my aeronautical engineering degree and another six months away from graduate school at MIT. My skin can fucking deal."

Her eyes latch onto something over my shoulder and I edge back. "Nina, this is-"

"Jake Ferrari," she finishes. "Pitcher, all-American, scheduled first round draft pick. Busted elbow."

He nods, but I see the cords of his neck tighten, his shoulders stiffen. "That's the one. You're Nina Torres, genius girl with a big mouth and pretty eyes."

She whoops out a laugh. "That's right — I forgot you were a flirt. Well, don't let Canfield see. He's crazy about me."

"Or just plain crazy," Jake mutters and I can't hide my smile.

"Bummer about your arm. Your chances of recovery are good, though, so all the books say. Don't let Canfield talk to you about it — ever since he's been accepted to med school he's been throwing knowledge around like he's already an M.D."

With this she gives me a light slap on the shoulder and heads over to Mia, embracing her friend in the no nonsense manner that can only be considered friendly when coming from her. Max steps up in her place and gives me a gentler hug, his foot barely landing on mine as he steps back again. Then he grins at Jake and holds out his hand to shake.

"Believe it or not, she was worried about you. Both of you," he adds with a small look at me.

I smile because I know, but the sensation is so unfamiliar that I don't know what else to do. Max motions to Jake's elbow. "How's recovery going? Your doctors tell you your prognosis?"

Though his shoulders are still stiff, I watch Jake's struggle to remain calm. "They say anything's possible. Though we both know that doesn't always mean probable."

"Hang in there, man, this surgery is a dime a dozen now. You'll be back before you know it." Jake doesn't say anything, just nods when Max wanders off to see Ryan. When Jake clears his throat, I turn look at him.

I'm almost tempted to ask him what happened, but I can see clearly enough that it's more than a bruised ego feeding him now. Instead, I smile. "So, you've known Ryan for a while, if you know Nina and Max."

He visibly relaxes. "I've only met her once, but man I'd forgotten how scary Canfield's girl is."

This makes me laugh because it's true. Nina's never been one to employ tact. Whatever she's thinking is what comes out of her mouth. I think that's the reason we've always gotten along — there's something refreshing about knowing someone who isn't going to lie or sugarcoat every word they say. If Nina has an issue with something, she's going to tell you.

When I see that Jake's still watching me, I lift my brow again. "Is there something I can help you with?"

His grin is lightening quick, and I'm suddenly aware that even at the top of my game this boy would have been hard to be in charge of. Now, when I've pulled myself from the game and have been sitting on the sidelines for almost a year, I understand that he's dangerous territory.

"I want to get to know you, Blue. What do you say we take a walk?"

"Even if I were interested — which I'm not — you'd have to do better than that to get me out of here."

"Are you calling me lazy?"

I shrug, relaxing a little as our banter progresses onto familiar ground. "Well, it doesn't look like you've had to work too hard for what you want, not with a face like that, so it's understandable."

"Ah, so you *are* interested."

"More like observant."

"Semantics." He leans closer. "You sure you don't want to take a walk? I'd put twenty on the fact that I could change your feelings from observant to interested in under a mile."

Under a half-mile if my body keeps reacting to him this way. Because I'm actually tempted, I smile and pat his cheek condescendingly. "You'll have better luck with the blonde over there in her daisy dukes and combat boots — she already looks primed. You might just get to keep being lazy."

With that, I turn and head toward Mia and Nina, letting out a slow breath. I know if I turn his eyes will still be on me and for that reason I don't, but I picture him in my head, all brown skin and dark eyes, that disheveled hair and tough body that speaks to who he is. Delectable, absolutely delectable. And bad, like most good things are.

Jake never makes contact the rest of the night, but each time I glance at him he's looking at me, and each time I feel his look as if it's his hands. Breathing deep, I turn away, but not without the slightest of shivers. Heading back to our hotel a few hours later with the Scientist and the bride in the car, I listen absently to their chatter, thinking that Wedding Week just got a whole lot more interesting.

Chapter Five

Jake

The warm desert air blows through the golf course and offers a slight bit of relief from the unseasonably warm late December weather. La Niña, they call it, though right now the heat might be from the lovebirds, I think as I watch Murph make up vows during this practice run, misquoting Shakespeare like an asshole. He's got both of the Angel's hands in his, and from the way she's looking at him, with both tears and laughter in her eyes, I'm guessing this must mean something to her, like it's their thing (though the English Lit major in me wants to pull Murph aside and let him know that *Macbeth* is most definitely not a romantic tale to be whispered to his bride).

When Murph finishes, Mia brings his lips down to hers, rising on her toes to meet him, to get closer, and the guy running the wedding has to break them apart so we can practice our procession off of the golf course and into the clubhouse for the reception. They laugh and out we go, the lovebirds first, followed by Max and Blue, who's looking gorgeous tonight in a pale pink dress that should be demure with its simple lines and fitted material that slicks down her body almost to her knees, and has instead ended up making me want to lick her like a piece of candy.

When that image makes me uncomfortably hard, I shift and take a deep breath, working to alleviate the need that seems to claw its way through me every time I'm anywhere near her.

We've been circling each other all week. I'm staying in Ryan's guestroom, and Cora's staying at Mia's house, which is conveniently located across the street. I haven't had much time with her since we've been pretty divided by wedding parties, girls to luncheons and fittings, boys to tee times and bars, but I've glimpsed her going for a run every morning, sometimes with company, sometimes without, and I have to say, watching her move is a real pleasure.

Like right now, as she strides confidently down the aisle in some sort of barely-there shoe with a sky-high heel, showcasing her legs and other assets in that pretty candy pink dress.

I hear the wedding coordinator chirp my name and say go, as if I couldn't figure out when to step next, so I tear my eyes away from Blue's retreating figure and step to the center aisle to grin as Nina clomps her way toward me from the other side, holding out my right arm for her, where she shoots her fist through it and begins dragging me down the aisle.

"It's not death row, Torres, mind easing back on the throttle? I've already got one busted elbow, I don't need you giving me another."

"Listen, pretty boy, if I don't eat soon, I'm going to rip some heads off. Knowing Mia's mom, she's probably already got a night of photos and toasts and God knows what else planned, events which will keep me from eating my dinner without being scorned with a look, so before she can do that, I'm going to get some grub."

The minute we enter the atrium with its high ceilings and sun washed tile floors, I spot Murph's future mother-in-law fussing with her daughter's hair, her mouth moving a mile a minute as she talks to them both. Murph looks amused, Mia patiently resigned. Stopping, I shed Torres.

"Better go fast, because it doesn't look like we're moving very far from this spot for the time being."

"Oh, Christ, what can she possibly want to do now? Isn't that why this is called a rehearsal dinner, because people get to sit around and drink and eat after rehearsing?"

"Your guess is as good as mine. This is my first wedding."

Nina scoffs and I see her eyes scanning the crowd, probably looking for an exit or a way to safely escape and get to the food that we can smell already being set up. My eyes are scanning, too, but I'm looking for that pale pink dress and chocolate brown hair. I tune back in when I hear a name tumble from Nina's lips.

"What did you say?"

She stops and looks at me, a scowl on her face. "Some partner you are. I said, this is my second wedding as an attendant, but I don't feel like Cora's counts because it was in Vegas and some guy dressed in a loin cloth pretending to be cupid performed the ceremony."

I feel like I've taken a blow to the head. "Blue's married?"

"Was. It's over now." Nina must focus on me because she scowls and gives me a thump on the shoulder that jolts me out of my shock. "Jesus, Handsome Jake, you okay? Maybe you need to eat."

I actually think I want to hurl, but instead I shake my head. "No, but I could definitely use a drink."

I turn and head in the direction I think the bar might be, ignoring the chirpy voice of the wedding coordinator whose been running us all through the gauntlet for the past hour. It's fucking walking and standing, lady, get a grip.

I hear my name called, but I ignore that too, striding through the archway that leads into a room filled with linen tablecloths and white china. It's clear this is our room, so I stop and look around, spotting the bar set up between the open doors that lead to the veranda which overlooks the golf course.

"Handsome Jake, wait a second."

"You probably need to let me be for a second, Torres. I'm not feeling very friendly right at the moment."

"Well, suck it up, this shit isn't about you," she snaps. I want to tell her to back off, but I can't because underneath whatever the fuck I'm feeling, I'm struck with how right she is. I blow out a frustrated breath and pause on my way to the bar, turning to stare at her as she leans on the back of one of the chairs and removes her heels, shoes that were no doubt picked out for her as she doesn't appear to be the fancy, high heeled, strappy sandal wearing kind of girl.

I scrub my hands over my face and give a wry laugh as I try to calm my speeding heart. "Christ, you're right, I'm sorry." Reaching out, I help steady her while she rubs at the arches of her feet. "New shoes?"

"More like torture devices. Crap, I knew letting Barbie pick out the dresses and shoes would bite me in the ass, but like I'm going to waste time looking at fabrics and colors when I'm in the middle of my senior project. Now, I'm trying to break in shoes that I'm almost positive were used as torture devices on my ancestors when their feet were still bound."

"The price you pay for not caring."

She glares at me as she finishes re-fastening the strap around her ankle (a slim, gorgeous ankle that as a man I appreciate seeing in the shoe. Not that I'd tell her that. I like my face the way it is, thanks). "The same could be said about you. Now, I'm guessing this little fit has something to do with whatever mating dance you've got going on with Barbie." I tuck my hands safely in my pockets and rock back on my heels. She nods. "That's what I thought. I don't know how I feel about that yet as I like both you and her, but I'm not sure you're best for each other at this stage in your lives. So we'll move past it and come back later when we have time. For now, let's go back in there and take this goddamn photo so we can come back here and get a drink. When we're done, I'll show you how to sneak out the side and we can sit on the green and look at the lights."

"You hitting on me, Torres?"

"You can't be that lucky, Handsome Jake. Besides, I know damaged goods when I see them, and you're definitely damaged. And it's not just your elbow I'm talking about."

I wince. "You don't pull punches, do you?"

"What's the point? You're still hitting someone in the face, you're just ultimately telling them they're too much of a pussy to handle the whole thing. Talk about insulting."

"Well, when you put it like that."

She smiles and looks at me. "You ready for this?"

I nod and hold out my arm again, waiting for her to loop hers through it before we head back to where everyone else is being arranged in front of and around certain sides of the entryway, the course, the atrium. I wait on the sidelines until I'm called, and then I go and do my duty of posing and laughing, of smiling my ass off and pretending that the cool tempered brunette in the edible dress isn't on my mind.

Chapter Six

Cora

I was nineteen when I met Rafe. Nineteen and hell bent on acting like I owned the fucking world. Trying to tell me I was young and naïve was a waste of someone's breath. I was struggling through fashion design school though I wouldn't admit it, and I was desperately lonely.

I'd never made friends easily, and though I'd always blamed it on the fact that I didn't like girls, the real reason was I didn't understand how to be around them. Girls were public enemy number one. I'd learned that at the knee of my own mother, though it had taken me a long time to admit that's who influenced me.

Girls were complicated where boys were easy. Girls needed honesty and attention and loyalty. And they weren't afraid to tell you to fuck off and get over yourself when you were acting like an asshole. I didn't want someone telling me I was wrong, so I shut Mia out as much as possible, which was easy since we lived in different cities, and I kept to myself, only partaking in relationships with someone who saw the world like I did: one big party that owed me something.

As a result, I was never lonesome for a drinking buddy or a clubbing partner, but I was lonely when it came to everything else. I ate alone, lived alone, studied alone. To avoid this, I started partying more, going out in the early evenings and surrounding myself with as many people as possible to block out the silence that was deathly frightening to me. Noise meant people, and people meant life, so I submerged myself in them to avoid listening to my own thoughts too often.

When I met Rafe, he was everything I had been missing in my life. He wasn't like the rich and spoiled that I had been seeking out. He was a hard worker with a plan; a bartender at night, a student during the day and when he looked at me, I felt like he actually saw a person, not just a thing.

I went home with him the first night we met, and rather than letting me sneak out the next morning, he drove me home and made me breakfast. Suddenly, my apartment wasn't lonely and I became addicted to that feeling. Just that small piece of contact filled me, and I never wanted to let it go. From that moment on, I ignored everything that wasn't Rafe — I altered my appearance to fit in with his casually trendy look, altered my class schedule to fit his work and class schedule, cut out my night time endeavors to sit at the bar with him before he took me home. My world was him, and a month after we met, I asked him to move in. A month after that we were rushing off to Vegas in a drunken stupor to get married.

For a little bit, we were happy. Whether it was contrived happiness or genuine, I still don't know, but I do remember waking up and thinking, *I did it. I'm not alone like my mother always warned me I would be. Someone loves me.*

Shortly after we got married, though, it became apparent that there was more to blending your life with someone else's than making breakfast and moving around some clothes in the closet. Rafe came from a blue collar family, and he was working to make ends meet while studying to obtain a degree in marketing, and no matter how many times I told him I had enough monthly money dropped into my account to take care of us, he didn't believe in living off his wife. His free time was minimal, and those exciting times of sitting at work with him and being home with him while he studied quickly became monotonous.

It never occurred to me to find something in my own life to fill my time. I had married him because I wanted something and someone permanent to entertain and adore me, and when it became clear he had other things that occupied his time, I got mad.

Two months into our marriage I was seeking out old acquaintances, finding parties, coming home drunk and belligerent. Not coming home. I don't know if that was the end or just a prelude to the end, but when it all crashed around me a few months later and Rafe moved out, I had never felt more alone.

The day he moved out, I remember standing there yelling at him, shoving any fear I felt to the back and relying on anger. "You're giving up? Just like that? Love me, my ass. If you loved me you wouldn't be walking away."

He stood in the doorway, a bag over his shoulder and another in his hand, and I'll never forget the look on his face when he shook his head. "It's not me who doesn't love you, Cora." And then he left, and I was alone. Again.

The silence was consuming everywhere I went.

I wouldn't answer Mia's phone calls, or any from the rest of her siblings. Even the Scientist called, but I ignored her too. I stopped going to class and failed out. I wouldn't go home and admit defeat to my parents, even when I was facing divorce and no career. The only thing I had was the person I'd been before Rafe, so I embraced her and everything she'd once been, partying harder, waking up in places I didn't remember going to, surviving severe hangovers only to get twice as drunk the next night.

It was Rafe who found me passed out after one of those nights and called Mia, one last act as my husband. He'd come over to give me papers and get the rest of his things and I was on the floor, passed out after taking God knows what and chasing it with the better half of a fifth of vodka. He couldn't get me to wake up. A trip to the emergency room and a phone call later, Rafe kissed my forehead and walked out for good, but not before telling me that I had to make a choice or I wasn't going to live.

One more thing that proved he was too good for me.

I don't know if it was that or the look of terror on Mia's face when she stepped into that hospital room, but I decided that enough was enough. And though I kicked and screamed more than once during the process, I went to rehab, got sober and learned how to stay that way, entered group counseling when I got out, shifted to AA when I hit the six month mark, and then I began the painful process of starting over.

Almost a year after starting, I'm a licensed cosmetologist with a budding client list and thoughts of going back to school to get a degree in business, though they are admittedly dire thoughts as I hate school.

I'm not sure I'm happier now than I was a year ago, but I do know I *want* to be happy, healthy, and free from the demons I let control me for too long.

~

By the time I'm done running herd on Aunt Margaret and doing my duties as maid-of-honor, the rehearsal dinner is almost over. I sat at Mia's side through the speeches, laughing with Max as he embarrassed Ryan, shedding an honest tear when Ryan's mother got up and started out with a teasing lilt and ended up crying a little as she said goodbye to her son and hello to her new daughter.

I held Mia's hand under the table as she cried silently during her older brother Joe's speech, laughing as he ended with, "And who knows, we could be marrying in the families again if Caitlin and Joshua keep going like they are." The brother of the bride blushed while the sister of the groom cheered, and everyone else laughed. I continued to hold her hand when the mood changed and her father stood to give a stiff, and somewhat detached speech about the blending of two lives. It was drastically different than the other lighthearted speeches, but the fact that he's here, that he stood and verbally congratulated his daughter, acknowledging Ryan as the man in her life, was a larger step than she could have ever hoped for.

Her genuine smile and embrace for him after was her acknowledgment of that.

If it made me think of my own father who was sitting and

talking with Aunt Margaret, I tried to do so objectively. He was here alone because she couldn't make the trip, my mother, the woman who might not live to see my wedding day, and even if she does, she won't remember it.

She'll always remember the first one, though, and I try to not care about that.

My father wasn't there, nor was she, but that isn't the point. They'll remember their daughter coming home with a stranger and showing them her ring, a ring that meant little more than the ceremony itself, little more than the man — boy, really — who had bought it and given it to her. They'll remember that same girl a few months later admitting that she was getting a divorce, and that she needed help. And they'll remember the satisfaction of being able to tell her they were right, that she was reckless, careless, thoughtless.

That she was desperate and it had finally caught up with her.

But only her father will remember what true desperation looked like as he visited his daughter in her first family session a brief three weeks after her divorce, facing her as she faced her withdrawals from every substance she'd ever used, and all of the people she'd ever surrounded herself with.

And only her father will remember how she looked at him and told him all she'd ever wanted was a mother who actually wanted her, and a father who actually stood up for her.

I jolt back to reality at the sound of a chair scraping on the tile next to me. Appalled, I look around and see that people are standing, leaving, coming over to our table to say their goodbyes to Ryan and

Mia.

Mia throws a glance my way even as she smiles at an elderly couple standing in front of her. I smile, motioning to the back as if I have something to do. I wave and then turn to disappear before she can make an excuse to follow me. I need fresh air and quiet and a minute to bring myself back together.

I skirt around tables as quietly as possible, smiling at people who call out my name, never stopping as I head toward the patio doors by the bar and out, away from the small fire pit that's lit with a few partygoers standing around it, around the corner of the building to the shadows where the edge of the golf course meets the stucco structure.

Leaning back against the rough side, I close my eyes and take a deep breath, sucking air in and out of my lungs slowly, waiting for the dread to cease and the memories to back off. Christ, I need to get a grip. I take another deep breath and open my eyes, relieved to see that I'm still alone.

In a minute, I'll go back and make sure that everything's being taken care of, that Mia's okay and still having a good time, but first I need to make sure there's no remaining panic or sadness, that the memories that snuck up are well and truly buried for the time.

"Sneaking out?"

It's not the voice so much as it is how close the voice is, close enough that a hand reaches out and steadies my arm when I jolt and stumble. "Relax, Blue. You look like you're about to crawl out of your skin."

I feel like that, though I'm not going to admit it. For the first time in months, I'm uncomfortable with my past, and whether it's because Jake brings out things in me I'd long forgotten or because he tempts me in ways I don't want to be tempted, I feel justified in turning that discomfort on the man next to me.

"When a person leaves a party and goes to find a quiet corner, the implication is that they don't want to talk to people."

He just raises a brow and leans a shoulder against the side of the building.

"When a person nearly sprints out of a dining hall filled with people she knows, she should expect those people to notice — and to worry. Mia was going to come after you when she saw you bolt. Instead of upsetting her, and possibly unleashing her mother on you when she followed, I offered to come and find you."

Guilt sneaks in and I blow out a breath, before leaning back against the wall. "You're right. Sorry, I just needed a minute."

"Yeah, I got that from the look of distress on your face before you bolted." He stands and holds out a hand, nodding his head in the direction of the course. "Let's take a walk, Blue."

Chapter Seven

Jake

"So, want to tell me why you were on the verge of a panic attack in there?"

She tries to pull away, but I keep her hand firmly in mine as we walk through the course. "Relax, I'm not going to jump you. I'm just trying to figure you out."

"Well, don't. If I wanted you to figure me out, I'd tell you things myself."

I nod my head. "That's a valid point, so we'll start there. If I ask you things, will you answer me?"

"Probably not."

"See, there you go making me want to figure you out again."

She lets out an exasperated sigh and stops. "Jake, it's been a long night, and if it was any indication of how tomorrow's going to go, I'm going to need all of my strength to get through the day. So, right now I need sleep and some quiet time, not some bumbled attempt at flirtation."

Maybe it's a male thing, or maybe it's just an ego thing, but when the word *bumbled* slips out of her mouth, along with that small sigh that falls just short of annoyed, everything in me snaps to attention. Bumbled?

Turning toward her, my hand still holding hers so I can bring her against me, I look down at her, letting her see everything I feel, everything I want, everything I've done my best to hold back from her this week as we danced around one another. The moon is overhead, lighting the green around us and highlighting that gorgeous skin of hers. This time I don't resist the urge to reach out a finger and trace it over that silky smooth cheekbone and down her neck to the hollow at the base of her throat.

When a shiver courses through her, I dip my head enough so our eyes are level and our mouths scant millimeters apart. I wait, watching her eyes flutter before closing, wait still as I watch her breathe in, taking some of my breath with her. When I see her tongue peek out of her mouth and wet her lips, the blood drains from my head and I can't keep myself from moving into her.

Our bodies mold together, pressing every part of me against every part of her and I take a second to thank whatever gods are listening for the fact that in her high heels we're only three inches or so apart, and then my mouth captures hers, absorbing the taste of her even as my body absorbs the jolt of recognition. Holy mother of God.

She's a banquet of flavors, spicy and sweet, intoxicating, and everywhere I breathe I smell her, taste her, feel consumed by her. I reach my hand around and cup the back of her neck, holding her firm while I change the angle of the kiss, taking it deeper, letting my tongue slip inside of her lips and tangle with hers.

Not for the first time, this girl has done the impossible and made me think of nothing but her.

I don't know what I expected when I kissed her. Whatever it was, I most definitely did not expect her response to be this uninhibited. Maybe a little shy, cold even, with an immediate attempt to pull away (which we both know I would have ignored). Instead, what I got was all of Cora wrapped around me, her fingers in my hair, her body arching against mine, and her teeth nipping at my tongue and my lips before she changes the angle and does it all over again.

Whoever Blue is, I now know my instincts were spot on about her secrets. She may dress and act like a choir-girl now, but after this moment, I know differently.

I cup her hips in my hands and pull her closer, flexing my hips into hers and dragging a groan from both of us. When I say her name, just her name, my fingers digging in possessively, I feel her body tremble and then still, and I know my time is almost up.

I hold on a second longer, drawing out the kiss even though she's stopped responding. When I pull back, I'm almost relieved to see irritation on her face. Too much longer kissing, and I might have begged her.

"What was it you were saying about a bumbled flirtation?"

She yanks her arms from around me and shoves against my chest. It's not because of her strength that I let go, but because I'm not quite steady and it's mortifying to realize how shaken I am after one kiss. *Jesus, Jake, get a grip, she's just another girl.*

Yeah, right, keep telling yourself that.

"I don't know what you heard about me and I don't care, but if you ever put your hands on me again without my consent, it won't be just your elbow that keeps you from ever playing baseball again."

Cora's arms are hanging at her sides and her face is pink with anger and (hopefully) desire. But her eyes are cold, lethal, as they bore into me and I acknowledge this, my own blood chilling at her words. "I won't apologize for wanting you, Blue, and I won't apologize for kissing you when you know damn well you were kissing me back. But," I say before she can interrupt me, "I will apologize if you think the reason I kissed you is anything other than the fact that I want the hell out of you."

She narrows her eyes. "I don't trust you."

"You don't know me."

"Exactly."

"But I want you to," I say and realize I mean it. "I want you to know me, Blue, because I sure as hell want to know you. Ten minutes. Give me ten minutes right now where you ask me questions and I answer and vice versa, and if your interest isn't piqued by then, I'll walk away and leave you alone."

She stares at me as if assessing whether or not she can even trust what I'm saying and, for reasons I can't explain, I'm starting to get annoyed. Finally, she relents enough to relax her shoulders. "Ten minutes, and then if I say I don't want to know you, you'll just leave me be, no more flirting, no more smoldering looks, no more kisses?"

I nod. "But you have to be honest. No ignoring me for ten minutes and then telling me to take a hike." Her lips tremble on a smile, and I relax a little, too. "To show how good a sport I am, I'll start by telling you I found out inadvertently today that you were once married."

I don't add that it made me want to put my fist through a wall.

She stares at me and then blows out a breath, slipping her beautiful shoes off before nodding and then beginning to wander barefoot through the spongy grass. I match my pace to hers and for a while, we just walk in the darkened silence, the moon overhead barely a sliver and the world around us quiet.

"Gonna tell me why you got divorced?"

She smiles, and shrugs. "Really, isn't it easy to figure out? I wasn't even twenty, and though age shouldn't be an excuse, I think I was a young and naïve nineteen-year-old trying to make a decision that showed just how mature I was."

"Who was he?"

"A bartender. I went out, he served me drinks, we went home together. Not that long after, we went to Vegas and made it permanent."

I can't help the shock that crosses my face. "Why'd you do it?"

"Why not?" she asks and sighs. "I was lonely, he was different from anyone else I hung out with at the time. When we were together it made me feel different, too, like I was a part of something important and that made me feel good."

I'm shocked by her stark honesty, and the way she's glancing at me, I can tell that's what she's hoping, to shock me into walking away. Not likely. "What happened?"

She shakes her head. "Nope, my turn."

"All right. Shoot."

I expect her to ask why I care about her, why I've been bothering her, whether or not I have a girlfriend, but instead she motions to my arm. "What happened?"

I could pretend not to know what she was talking about, draw out the question further so I have time to get my wits about me, but then I remember that I'm the one who started this conversation. "UCL surgery."

"What does that mean?"

"You want the medical jargon?"

"I wouldn't understand it even if you had it."

"Then the gist. I overworked my arm, the tendons got overstretched, too overstretched to keep the bones together or for me to throw worth a damn. The end."

She stops and looks at me. "Is it? The end, I mean."

I shrug because it's something I've been trying not to dwell on. "I don't know. They say it's not, but then I'm in a weird position. I'm not finishing my college career, but I haven't been drafted yet, either. I guess you could say I'm in limbo because there's really nowhere I belong."

Her eyes stay on mine and for a second I see understanding in them. "That's a hard place to be."

I nod. "Something tells me you've been there before. With this husband of yours?"

"Ex-husband, and no. Rafe was… the one time I thought I was actually somewhere that mattered."

My gut clenches because this is not what I wanted to hear. I wanted to hear that she didn't love him, that he was a mistake, that he wasn't the person for her. I have no right to her, and yet I want her to look at me and tell me all of those things so I can take her.

"Ever been in love, Handsome Jake?"

I snap back and see her watching me. "Uh, yeah, I guess you could call it that."

"What happened?"

I run my hand through my hair, wondering if this was the smartest round of questions to start. "Isn't it my turn to ask?"

"Afraid to talk about your feelings?"

Dammit. "Nope, just thought you wanted to make things fair."

She laughs like she's knows what I'm doing. "You wanted to know me, and so far I've already told you things most people don't know. But I can't trust you with more until I know you. So, tell me about the time you guess you were in love."

"What do you want to know?"

"How long did it last?"

"A year, give or take a couple of months."

"Why'd it end?"

"We realized we weren't in love enough to actually fight for what we had."

"One word to describe how she made you feel."

"Comfortable."

I pause because it's unflattering, and not what I thought I was going to say. As descriptions of serious lovers go, comfortable is insulting, like a comparison to a nice pair of shoes or your baseball glove.

Blue raises her eyebrows. "Was comfort what you were looking for?"

"I wasn't looking for anything, not like you mean. Hooking up with Lise, then dating her, wasn't planned. It just happened."

She nods. "A year is a long time for something unplanned. How did you meet?"

"Russian lit, my sophomore year. We partnered up for a reading seminar and ended up in bed. Since we liked the results, we kept ending up there."

She stares at me and I can see the wheels turning as she tries to comprehend what I'm telling her. Since I barely understand what Lise and I were together, or what my feelings for her were, I stay quiet

"Did you see other people while you were together?"

Her question isn't uncalled for, especially with the description I've just given her. Hell, I might have assumed the same thing, and still, my mood darkens slightly.

"No. I don't share, and I don't cheat. If I'm in a relationship with a girl, or even just in bed with her, she's the only one I think about. When either of our minds start to wander, it's time to call it quits."

"Is that what happened with you and Lise? You decided you wanted freedom?"

I blow out a breath and drop to the manufactured green grass that one can only find on a golf course in Arizona, not looking at her when she folds her legs under her and sits next to me. Even though I started this conversation, I'm suddenly wishing I could pull the plug. "Yes and no. We were friends, Lise and I, and we liked each other. For a while, sleeping together and talking literature was satisfying for both of us. I gave her the break from the perfect pupil mold she always wore, and she reminded me that there was more to life than baseball."

Blue waits, and then prompts me to finish when I trail off. "And then…"

I shrug. "And then she fell in love with someone else. The real deal love. Passion and jealousy and aching when you're not together. I got home from a road trip and she was waiting for me. She told me, I kissed her goodbye, and that was it."

Except, it wasn't, not really. Lise hadn't cheated, not physically, but she had done the one thing I'd feared since my mom walked out before I was a year old: she'd stayed with me until she found something more permanent, or just something better. Blue's watching me like she knows what I'm thinking and I clear my throat.

"Is that really it?"

I nod. "It was a surprise because like I said, I was comfortable, but if you're asking if I wanted more, if I was heartbroken because she left, then no. It was the opposite, actually. She fell in love with someone else, and I let her go because, although I cared about her, she wasn't someone I spent my entire day thinking about."

I turn to her now that she's quiet, and I hold her eyes with mine so she can't doubt any of the words I'm about to say. "Not like I've thought about you every day for the past week, Blue. Just hear me out," I say, as she starts to shake her head and stand. "The minute you walked into that party I was hooked. I couldn't look away. Now that I know a little bit about you, now that I've tasted you and spent time with you? You're all I think about, Cora, and after the last few months of not wanting to think, it feels really fucking good."

"This isn't smart," she says and I talk over her protests.

"Mia's moving out. Who's going to move in with you when she does?"

She blinks at my odd transition. "What?"

"You're going to be alone, and I need to get out of Arizona and everything my life used to be. Since Mia's moving back here to take up residence in my apartment, why don't I move to San Diego and live with you?"

Now she does stand and I can see the panic on her face when I stand with her. "No. Are you crazy? We just met, and even if I was looking for a roommate, it wouldn't be in San Diego. I'm moving back to Portland," she says. "There're some things there I need to take care of and I think it's time I got out of San Diego and started my own life."

"I can do Portland."

"I wasn't asking," she snaps and I grin, unfolding myself and standing with her.

"Think about it, Blue. I haven't lied to you, and I'm not a stranger, but I'm not a part of your past, either. You can say whatever you want, but I know you, Cora. For whatever reason, the minute I saw you I knew you and, despite what you tell yourself, you know me too."

"Jake," she says, but this time it sounds more like a plea.

Reaching out, I ignore her skeptical look and take a piece of hair that's slipped from the pin she's used and tuck it behind her ear. Her eyes never leave mine, and her breathing is too fast. I can see that she's panicking a little, that I'm pushing her too hard. Murph's warning from the first night after he noticed my interest in her floats through my brain, but I can't focus on it right now. Knowing I'm asking for too much doesn't matter.

I can't stop myself because there's something pushing me, telling me that it's this girl who's going to save me. Hating that doesn't make it less true, so I've given in and am now convincing myself that, once she agrees, I'll think of her first from then on out.

But she has to agree first. Taking a chance, I trail my finger down her arm until I've linked our fingers together.

"I need to get out of here, Blue. Things have changed for me and I need something new. You're starting over, too, or you wouldn't be moving. What do you say we start over together?"

Chapter Eight

Cora

Over the past year, I've turned a lot of corners, erased a lot of lines I had drawn in the sand before, and become a different person. Some of it had to change because what I was doing (or sometimes who I was doing, if you want to get technical) and who I was becoming was destructive and harmful. And some of it changed because once you stop partying, stop thinking about where you're partying, about what you're wearing, who you're going out with, and how you're getting over your current hangover, there's a lot of fucking time to fill.

After my thirty days of counseling, sobriety, and reflection, which were some dark days, let me tell you, and then the subsequent group counseling that followed, I figured out two things. The first was that I needed friends, and if not true friends, then at least people I could hang out with who didn't make me want to punch them in the face or go one further and drink a bottle just to get away from them.

I know, my life is gorgeous. What I needed was someone to help me quiet the craving for life, noise, excitement in my head that I had begun to associate living with.

The second thing I learned, perhaps more necessary than the first, was that I needed a hobby, one that could take up a considerable amount of time as now that I was sober and aware of my life twenty-four hours a day, I was also aware of the fact that I didn't really do anything (other than boys, but new leaf and all that).

So, in an attempt to not just be clean and miserable, but clean and healthy since happiness is overrated in my book and will come when it goddamn feels like it, I did what the counselor called trading one obsession for another, and I began to work out. After one week of burning lungs, overused muscles and intense physical pain, I gave in to Mia's suggestion and hired a trainer to actually show me what I was doing instead of continuing to rip myself to pieces each day.

After that, it was still tough and painful, but it was manageable, and after the first month of pain, embarrassment and downright horror that the sixty-year-old woman next to me could lift more weight and run longer on the treadmill than I could, it got better. The first three months were all about training my body to stretch, lift, climb, run, and move, when previously all I'd done for it was drape clothing over it and consume substances that weren't quite this side of legal.

After those twelve weeks, I spent another twelve shedding the excess flesh that I had gained when I replaced my alcohol with sugar. I lost ten pounds and put on some muscle. My body started craving things that I had never eaten, so along with my fitness craze I added a health craze, learning how to cook, how to eat, how to grocery shop instead of just ordering off of a menu.

Through it all, Mia was with me, going to the gym when she wasn't in class, taste testing my meals, though some were undeniably inedible.

She never let me down, never teased me for finding myself consumed with something so clichéd. Instead, she joined me so at month six, when I was getting bored with the inside of the fitness club and the monotony of the same routines each week, she found us the outdoor club that provided a new challenge each day.

We've climbed hours of stairs in every stadium in and around San Diego, we've run hills, done sand relays and beach yoga. Despite the awkward and painful learning curve I endured, I kept going because, for the first time in what felt like forever, I wasn't just drifting anymore. I was determined; I had a goal, and it felt good.

Which is why at just six a.m. on the day of my cousin's wedding, I'm awake and tugging on running shorts and a sports bra. We have a full schedule of hair, make-up, nails, and everything else that my life used to be about, but before the whirlwind, before the hurricane and the fluttering and worrying that can be my Aunt Margaret, I'm going for a morning run. I'm replacing my normal sand and surf with the dry desert.

In my room at The Authentic, the inn in Verrado owned by Mia's parents, I slip on my running shoes and make quick work of the laces before easing open my door. A second before it closes behind me I think of my key and slap a hand on it, wincing at the echoing sound it makes as I dart back inside. I spend ten minutes looking for my room key, which I find in the bathroom drawer with my toothbrush. Puzzled, I try to recall events from last night that would have landed them there, coming up with nothing.

Ninja bastards are getting more creative in their disappearance acts.

Armed with a way to get back inside, I finally exit my room, slipping past the other doors I know to be occupied by family as I make my way down the hallway and toward the stairs. My stealthy actions are more out of self-preservation than courtesy, as my biggest fear is that someone will wake up and want to talk to me or worse, come with me, before I take this one hour to be selfish.

I'm almost to the top of the stairs when I hear another door open, followed by quiet voices and a light laugh — a laugh I would know anywhere. Tongue in the side of my cheek, I turn to the left instead of heading downstairs, and low and behold, standing at the entrance to my cousin's suite (where I stupidly assumed she would be getting her beauty rest for her day as the bride) is one hot piece of ass kissing the lights out of his fiancée.

"Jesus, get a room. Oh, wait, you have one. Try going back inside of it."

Even though I keep my voice down, Mia startles enough to break away from the kiss, but I give points to Ryan since he just turns and offers a lazy smile before attempting to get back to his business. Mia slaps at him, but he keeps going, leaning into her until she has no choice but to grab onto him or topple over into the room. The kiss he gives her is brief, strong, and everything a girl who's loved understands, I'm betting.

It says *hold onto that, because there's more to come.* For a second my body tightens and I wonder what it's like to feel that amount of affection from someone. Shaking it off, along with any lingering thoughts of love, I raise an amused brow and cross my arms as dopey one and two stay wrapped up in each other.

"You better put a move on, lover boy, since I'm guessing Auntie Mags didn't lock her daughter in the tower so you could scale the walls. In fact, I think the purpose of moving us all here was so your bride was further away from you, not in the same bed."

"No tower's keeping me away," he says, as he sets her down. He kisses her again and she raises to her toes. I look away because, Jesus, it's a little much. "Two o'clock. Then you're all mine."

"Two o'clock," Mia repeats.

Ryan grins at me as he walks quietly past. "Take care of my girl until then."

"You got it," I say and smile as she watches him disappear.

Sighing, I walk toward her. "Cousin, how the tides have changed. Here I am, getting up after spending the night alone, responsibly going over the itinerary I was given, making certain I have the schedule for the day burned into my brain so nothing could possibly go wrong. Then I find out you've not only been harboring a boy in your room, you've kept him here to the day of your wedding, a day he's not supposed to see you on." I tisk at her as we walk inside and close her door.

Her room is the suite, an extravagant affair made up of white fabrics and what appears to be reclaimed beach wood — something more suited to the sand and surf than the desert — but it also feels like an oasis from the harsh landscape, an invitation to sink in and forget the dry and dead outside. The bed sits dead center with its magnificent wood headboard, the plush covers all done in sparkling white and thrown everywhere, the adornment pillows in white and gray scattered on the floor.

She's smiling at me, her head shaking back and forth as she walks into the bathroom and begins to change into shorts and a running tank similar to mine. "We don't care about that. And since we're not going to get a ton of time together once baseball season starts, we're taking what we can now."

She pulls back her mane of hair in a ponytail and walks out to slip on running shoes. "Three?" she says and I nod. "Together or alone?" she asks and I know if I said alone, she'd point me one way and go another. That's the thing about Mia, she doesn't push, she doesn't smother, and she doesn't criticize. But she's always there.

"Together," I say with a smile, following her out and down until we're outside in the mild December heat.

"You doing okay with that? The fact that once he finishes with this season he'll begin another right away, for a team that might not be anywhere near here?"

She nods and we begin out of the inn parking lot, hitting the running trail that goes through the small town. Following it, we take it all along and through different housing complexes, switching between trail and sidewalk until we reach Lost Creek Road and head up into the stark brown hills of Arizona wilderness. We don't talk, not just because we're both concentrated on breathing through the altitude and the almost consuming dryness, but because it's part of who we are, who we've become as a unit.

This used to be Mia's thing, running, getting away, getting out.

I never took the time to go deeper, to understand that she needed this because it helped her release those things that she felt bound by, those things she couldn't control and needed to.

Now that I run with her, we rarely talk because I see the value in getting away from the noise and the people, the constant communication and attachment that I once craved like a junkie. Even if it's for only an hour a day, I detach myself, disengage, and I focus only on the next step I need to take to move forward.

When we get to the top of the hill, we're both breathing hard, chests heaving, sweat glistening off our skin. In San Diego, we run a five mile circuit on the beach that we usually try and end with a quick swim in the ocean. Now, I mourn the loss of that beautiful piece of my morning as I squint and try to breathe. Christ, it's brutally dry here, and try as I might, I can't work to find it beautiful in its sparseness.

"God, are you sure you're ready to be back here? It's so ugly."

Mia smiles and bends at the waist to stretch and catch her breath. "If you're asking am I hoping that one day Ryan gets drafted and it's anywhere but here? Yes, but for now, he's here. We won't get a lot of time together once we get back to school, and after this season… well, he'll be somewhere else playing and I'll be working on my graduate degree. So right now? It's worth the time we'll have, and moving from our place back to here."

I nod because I get it. She doesn't see brown and deserted when she looks out anymore — she sees a future and some time with the man who *is* her future. It's almost second semester for both of them, but Mia won't be going back to USD in January. She's transferred to ASU so she and Ryan can live together and spend as much time as possible being a married couple before their futures take them in different directions. But always back to each other at the end, that's the way their love story works.

"Are you going to be okay by yourself?"

I don't pretend to misunderstand her, though a part of me wishes I could brush off her question with a grin and a promise that being alone has always suited me. We both know what suited me before is no longer what's good for me now. An image of Jake and his proposition from the night before slams into me and I knock it away. The fact that I was tempted for even a second, and that I've thought of him all night and into the morning, tells me just how dangerous he is.

Pushing him out of my mind, I stop stretching and so does she, both of us standing and resting our hands on our hips as she waits for me to answer. She's small, petite, a girl who carries her strength without showing it. Her hair is golden, darker than the platinum I used to rock, lighter than her sun-kissed skin, but not by much. Her eyes are a clear blue, and her skin is flawless, stretched over high cheekbones, a pointed nose and a perfectly sculpted chin.

I used to think that she was the one who needed to be protected, sheltered, saved, because she was the one who felt everything. Every failure, every loss, every angry word shared by someone touched Mia until she was driven to fix it. It wasn't until she was saving me from myself, going down to Los Angeles a year ago and gathering me up, taking me to The House and visiting me every chance she got that I realized in *not* feeling, I had broken myself.

The person I had been three years ago was someone who refused to acknowledge anything that hurt — instead, I pretended to be a warrior, wearing armor that I had made out of careless looks, careless hook-ups, and chemical induced memories.

I thought I was so grown up when I moved to Los Angeles alone, that I was going to take the fashion world by storm, a naïve eighteen-year-old from Portland, Oregon, who graduated from high school online because she was too impatient to wait and graduate in June, and who thought that everyone else would be amazed by her grand vision when she met them.

Instead, my life went from confusing to awful as I struggled to find myself, began and ended a marriage and discovered that my mom, who I had never been close to, had become a victim of early onset Alzheimer's. Our already rocky relationship became volatile as she pushed hard against any weakness and I fell into it. It was then that I decided the best way to mourn what she was losing was to give my life away to whoever wanted it. Until Mia saved me, and then taught me how to save myself.

So, the answer that I'd like to give isn't the answer I do, because I long ago stopped lying to Mia, and to myself. "I'm not sure, but I know that it's time I try. You saved me, Mia, and gave me a place to feel safe. Now, I need to learn to stand and find my own place, and you need to go and be married to that gorgeous man. I'm happy for you, cousin," I tell her and see her smile. "I didn't understand how you could trust Ryan, or how you could trust that he's always going to be there, that he loves you even when he's not with you, but every time I see you guys together I know it's true. And I want that for you."

She touches my arm briefly. "What about for you? What do you want for yourself, Cora?"

Love. It pops into my mind and almost rolls off my tongue before I catch myself. The fact that Jake's face comes with it is twice as terrifying. Irritated, I swallow the thought back and smile. "Well, I wouldn't mind a handsome man with abs like the one you've snagged, but if I can't have that, I guess I'll stick with contentment. I want to feel satisfied," I tell her, and know it's the truth. It might not be the only thing I want, but it's definitely one of them. Knowing she'll keep pushing if I don't move this conversation elsewhere, I smile at her then turn to head back.

"Enough serious talk — you're getting married today and we still have to devise a plan as to how you avoid your mother for most of it. I think we use the Scientist; she's just bitchy enough that Auntie Mags doesn't know how to respond. We'll have Lily throw a tantrum about refusing a hairdo or something equally horrifying, and that should keep her occupied long enough for us to get you made up and dressed before she can offer advice and last minute additions."

Mia laughs and we head away from the horizon and back down toward the city, but I don't shake that feeling for a while, the one that says I want too much, and what I want could be the very thing I'm incapable of getting.

Chapter Nine

Jake

I'm sitting in a lounge chair on the side of Ryan's pool at just after six a.m. on his wedding day when I hear the side gate open and close. Since the groom slipped out of the house last night after everyone returned from dinner, I can only suspect that's him whistling his idiot head off as he saunters around the corner. One look and I grin, holding out my middle finger.

"Maybe try not rubbing everyone's face in it that you're getting some on the regular these days."

He grins back and plops down into the chair next to mine. He's shorter than me by a few inches, topping out at just over six feet. He's a fast little bastard though, lean with the agility of a leopard. The way he steals bases makes me wonder if he's part ninja sometimes. Athletic doesn't begin to describe him, and when we first became friends during our sophomore year, both getting our shot to play more than a few innings, I learned what dedication was from him. Of course, knowing you had a girl like Mia probably helped with the focus.

Why focus on a party and females when the angel was already yours?

Blue pops into my mind unbidden, along with her reaction to

my proposition last night. I hadn't been planning on asking, had actually planned on leaving her alone, heeding the warning that Ryan had given me that morning. *Cora's been hurt, she's been tossed aside, and she's just getting back on her feet. Now isn't the time to mess with her.*

I let him say it because she deserved to have someone looking out for her, and from what Ryan has told me, not a lot of people do. I don't begrudge him his protectiveness, I just don't have the power to resist her either. Since I not only respect Murph, but consider him one of my true friends, I'm going to have to talk to him about the plans I've been making. Plans that include one blue-eyed siren.

"You already work out, Handsome Jake?"

Murph motions to my sweat covered T-shirt and the medicine ball at my feet. I've done my workout for the day, and I'm just about to start the throwing motion exercises I get to go through with a one pound medicine ball. Admitting I'm scared won't change the fact, so I just shrug and play it off.

A few months ago — just over four, to be exact — I had major reconstructive surgery of my UCL ligament — that important one that keeps your elbow where it's supposed to be so you can do things like throw a baseball. When they told me I had the commonly feared Tommy John injury, I thought I'd never throw again. Even after they said they could fix it and give me back my pitching arm, I wondered if I'd ever *want* to throw again. The first months after the surgery were all wrist modalities, lifting and extensions, teaching my arm how to move now that there was a foreign ligament replacing the one I'd overstretched and blown out. Then, it was forearm weights and shoulder motions and wrist and elbow movements, until I could finally move the arm without pain or awkwardness.

Every exercise since has been a gradual increase in movement and weight and such, leading me to the moment I'm at now. I've swung a golf club repeatedly in the last weeks to remind my body what it knows how to do, what motions it needs to bring back, etc., and in two weeks, if everything stays on track, I'll begin a new throwing program. It will be the first time I've thrown a ball since last July. And still, I'm almost five months out of surgery and I feel less like an athlete now than I ever have before.

Because I can see the curiosity in his eyes, because we both know I'm working out and doing everything the doctors say even though I refuse to acknowledge a possible future in baseball, I shrug.

"Yeah, you know, took my little jog, did my lunges and core, worked hard to make sure my ass will look good in those pants your girl picked out. Of course, she thinks I look good in everything, so it won't be hard."

"Just give it five years when you're in the majors and your running is minimal and the body you're so proud of now becomes thick and flabby. You might just lose your Handsome Jake superpowers."

Murph's grin remains as he throws the banter at me, but I freeze. I know what he's doing, refusing to accept that I'm done, refusing to let me accept it. His eyes are steady on mine but rather than amused, they're set in a challenge.

Go ahead, they say, *try to walk out on all of it.* Fucking Murph.

This kid shits happiness because that's what his life is, fucking happy. His girl is perfect, his parents are actual parents, the ones who appear to feel pride and actually enjoy being with their kids, and his career... Christ, his career is just beginning.

There's no stopping the Murph, and for some goddamned reason he doesn't believe in allowing anyone else to stop, either.

Because it's his day, and the fact is that I really do care about him, despite my deep seated envy of everything he's got going, I try to stay calm as I shake my head. "Let it go, man. I'm doing the rehab, I'm following the orders, but you and I both know eleven months to a year off with an un-played college season makes me less and less desirable."

"Neither of us knows that, Jake, but what we both *do* know is that this shit happens and people recover. You tore a major ligament, now you've replaced it and are rehabbing. You're following the orders of some of the best sports doctors there are. The timing is shit, but your arm is going to heal, man, and when it does, you're entering next year's draft with me."

"To do what? Spend a half a decade or more in the minors working my ass off just to be told I'm not quite good enough?"

Murph just shrugs his shoulders when I push off the chair to pace. "That's a chance all of us take. With or without surgery you would have gone to Short A just like me and every other prospect that's coming out of college. There are still three levels we've got to move up before we really get looked at, possibly four. So no, it's not a fucking guarantee, but you knew that last year, just like you know it now."

He stands with me, watching me as I pace, his voice like a whip. "You're scared, I get it, but don't quit because it's easier than admitting how much you care. That's bullshit and you know it."

The problem with someone like Ryan is they make you want to believe. They're the optimistic prick that sees the glass as half-full, the ones who know that if one dream doesn't work out, another will come along because life's just that good to them. The rest of us know that getting to taste even a little bit of one dream is pretty fantastic, but to get two chances? No way.

"I'm moving to Portland. I asked Blue to think about taking me on as her roommate."

He stops, his eyes going wide, his breath heaving in and out. For a full thirty seconds he stands there staring at me, neither of us talking. "What?"

I feel the calm wash over me and I stop my pacing to stand face to face with him, to look in his eyes. I know his fists have clenched at his sides, just as I know that if he sees good reason to use them, he will. Murph might be a happy guy, but he's also a loyal one and if he thinks I'm a threat to someone he loves, especially if it involves his angel, he won't be afraid to lay me out.

"What did you say?" he repeats.

I lift my brow and cross my arms over my chest, reveling in the pain free feeling of being able to do that. "I think you heard me. I'm transferring. It's almost second semester, Mia's moving into the apartment with you. You guys aren't going to want a roommate hanging around during the few days that you might get to see each other."

"Jake, you know we wouldn't kick you out. You're family."

Just that easy. For Murph, family means something — whether they're blood related or not. As for the angel, Murph's told me enough about her situation that I can understand that, for the two of them, they're building their own family, one they can depend on. It shocks me when I feel a tremor of regret that I'm walking away from it.

"Yeah, man, you know I feel the same, but I can't stay. I can't," I tell him when he goes to open his mouth and argue. "I've already called the doc at school and had him make arrangements for my treatment to be transferred. There's a trainer lined up in Portland that can finish my program. I've already emailed my counselor and started the process of figuring out whether my scholarship will cover the four classes I have left online, especially if we claim medical necessity, or if I have to apply somewhere else and forfeit the rest of it. I need to go," I finally say, and I see his sails deflate.

Murph will push when he thinks he can win, but he also knows when to step back, when to let the runner take their base instead of trying to make the play and throw them out. He's got a level head, and I know he can see that I'm not messing around. I need to get out. I might suffocate if I don't.

"What about what the doc said about team cohesion? Staying mentally tough by staying a part of it? How are you going to do that if you're in another state?"

It's why I'm leaving.

"Murph, I'm not playing this season, I'm not going to be traveling. You and I both know that my time with the team is done. It would be different if I was coming back, but this was my last season and it's over. I only have a few classes left to finish my major. I'm doing everything else the doctors have said, but I have to do them somewhere else."

Somewhere it doesn't hurt to fucking breathe. Somewhere there isn't a reminder around every corner of what I'm missing. Somewhere that I can see Blue.

"Why Cora?"

I snap my eyes back to Murph's and I can see the struggle in him. "What do you mean?"

"Come on, Jake, we've known each other for almost four years. I haven't seen you take more than a passing interest in a girl since you and Lise broke up end of sophomore year, and even then you weren't brokenhearted when she left. The carpet's worn from the girls trekking to and from your room in the past year. What makes you want to be close to Cora?"

I need her.

The words are there again, without being prompted, and it scares the life out of me that I'm not sure I have control over my feelings or her. Fuck if I'll tell him that and try to explain what I barely understand. Something about her makes me want to believe that there can be something out there, something that I've never thought of before, something that can make my life feel like mine again. I don't say any of this to Ryan though, partly because it scares the shit out of me and partly because it's none of his business. I respect that he cares for her, but he's got his own girl and Cora's an adult.

When I stay silent, his brows lower and I can see the struggle in him. "Shit, Jake, what are you thinking? She's Mia's cousin. She's not just some girl you can use to make yourself feel better."

"Don't you think I know that?"

"Do you?" he snaps back. "Jesus, you're a mess, and Cora just got herself back to a place that she can be safe. I love you like a brother, dude, but if you mess with her I won't be able to take it. She doesn't deserve that."

I'm momentarily sidetracked as I get hung up on that one word. *Safe*. What the hell happened to Blue that safety was a concern?

"It's not like that, Murph." When he narrows his eyes at me, I concede enough to run the hand of my good arm through my hair. "I can't explain it, but have you ever just seen someone and felt something for them, something that scares you and pisses you off and makes you want to walk in the other direction even when you know you can't?"

He nods. I can tell he's still wary, but I accept that. "The minute I saw her I knew she was someone that I needed. It might be selfish, it might be crazy, but I can't stop thinking that she's someone I need to know. And even if I didn't, I need to get out of here, and she's packing up and leaving, starting over. She said something about looking for a room when she got up there, or maybe finding a place and looking for a roommate. Wouldn't you rather it was me living with her than someone off the street?"

He's struggling with the urge to yell at me, and I know he sees my point about the stranger. If whatever he's saying about Cora is true, then she does need a roommate, not for the financial help, but because she needs someone to ground her, and she needs someone she can trust. I might not be a saint, but I'm not going to hurt her.

"Be careful with her," he finally says on an expulsion of breath, and I feel the tightness in my chest ease. "She's tough, and she acts like she's not afraid, but Cora needs someone who thinks of her first. I need you to think of her first, Jake," he says and I know he's asking me as much as he's telling me. That he trusts me to do what he's asking.

I nod. "I won't mess with her, Murph. I would never do you like that."

He stares at me for a minute and then he grins, quick and lethal. "Shit, Jake, I'm going to miss you. Let's go get me married then, so I can send you off with one hell of a party."

And just like that, the son of a bitch is happy again.

Chapter Ten

Cora

Everything is choreographed and scheduled down to the last minute. The bride and groom have said I do and kissed each other senseless. We've processed back down the aisle to the side of the golf course, taken all of our photos and been ushered into the dining area to mingle and enjoy cocktails and hors d'oeuvres while Ryan and Mia finish up their final photos.

It was a relief to be released for a while, since I'd been paired up with Jake so the Scientist and Max could stand next to each other after the original procession. Standing there pressed against him, his broad chest against my back as we smiled for the group photos was almost too much. Not that he acted any differently.

When we were taking the photos, he was relaxed and happy, and now that we've been freed he's removed his jacket (an act which I can only hope Auntie Mags skins him for) and is talking intently to Ryan's sister, Caitlin, and Mia's brother, Joshua, the other Murphy/Evans love affair.

He hasn't tried to talk to me once, only making funny little comments as Auntie Mags and the wedding coordinator fluttered around us making certain we were all put together perfectly for each photo. When we were finished, he squeezed my shoulder, gave me a small smile, and walked a little bit away to where he is now. He never even mentioned living together, and goddammit, wasn't it his idea?

To say I need a distraction is an understatement of epic proportion.

Even after my run this morning, I haven't been able to clear my head enough and rationalize why Jake living with me is the worst idea on the planet. I mean, the boy screams player and I just got out of the game. Wouldn't living with him be like settling a sugar addict in a cake shop and telling her good luck?

Which prompts me to wonder if cake can be that horrible for you. I mean, really, is sugar the worst addiction a person can have? It's not crack.

Christ, I'm even attacking my analogies.

When my father steps up next to me, I wish fervently that I was still outside suffering the tortures of the photographer, wedding planner, and Auntie Mags. At least then I was simply expected to do as I was told without responding. One look at my father's face tells me he won't be as easy to be around. Which is promptly followed by feelings of guilt for being such a bitch.

He's not a bad man, he simply had the bad luck to be flexible in a marriage where his partner was anything but. As a result, we both suffered, and after a while, that suffering was no longer something we bonded over.

"Cora, you look beautiful." He leans in to kiss my cheek and I keep my hands clasped in front of me, though I tilt my chin for him.

He steps back and for a second I'm thrown into the past and the memories of the many social functions my mother dragged us to. I would stand in the corner and pout, wearing whatever hateful and overly fussy dress she had forced on me, vowing revenge on her for plunking me down in her social life as a prized pony and then ignoring me. Before long, my father would sidle up to me, hand me a Shirley Temple and stand next to me. We'd never really speak, no more than a comment here or there, but by the time he walked away, I was no longer unhappy.

It went on like that until I got old enough to stop caring what my mother wanted, which was about the exact same time she stopped caring what I did. My father never stopped caring what she wanted, and in the end, he chose her and I chose to go my own way. The road back has been hard on both of us.

Tonight he looks almost as I remember him, though, dashing as ever in his perfectly tailored suit, his brown hair now almost fully gray. Though he's just over sixty, older than many parents of kids my age as I was the one and only baby my mother conceived and kept from giving up in the womb after years of trying, he's an attractive man, with a strong jaw and broad shoulders, a long frame that he handed down to me. The only real difference comes from the fact this his normally content face is much thinner with deep lines, that weren't there even last year, etched into it. And still, he smiles at me. I don't know if it's that or something else that prompts me to speak first.

"How is she?"

He doesn't flinch, but his smile falters a bit before he clears his throat. "As good as can be expected, I guess. You know your mother."

"Not really," I say and feel like a child. Since it's the truth, I refuse to feel badly about saying it.

He clears his throat again. "She just finished a round of tests with the doctors again, blood work and all of that. They're still trying to pinpoint the exact stage she's in based on memory loss, gaps in social habits and other things in order to complete her overall timeline. They say this will give us a clearer view of expected years."

It takes me more than a minute to process his words, and finally it hits me. Expected years. Life. My mother isn't battling a disease anymore; there is no battling this. What she's battling for is time, for life. And it's a battle she knows she's ultimately going to lose.

Almost two years ago, my mother was diagnosed with early onset Alzheimer's disease. The only reason it was even detected was because she went in for her routine physical and her doctor discovered there were holes in her answers; lapses of time where she was fuzzy, incomplete in her memories of what had happened. When he asked if she'd had a concussion recently, she couldn't answer him.

This led to tests which led to more tests and finally, at the end of it all, their diagnosis was confirmed: early onset Alzheimer's, a disease that is usually fatal within ten years of the first sign. Only, those estimated years don't take into account the actual living years for the person suffering. They don't explain what it's like to live with someone who's so afraid of not remembering you, she chooses to forget you before her mind does it for her.

I haven't seen my mother in almost a year, not since right before I went to rehab and she was beginning her slow transition away from the world and into solitude. I was broken from the divorce, devastated from the failure I felt surrounded every choice I'd ever made, and she was the person to tell me that being disappointed was what living was about. She looked right at me and I knew what she wasn't saying: I had disappointed her, so it was only fitting that life handed some of that back to me. And then she walked away, just like Rafe, and I decided giving up on life was easier than feeling as useless and unwanted as I felt at that moment.

Looking at my father now, all these months later, I wonder what it's been like for him to watch the woman he's loved and cared for his entire adult life, fall victim to her memories, growing angrier with every one that fades.

"I'm sorry," I say and feel like a failure. I don't have the words to express what I feel; an inherited trait from the very woman we're speaking of. My mother could never talk to me unless it was to tell me exactly what I was lacking, and I had followed suit. By the time I turned eighteen, we could go days on end without uttering so much as a word to one another, and if one slipped through, it was always hostile.

My dad doesn't call me on my absent response, though, he just nods. And then, as if he's just remembered who I am, he reaches out and places his hand on my shoulder. It's a small gesture, one that shouldn't hold so much weight, but in my family, touching — like communicating — isn't something we do.

"I'm sorry, too, Cora, for a lot of things." He clears his throat and drops his hand, sipping from the glass he holds in the other. "Margaret tells me Mia's moving back home."

He doesn't ask and I get the feeling it's because he doesn't think he has a right to, but I can sense the question that statement prompts: will you be all right by yourself?

I nod. "Next month, actually." He nods and sips from his water again. I clear my throat this time. "I'm thinking of moving back to Portland."

His expression clears for just a second, but in that timeframe I see what appears to be genuine happiness on his face before he schools his features back into quiet interest and he's just a polite stranger again. It's odd how for that small space of time, I wanted him to be happy that I was moving back, and more, I wanted to throw my arms around him and tell him how sorry I am. For nothing, for everything, just, sorry. But I don't and we move on from the moment.

"Will you be moving next month as well, then?" I nod. So does he. Then he takes a deep breath. "You know you're more than welcome to move back… we haven't changed your room. It's there if you want it."

Uncomfortable, I nod my thanks. "I'm actually going to live with someone. A friend, sort of. He's more like Ryan's friend, but he's moving, too, so we thought it would be a good idea to go together."

My dad's nodding before I finish speaking, his head punctuating each of my words. "Of course. Well, it will still be good to have you close. We've, uh, we've missed you. I've missed you," he says, and I hear the sincerity in his voice.

Wishing again that I was more, that I could give him more, I reach out and touch his arm, waiting until his eyes meet mine. "I've missed you, too, Dad. I'll come by the house when I get there. We can have dinner and you can tell me about the new mansion Uncle Tommy has commissioned you to build."

"I'd like that."

A few minutes later, the bride and groom are announced and I say goodbye to him before walking over to take my place around the dance floor and watch them. They've chosen something old for their song, with a hint of blues to it, and while the female vocalist croons about never letting go, I watch the couple sway. Mia chose a simple strapless dress in white, with an empire waist and sweetheart neckline. The sweetheart top is lightly jeweled, separated from the skirt with a sheer white band, and the skirt is full and flowing without a train. Her hair is pinned back from her face with a Swarovski hair comb that was our grandmother's, and then left to flow down her back in heavy waves. She's a vintage princess, elegant in her simple dress and hair.

Ryan went for a tie instead of a bow tie with his tux, and the slim fit of the jacket makes him look twice as sexy as normal. Together, they make a breathtaking couple, only more so when his fingers slide from her waist to lose themselves in her hair while he brings his forehead to hers. It's such an intimate moment I almost feel like the rest of us are intruding.

"She really is an angel," Jake says in my ear and I hate that goose bumps pop out over my skin. "Though, I have to say with everything I've heard by way of wedding torture stories, I'm not understanding the rumor about ugly bridesmaids."

I smile because it's true. Our dresses are strapless tea length champagne silk that nip in at the waist and flare out into a skirt. Auntie Mags almost had a coronary when Mia told her we weren't wearing floor length, but that didn't stop Mia. Just as she didn't give in to the heavy pressure to have the wedding somewhere more formal or somewhere exotic. She and Ryan met in Verrado, that's their place, that's where they wanted to be married. While I myself would rather be on the beach, I can appreciate her sentiment.

When the bride and groom dance ends, the father daughter dance begins and I watch as Uncle Thomas takes Mia's hand formally and begins to waltz her expertly across the floor. Halfway through, Ryan bows to his mother lavishly before leading her onto the floor. Soon, the rest of the wedding party is joining, another request of the bride and groom that was met with parental resistance at first.

At his cue, Jake holds out his hand to me. "It's our turn, Blue, what do you say?"

I nod, having known this moment was coming. When we're on the dance floor, I try to ignore the heat from his body, and his smell, as they wrap around me and draw me closer to him. Something about Jake makes me want to lay my head on his shoulder and let him take the lead — or just take me, which is as dangerous an image as it is a delicious one. Even when I was having sex I didn't think about it this much.

"So, have you thought about living with me yet?"

For the last twenty-four hours straight. "A little."

He smiles but lets my lie go. "Come to any conclusions?"

"That it's the worst idea on the planet, not just because we hardly know each other, though that's definitely one of the reasons."

"Worst idea on the planet? You've heard of our recent health care issues, right?"

I glare at him. "Then there's that. Can you take anything seriously?"

"Maybe I would if you didn't take everything so seriously. Come on, Blue, lighten up. I get that you're hesitant because you have a hard time resisting me, but I promise to respect your boundaries while they're there."

"You say that as if they'll be disappearing."

"I said respect them, not give up getting around them."

My laughter escapes before I can contain it. Dropping my head on his shoulder, I let it come because it feels right and denying the decision I've already made is pointless. I feel good about the idea of living with Jake — though I know it's bound to be a stupid choice. Right now, the thought of going home alone isn't appealing, but the thought of reclaiming my city and having Jake there to help, or at least distract me, *is.*

"Is this your way of submitting?" he whispers in my ear and I shake my head, ignoring the shiver that races across my shoulders.

"I'm never submissive." The words are out much like the laughter, without thought, but once they are, I admit that they feel natural. This banter, this friendship, it feels natural, too. Dangerous tomorrow? Who knows, but right now it's enough to be pleased with what I feel like. Almost like a blend of who I was with who I've become, the darkness shaved away to make room for the laughter. I know that for some reason Jake's an intricate part of that. Why's another question altogether, one I won't be attempting to answer anytime soon.

"Okay, Handsome Jake, pack your stuff. I'm picking the apartment, so no complaints about rent and location."

"I want the master bedroom."

"Keep dreaming."

"In that case, I'll share it with you, Cora, but you have to respect my boundaries."

I laugh again, and so does he. The song changes and more people come on to the dance floor, but we don't stop dancing, my hands around his neck and his on my hips. For a long while we sway and we laugh, and inside I feel myself start to come alive again.

Chapter Eleven

Jake

I arrive in Portland at rush hour and spend over an hour battling bridges that take me in the wrong direction and rain that continues to pour down and make everything more difficult to navigate. Yogi is sprawled in the passenger seat next to me, his blanket beneath him, one eye open and on me. He's refusing to look at the scenery, and I can only imagine it's because he's mad about two days of travel and the dramatic climate change.

He might have started off as an abandoned cat, happy to just have a warm place and a full belly, but in the last year he's really turned into a diva.

When I finally arrive at the downtown apartment that matches the address Cora texted me earlier in the week, I spend another ten minutes searching for my parking spot, only to find it's on the top floor in the uncovered part of the parking structure, approximately three floors above where our apartment actually rests. Awesome.

Grabbing the cat and my phone, I tug on my hood and sprint through the rain, grateful that the stairs are covered. When I get to our door, I knock and scan the area as I wait. Unlike my outdoor apartment that I shared with Murph, with its individual walkways for each condo, this is indoor, much like a hotel, and is going to cost an easy thousand more than the apartment in Arizona that I shared with Murph. When Blue opens the door wearing athletic pants that fit like a second skin, and an oversized T-shirt the color of sunset that's slipping off one shoulder, I think it could cost two grand more and I'd still pay it.

She is a mortal danger to all men. The line from *Cyrano* runs through my head and before either of us can think too much, I lean in and press my lips to hers, quick and firm. My free hand reaches up to cup her cheek and I angle my head a little to the right, my tongue sweeping out and over her lips, drinking in the taste of her that's haunted me for the past month while we've been apart.

Her hands come to my chest and I release her, but not before I place another peck on her lips. I lean back and grin, happy despite her narrowed look.

"Hey, roomie."

"Don't expect to come home to a greeting like that again."

"I wouldn't be opposed."

"Well, I am. I'm serious, Jake," she says. "If this is going to work, you have to respect those boundaries we talked about. That means not touching me."

I hold out my hand. "I know, and I promise, I will. But it's been a long damn month, Blue, and I've been on the road for two days. The sight of you was just too much."

As if to punctuate my words, Yogi mews and Cora's eyes zero in on him. They widen briefly and then come back to mine. "What the hell is that?"

"Blue, meet Yogi. He's been with me since last year when I found him outside of the stadium in a cardboard box. He was the only one left and I couldn't leave him." When she just continues to stare, I bend down a little so I can meet her eyes. "You're not allergic, are you?"

She shakes her head no. Then she looks back at Yogi and I see that small smile. "A cat? Jesus, Handsome Jake, how did you ever get to player status while harboring a feline friend?"

I leave Yogi and Blue to get acquainted while I make the trips to and from my old Rover to bring in my clothes and other things. The big stuff was already shipped and moved into my room. I don't know if Cora told the movers where to put everything or if they decided on their own, but the bed in the center of one wall, facing the desk that's against the window works fine for me, and I start dumping stuff on the floor around it.

As I walk through the apartment each trip, I take in a little bit more of the space and the décor and I'm grateful for what I see. Nothing is overly girly or fussy, and the color scheme appears to be neutral with bold slashes of royal blue and some lighter grays in fabrics and paint. There's an overstuffed chair with its back to the door, with a couch parallel and facing a wall where I assume the television will go (my television, as Cora's is only thirty inches. Please, my computer screen is bigger). Both are oversized and done in some light fabric back cushion with a leather seat.

I saw them in the picture Blue sent me, and I'm grateful to see now that they're as big in person as they looked on the phone. Dainty furniture doesn't really fit me, literally or figuratively.

After my last trip, I close the door to my room, knowing that until I get to unloading the boxes and putting it to rights, Blue will probably appreciate not staring at the mess. Stripping off my wet jacket, I set it on the coat rack near the door and head into the kitchen where Yogi is digging into his dinner. Cora's standing at the stove stirring something that smells suspiciously healthy.

"If I'd known you cooked, too, I'd have been here ages ago. Ryan makes fun of his mama, but he's no wiz in the kitchen."

I open the fridge and take out a beer I crammed in there earlier. When I offer one to her, she shakes her head and I close the door, popping the top and draining half before I turn and lean against the counter.

"What's in the pot?"

"Kale, white bean, and carrots with some rosemary and onion."

"No meat?"

"When you cook, we can have meat, though I should warn you, I only eat happy meat."

I smile. "Who doesn't? Every cow deserves to have a smile on his face."

"*Organic, grass fed,* that sort of thing. I don't eat meat from farms or slaughterhouses that abuse or mistreat their animals or inject them with hormones."

"Does it say that on the packaging?"

"It'll say if the animal was humanely treated."

I sip from my beer and try to hide my smile. Can't, I just can't. "Aren't they slaughtered and eaten no matter if they see a cage or a field?"

Her eyes flash fire and I hold out my hands. "Never mind. Happy meat. Got it. Anything else I should know before we get too far into this relationship?"

"It's not a relationship, it's a lease."

"Semantics again. We're roommates, Blue, which means we're going to get to know each other, whether you want to or not. Living in the same space is intimate no matter who it's with."

She releases a breath and turns away from the stove to face me. "You're right, and I'm sorry, I know I'm being a bitch but I can't seem to help myself. You scare me, Handsome Jake, because you make me feel things I don't want to feel."

I grin. "Tell me where you feel them, maybe I can make it better."

"Interested," she says on a laugh. "You make me feel *interested* in whatever it is you're offering me, and I don't want to be interested."

I cross my feet at the ankles to keep my stance relaxed and non-threatening, but my body is humming. My feelings shot past *interested* the first time I saw her, but it's nice to know she's catching up. "Interest isn't a bad thing, especially when it's reciprocated."

She shakes her head. "It is when you're me. Interest often leads to intent, which leads to action, action I'm not ready to take."

Not ready. That's a whole lot different than *not willing*, but I don't call her on it. Instead, I nod. "Well, why don't we try this? Let's get to know each other, not because we're roommates, but because I want to be friends too."

She watches me for a minute and then inclines her chin. "I can live with that. Where do we start?"

Chapter Twelve

Cora

"I'm not answering that."

"Blue, the game is *questions*, you can't pass on every one I ask or it's not a game, just a replay of my seventh grade year."

I laugh and stand up from the small table at the window to take our bowls to the sink. He grabs the rest of the dishes from the table and follows me. "Were you an awkward thirteen-year-old, Jake?"

"I was smart and nice and I actually read the Harry Potter books instead of just seeing the movies and making fun of them, so it's more like I was an oddity. If it wasn't for baseball, I would have gotten my ass kicked regularly; instead, I was just shot down a lot. Mostly by your kind."

I laugh again and turn on the water to rinse, unsurprised when I feel him next to me, opening the dishwasher and holding out his hand for the dishes I've just cleaned. "How did you go from being rejected all of the time to raking them in?" I ask, and his smile is slow and satisfied.

"By realizing early on that girls thought they wanted a bad boy when really what they wanted was a boy who knew how to talk to them, to make them laugh and actually hear the things they said while still being a bit of a badass. The whole voice-cracking thing quit by sophomore year — praise Jesus — and my dad got me into karate to help me control my limbs that were growing pretty rapidly. By my junior year, I was coordinated and weighed a hundred and sixty-five pounds instead of the hundred and twenty I had arrived at high school weighing. I made varsity as a sophomore and threw the ball just over eighty miles an hour. The fact that I could quote poetry and remember what a girl said was really just icing on the cake."

"And so the legend was born."

He wiggles his eyebrows and I can't help but laugh. When I opened the door and saw him standing on the other side of it earlier, my heart actually leapt, which was probably why I didn't see his move coming until our lips were fused — or why I didn't reject it even when I did see it. I'd missed him, which is insane and the reason for the cold shoulder I then doled out.

Jake Ferrari is everything I shouldn't want, mostly because he's everything I've convinced myself is no longer a part of my life. He's fun, appears frivolous, though in the past hour he's proven not only to be intelligent, but motivated, as he explained he's only got four classes left to take in order to graduate with a BA in English Literature, a degree he promised himself he'd get, no matter where his future led him. He's laid back, but I've seen the serious side a few times, enough to know that when Jake cares, he cares with all of himself.

His words from our conversation after the rehearsal dinner flit though my brain as they have multiple times in the past month. *When I'm with a girl, she's the only one I think about.* It's not hard to see that whoever he is, Jake isn't careless with people's feelings, especially those he considers important. I can't explain why I already feel important to him, any more than I can explain the absolute elation that thought brings.

"Seriously, where do you get your pants?"

I'm shaken out of my reverie when he repeats his asinine question. "What is this fixation with my pants?"

"You have a mirror, right?"

I raise my brow at him, both impressed and a little irritated that he can deliver lines like that and not sound like an asshole. "Lululemon."

"What the hell is that?"

"Is that another question? Tell me, does this game ever end or do we just continue asking questions willy-nilly the entire time we're roommates?"

"Never ending, though it's not really *willy-nilly*. I'm building up here, making you comfortable. The purpose is to get the easy stuff out of the way so we can eventually get to the hard stuff that requires more than the name of a grocery store."

"It's a clothing store. What if I don't want to answer the hard stuff?"

In the past hour we've talked about everything, asked silly questions, answered them, shared silly stories. Being with Jake has reminded me of everything I missed out on the first time around — the conversations, the jokes, the comfort. And it's reminded me just how lonely I was before he walked through that door today.

A year ago I was a wreck, a shattered mass of bad choices and even worse outcomes, and when I stopped being that person, when I learned how to make better decisions and actually think about what my choices would do to me and others, I promised myself I would never lose myself to my need for intimacy and connection again.

Standing in the small kitchen with Jake while the late January rain continues to pelt the windows and the city lights illuminate the streets outside, I know he's someone who could make me go back on my promise. And as much as I want to just let go and enjoy this time with him, whatever it brings, I don't ever want to fall back into the person I was, the one that latched onto a boy and a marriage because she was too lonely and insecure to find something for herself. I don't know if there's a balance here, but I *do* know that something about Jake makes me want to look for one.

"Well, I don't believe I've asked you anything hard yet so you're safe."

"I'm not so sure anymore," I mumble and turn off the water. Drying my hands on the towel that hangs over the oven, I take a deep breath and remind myself I'm in charge of my actions. No one can make me do things I don't want.

"I think I'm going to head to bed. Welcome to Oregon, Handsome Jake."

I'm halfway out of the kitchen when he says my name and stops me. I turn my head and look at him, and for a second we're both staring at one another and I feel that familiar pulse begin.

"Being with you, it's the only thing I've thought about in the past month." He says the words simply, and still, I feel the world change around me. I want to deny them, to ask him to stop and think of what he could do to me, but that feels weak, and that's one thing I don't want to be anymore. Since I can't think of any way to respond, I do nothing. He acknowledges this with a jut of his chin. "You might not be the one to ask the questions, Cora, and you might be able to convince yourself you're better alone, but we both know I'm here because the idea of being alone isn't as appealing as it once was. Not for either of us since the night we met."

I nod once and then turn and walk away, hardly breathing until the door to my bedroom is safely shut behind me. Only then do I let out an expulsion of air and sink down onto my bed, breathing through the trembles that prove I'm anything but immune to him, anything but strong. Jake Ferrari wants me, and he just insinuated that I want him back. Closing my eyes, I cradle my head in my hands, thinking he's exactly right.

Chapter Thirteen

Jake

I'm relearning my throwing motion and I feel like a fucking toddler.

This is when rehab feels like too much work, like a lost cause and a heartache waiting to happen. I want to rage, I want to smash things, I want to punch someone. And then I remember that I'd be more likely to break my goddamn arm than actually hurt anyone or anything, which just pisses me off more.

I'm a couple of weeks behind on my rehab program, though the doc I'm seeing here (along with the one I was seeing in Arizona) swears that the estimate they give after surgery is rough. Some players heal within the allotted twelve months, some take longer. He also swears that healing slower doesn't mean anything different. Healing is healing, he says, but I can't help but want to call him on his shit. Healing? I'm five months in and I've just gone from *practicing* (so not actually releasing) my throwing motion with a fucking one pound medicine ball, to what's termed a *soft toss* from less than fifty feet away from my target. The fact that it's actually pretty difficult to reach the target is where my rage is coming from.

Underhanded tossing, that's what I'm doing, and that's what I'm struggling with. How the fuck am I ever going to throw a ninety mile an hour fastball from sixty plus feet away?

Baseball players in general are considered arrogant, and for good reason. There's a certain amount of arrogance needed to go one on one with someone in front of your team and theirs, knowing that the victor earns points (be they actual points or just emotional points, which are just as important sometimes), while the other has to continue the rest of the game with the loss in the back of his mind. Baseball isn't just about the end score; it's about runs stolen, bases stolen, pitches snuck through, and those forced through. Sometimes it's about luck.

I analyze my batters, their percentages, their weaknesses, and I go through them systematically with everything I've got. When what I know doesn't help me, I use what I am and I work to make every batter's life a living hell when he steps up to that plate. Until seven months ago, I was renowned for facing down batters and taking away their confidence, so when I heard that today was the day I got to start my throwing program, I ran through my morning workout with the knowledge that the minute I picked up the baseball, my life would fall back in line. Which makes me an idiot. Or an asshole. Quite possibly both.

Not only did nothing fall back in line, I think I may have regressed a couple of steps emotionally, and the doc was more than happy to point out that counseling was recommended since I'm so far away from my team, something that *isn't* recommended.

Counsel this, I think and swing through the outside door and down the hall to our apartment. The sight that greets me when I unlock it and enter is one that improves my mood significantly faster than any medical interference could.

Christ, is there anything greater than yoga pants and the women who wear them to actually do yoga?

Cora's pushed the low, refurbished yellow table that usually sits in the center of the small space off to the side. In its place, she's rolled out a mat that she's currently twisting away on, in a position I'm pretty confident has the word dog in it. *Thank you, Jesus.*

Hands flat on the ground, superb ass in the air, legs straight and feet planted so she's in some sort of upside down V, Blue doesn't notice me as she balances on one hand and reaches for her opposite ankle with the other, showcasing not just her fabulous assets, but her extreme strength and flexibility, too. There's music pumping through the small Bose speaker that sits on the shelf perpendicular to the window. It's more like dance music than relaxing meditation music, and it's the throbbing bass combined with the erotic poses that have my body tensing for entirely different reasons than the one I carried in twenty seconds ago.

Christ, I want this girl.

Because my instincts are telling me to take, to walk up behind her and grab her and show her everything I want, I shove my hands in the pockets of my sweats and lean back against the door to enjoy the rest of the show from a safe distance. Yogi is sitting on the desk chair, and he slits his eyes at me as if he knows what I'm thinking. In the month that we've lived here, he's taken to Blue and become her shadow when she's home, following her from room to room, curling up in the corner and watching her while she cooks, cleans, peruses the Internet. As if he senses my jealousy at the fact that he can be close to her and I can't, he's always staring me down, and if a cat could talk shit, I know just which words would be coming out of his mouth as he eyes me from his seat right now.

I glare right back at him and finish the show, admiring each new pose and the fluidity with which Blue goes through them. Our relationship has been a little rocky in its beginning. Rather than feeling closer now that we live together, since that first night it feels as though Blue's put a wall up between us, one that she stays safely behind. She's polite, friendly even, but never forthcoming and playful, never spicy and confrontational like she was when we first met and she told me in no uncertain terms to back the hell off.

It's been four weeks since I got here, and other than polite conversation, she's hidden behind her imaginary wall, finding things that keep us at a safe distance, finding solace in her room or the excuse of a busy work schedule to keep her busy. I've let her breathe because I realized that first day that she needed to be the one to make the next move or this relationship — at least the one I want — is doomed.

She hasn't made a move, and as I watch her roll up and out of her last pose, I wonder if I've just fucked myself into wanting her even more while she's still maintaining what she considers a safe distance. Knowing I'm close to begging, hating myself for it even though I know I can't stop it, I clear my throat and wait for her eyes to meet mine.

She doesn't flinch or jump, which makes me almost positive that she knew I was here while she finished. I don't know whether it's good or bad that she didn't acknowledge me.

Trying for light even though my whole body is tense with this need for something, whatever it is, I smile. "I like your workout routine, Blue. And your pants. Have I mentioned before how much I like your pants?"

Her smile is slow, but it comes eventually and some of the heaviness inside of me eases.

"You know, I think you have," she says and reaches over to lower the volume on the speaker, so the music falls to a low pulse. There's a ray of sunshine pushing through the rain, illuminating the small spot where Yogi sits and, looking at it, I can't help but think that's how Blue is for me. She's my port, my piece of sunshine when all I want to do is wallow in the darkness and sink.

Knowing I might not be good for her doesn't change my need for her, which probably makes me a bastard, but there it is.

"Rough day?" she asks and I meet her eyes. She's standing with her mat rolled up in her arms staring at me. The light's still pouring in behind her, and I wonder if she knows what I was thinking, or how badly I needed her to ask.

"It wasn't great."

Her hesitation is minimal, just enough that I can tell she's not one hundred percent sure of her moves. I wait, and eventually she makes her decision and takes a small step forward. "Want to tell me about it?"

My shoulders unwind instantly, and a large breath exhales from me. "Yeah, I really do."

~

"Tell me about baseball, what it's like to play in college, to know your career might go beyond that."

"What do you want to know?"

She shrugs and sips from her coffee. She's sitting in the corner of the couch with her legs curled under her and I'm sitting next to her, a beer in my hand. We've finished dinner and are capping off the night together, something that we haven't done since the night I moved in. Over dinner, I told her how training is frustrating and slow, and that even though the doctors and trainers and therapists all say that people heal at different speeds, it's making me crazy. I want to be done, to know where I stand, where my future and my baseball career stand.

Talking to Blue and being with her for the last hour has made that itch, that impatience, die down a little.

"Start with college life. I didn't do the whole college thing and though I went to my fair share of college parties, I wasn't on campus day-to-day. What's it like being a scholarship athlete for a major university? Tits and ass and alcohol every day?"

Her voice is lighthearted, for me I think, to make me remember the fun while I'm still digging myself out of the bad, so I laugh and sip my beer again, trying to figure out how to explain what it was like.

"You're both wrong and right," I start and she rolls her eyes, annoyed, most likely, by the fact that I can't just give a yes or no answer. "I never thought anything would be better than the day I signed my letter and knew I was making a future for myself, and then I arrived on campus and went to my first training session and I was proven wrong. Everything was better than I'd imagined, and I'd imagined some pretty great things."

"Like what?"

"Well, I thought I'd get some gear, a room, and some food and have someone take care of me while I majored in something I loved and played the game I'd dedicated my life to since I was little. I got all of that in a much larger sense. I lived in an apartment style dorm with three other teammates, the same but larger than the rooms other people on campus lived in, and in the first four months I was there I had two Christmases — days when I walked in and in front of my locker was a bag stuffed to overflowing with shoes, shirts, sweats, socks, shorts, hats, batting gloves, and loads of other swag." I shake my head at the memory, still a little awed even after three and a half years of the same treatment. "The gear, the stuff, it was unending, and for a kid who had come from nothing and was just looking for a way to never go back there, it was very clear that I was no longer going without like I once had. From the first day that I walked into that locker room I was someone, and it felt really good."

"That's what she said," she quips with a wiggle of her eyebrows and I laugh, appreciating the light banter as it pulls me away from the frustrations I walked in with. "Seriously, though, I've spent time with enough people like you to understand that you're not a normal person on campus. There had to be more to the perks than an extra T-shirt or two."

I nod, thinking of my last three years, the people who supported me, loved me, shouted my name even though I had no idea who they were. "Let's just say that being on the baseball team definitely gave me certain advantages in the social world. For instance, you weren't wrong when you called me lazy the first time we met. The fact is, even with Lise, I didn't have to do much because girls came to me. So did the guys, in reality. Everyone is more interested in helping you, tutoring you, talking to you in the hopes that they get to be your friend and embrace the extras that come with your position on campus. And when it becomes apparent your career might take you further than college, your friend count doubles because even if you fail at your attempt at the majors, people love nothing more than being able to drop your name into party-time conversation and talk about how they shared beers or a class with you way-back-when."

She frowns. "Sounds like people are assholes."

"Maybe, but if you do make it, they're also you're biggest fans, and that can't hurt in a world where less than one percent of most college players ever get to go."

"What did you do when you weren't playing baseball?"

"Train to play baseball," I say. "People call baseball players lazy, which is partly true because our bodies don't take the daily beating that a football player does, so a few beers after a game aren't going to kill our recovery. But," I add, "we also have longer training year round, with expectations that most people don't see."

"Like…"

"Like, I went into college weighing one hundred and eighty-four pounds with around thirteen percent body fat. At the end of my freshman year, I weighed just over two hundred pounds with eleven percent body fat. It's only gotten better from there. Outfielders and infielders lift all season, and all of us conditioned from the start of the school year through the start of the season and work to play well into June and make it to Nebraska. And then we play summer ball."

"So I was really only half right when I called you lazy the first time we met."

"With baseball, I was never lazy. With girls... you weren't wrong," I say again, and her smile is triumphant. "I'll admit that after a game, when frequenting an establishment that served alcohol, if I met a girl, a conversation may have gone something like 'Hey, I'm Jake,' to which she would respond, 'OMG like in Twilight?' We'd then discuss the mythical wolf creature and his many flaws — none of which I possessed, of course — and then girl, whose name I've most likely forgotten by this point in the conversation, would ask what frat I was in, to which I would promptly reply, 'I'm not in a frat. I play baseball.'" My grin is back as the memories of my first year swarm through me. "Things got infinitely easier and more guaranteed after I dropped that tidbit of information."

"Ah, one of the many perks of being an athlete."

"Other than per diem, I'm pretty sure it's the biggest one."

"Per diem?" she asks.

"Like grocery money — the payment you receive for being an athlete on away trips and vacation times that you have to stay on campus. Meal money, but for those programs who are big enough, or supported enough, it can be excessive."

She stares at me for a second and then laughs and sips her coffee. "One last question."

"Shoot."

"If you were having such an easy time finding females ready to spend the night with you while someone else footed the bill, why did you come here? I'm guessing they had to honor your scholarship, at the very least, and I know for a fact that a broken, dark soul is almost more appealing to girls than a happy one."

"Is that right?"

"Yeah, bitches be crazy," she says and I smile again. "Seriously, they think they can fix you and so they sleep with you thinking you'll let them try."

I remember my last few months at school, the drunken haze I walked around in, the females I found solace in only to wake up and not quite remember who she was or how we had gotten to my bed. The irritation that Murph would try to hide as he escorted them out so I could nurse my hangover in silence and try to piece myself back together enough to function for the day.

Cora's still watching me, so I shrug and give her the truth, hoping it doesn't close the door on the conversation we just got back.

"Sometimes, you realize that however fun the moment is, you want something more. My future is more than I was giving it when I was at school those last months. Since one look at you made me realize that, I figure you're the more I needed too."

Chapter Fourteen

Cora

The mind is a funny thing, shaped it seems, not only by what it experiences and remembers, but by our desires, fears, needs, and perceptions of everything around us. Memories take on different hues as time progresses, manipulated further by what we observe throughout our lives, who we meet, and how we view ourselves.

Although I've always thought of myself as a confident and strong woman, which I showed through unwavering opinions and a fuck you attitude, counseling taught me that hindsight is much clearer and, in actuality, what I saw as confidence was an innate fear that no one would ever love me, therefore, I refused to let anyone try. (Therapy can be a real bitch when it works.)

During my childhood and teen years, I thought my mother to be overly confident. She was demanding, opinionated, rude when she thought it was her only option — or even just a viable option — and needier than any toddler I've ever come into contact with. When Suzanne Whitley wanted something, she did anything she could to get it, and most often what she wanted was for everyone to think she was a raging success in life.

Anytime she didn't get her way, she would throw a tantrum of epic proportions, screaming, tossing things around the house, slamming doors, until she eventually broke down in a fit of needy weeping, where my father would scoop her up and she would cling to him as if he were the only life raft after the Titanic had done its thing. It's that memory, and the ones that follow it like the shifting forms of a shadow in the dying sunlight, that show me my perception about my mother was just as inaccurate as my perception of myself.

My mother was an easy target for my unhappiness growing up, because she and I have never gotten along. She wanted a quiet, demure daughter who would rise with her in the social ranks and keep a beautiful home. I wanted to be someone, *anyone*, important and I didn't want to worry daily about what other people thought. Where my mother envisioned her little girl growing up as a mirror image of herself, I imagined growing up as anything but and soon all my mother had was a younger, sexier version of herself who threw that fact in her face daily. The results of our dislike were disastrous and, after several volatile years, we came to a cease-fire that was much worse.

The silence between us widened the already existent emotional gap at a rapid rate, therefore compounding that anything we did say to one another was cold and short, critical in nature and lacking in any feeling. I dealt with this by being loud everywhere else in my life — my clothes, my friends, my social life, and she dealt with this by trying to be a younger, more gorgeous version of herself to prove that I wasn't special.

In the end, we both lost ourselves. The only difference is that I came back, and she'll never get to do that.

~

I've let two of the other stylists from the salon I work at talk me into grabbing a drink after work. I'm not sure how it happened, except one minute I was sweeping up my station, wiping down my tools and cleaning my counters, mentally going through my few scheduled appointments for tomorrow, and the next I was walking out the door and down to a trendy little bar in the Pearl.

We snagged a booth pretty easily, since it's a Wednesday evening, and now I'm sipping my sparkling mineral water and lime while A.J. and Liam are tossing back a pair of shots and chasing them with some sort of import beer. I cringe, wondering if the burn of tequila is the same.

Jake texted me to let me know he was on his way home (since my ninja keys have disappeared again and I'm without them and, therefore, without a way into our apartment) and, for some reason, I told him to come meet us. I'm half listening to A.J. talk in her short, rapid sentences about everything around us while I click the power on my phone and check to see if Jake texted back.

"Okay, Snow White, spill your story. What's with the beauty on ice routine? The eyes that speak volumes and the mannerisms that tell me you're a lady, when we both know you're not. The water instead of alcohol?"

"Jesus, A.J., this was a friendly invite, not an interrogation," Liam says and throws his arm over the back of their booth.

"What, friends can't ask questions?"

A.J. is what one might consider a ball buster — which is odd since she's gay. Or maybe not odd considering. Either way, she's beautiful in a unique way, with her dark hair shaved short on one side and left to flow over on the other. Her nose is pierced twice and she wears two tight gold hoops through it, plus one through her opposite eyebrow and too many to count in her ears. She's got beautiful skin, attributed to her Indian heritage I would bet. She's petite, has the voice of a foghorn, and a personality as stealthy as a bulldozer.

Liam is her polar opposite. He's quiet, beautiful in a pure way, with clear skin, blond hair, and brown eyes fringed with dark lashes. His hair is short on the sides and styled on the top in the ever fashionable gentlemen's cut, his wardrobe is trendy without being over the top or flamboyant and, despite his profession as a hairdresser and the stereotype on sexuality that goes with it, I think he's straight. If I didn't know A.J. batted the other way, I would consider them a beautiful match.

"Are you gonna answer, or do I have to guess?" A.J. asks and I smile.

"It's a long story."

"Give me the basics."

I smile and take a sip of water. "Grew up in Portland, moved to California after high school, lived with my cousin this last year, but she just got married and moved so I decided it was time to come home. There was a stint in rehab somewhere in there and, since I don't want to go back, sparkling water is as hard as my beverage choice gets." I smile as I say all of this, not even changing the tone of voice on the last part, hoping she'll take it as I've said it, a thing that's no big deal.

A.J. studies me for a minute and then leans back, her beer in one hand and her lips pursed. Liam gives a supportive smile and head nod.

"You're a Snow White all right. No worries, I'll figure you out. One question, and you have to answer."

"I don't have to do anything," I tell her, but she only grins.

"Boys or girls?"

My mouth kicks up on one side, and I can't help myself. "Neither. Men."

Liam lets out a laugh and A.J. smiles her approval, before saluting me with her beer. Talk turns lighter and though I've found that my new personality likes to hang back, I find myself laughing and even adding tidbits to the conversation every now and then because A.J. makes it impossible to do otherwise. She's a firecracker, or a sparkplug, engaging, entertaining, exploding everywhere so everyone around her is invested in what she's talking about.

Halfway through a story about when she came out to her mother, I have to hold my hand over my mouth to keep the laughter in.

"You lie."

She shakes her head. "No need to. When you meet my mother, you'll understand. Everything she does defies logic."

"In fairness," Liam interrupts, as he has been all evening, "you aren't exactly tactful or gentle in the way you present information. It's just one day 'I have a boyfriend', and the next, 'meet my girlfriend, I'm a lesbian'. It tends to throw people, especially people like Didi to whom the world is very ordered."

"Not you," A.J. says and I realize their relationship extends way beyond that of comfortable co-workers. "You just patted my shoulder and told me liking what a man liked didn't mean I had to dress like one too. It was rather poetic."

This elicits a number of other stories and memories that A.J. begins to work through, and though I've been entertained all night, the picture on the opposite side of the table is so beautiful and comfortable that I feel suddenly lonely. Mia's the closest person I have that could be considered a best friend, someone who knows me better than anyone else, and yet our relationship isn't like A.J. and Liam's. Mia saved me, and we were always close growing up, but her family moved to Arizona before we started high school and, even before then, we didn't spend our time together. She was a student and an athlete who wanted nothing more than her parents' approval. I was a party girl who spent her days shopping and her nights worrying over my boy of choice, usually settling on the one that would shock my mother the most.

It hits me hard, here and now, that I don't have this, the bond of a childhood friend who's watched you grow and had your back. I don't have the shared stories and memories that A.J. and Liam do, and the affection that underlies everything we say to one another. I have the regret that comes with being a surface friend for most of my life.

"Hey, are you okay?"

I nod at Liam, though I feel hot and a little sick right now. "I think I need some air. I'll be right back," I say and slide out of the booth, but not before I see the look they exchange. I instantly hope they think I'm leaving to break the temptation to drink instead of because of the fact that I'm jealous.

I feel stupid, but I can't make myself go back yet, can't make myself brush off the feeling of absolute isolation that has washed over me in the last ten minutes. I step out of the bar and lean against the side of the building, taking out my phone. I've been trying to prove to myself and everyone else that I'm strong enough to live without constant support, and as a result I haven't texted or talked to Mia or Nina in a few days. They call or text me, but I wait for them to initiate because I don't want to be needy. Now, though, I text Mia because I can feel myself wanting to sink, and I know she'll pull me out.

Her response is immediate, but rather than text, she calls.

"Is it raining still?" she asks when I answer and I smile, knowing she would never mention the desperation in my text unless I brought it up.

"Nope. It's a balmy sixty degrees right now. How's the desert, dry and suffocating?"

She laughs and I feel myself relax. We might not have the history of shared moments like Liam and A.J., we have a connection nonetheless. We chat about the salon, my new friends, the apartment, a little about Jake. When she asks about my mom, I pause.

"Good — I see her, but she doesn't really talk to me yet. I think I might be wasting my time."

"You're not, Cora. Do it for you, and for her. Keep trying, I promise you aren't wasting your time."

I nod, but don't say anything and we sit in silence for a minute.

"I'm glad you texted," she says, and like she can read my thoughts, she adds, "I miss you, Cora."

I blow out a breath and feel my shoulders relax. "I miss you, too. Tell your husband I say hi. I have to get back."

"I will. And Cora?"

"Yeah?"

"I'm always here. Don't forget that."

I close my eyes and nod. "Thanks, cousin." I hang up and stand there, bringing myself back together. I'm watching people pass by me on the street when I hear his voice.

"If I'd known you were waiting outside for me, I would've tried to get here faster."

Jake finishes walking toward me and I turn my head to watch him. His hair's damp and he's no longer in practice clothes, so I can deduce that he went home to shower after his training session. He's wearing what I've come to understand is pretty standard attire for him, with his dark levis, white long sleeve Henley that's pushed up to his elbows, and a pair of worn brown boots. His hair is long enough that it curls damply around his face, and his jaw holds a day or two worth of scruff.

The sight of him brings a tingle low in my belly, but it also brings a slight relief from the loneliness that was sucking me down so instead of looking away, like I've done the past month, I keep staring at him. He stops next to me and leans back, his hands stuffed casually in his pockets.

"You okay, Blue?" I nod. "Then why are you out here? Aren't your friends inside?"

"I needed some air."

"Too hot in there?"

I could say yes and take the lie he's offered, but I don't. The other night was a kind of truce for us, a thawing from the freeze out I had employed to safeguard myself against him. For whatever reason, when he'd walked in the door I'd known he needed something — and I wanted to be the one to give it to him. We talked about his arm, but after his initial frustrations were vented and after we made dinner, we moved onto different topics, things like favorite movies, books (of which my list was pathetically short and somewhat contrived as I've only heard of some of the books and never actually read them), music, and food. And then back to baseball, which he clearly loves and misses. He didn't make a move all night, not even when we went our separate ways to bed. Which shows me that we can be friends… and I think I want to be. Whatever else he wants, well, I try not to think too hard about it, because I know my answer is definitely not the one I want it to be.

"Have you ever had to change who you were, and in the process realized just how much you missed out on the first time around?"

He nods slowly. "I think I can relate to what you're saying."

I think about his arm and feel like an asshole. Of course he can. "Sorry."

"Don't be. We both have a past, Blue, and neither of us wants to rehash it, but that doesn't mean that shit won't sneak up from time to time, shit that a friend can help you deal with."

It's the perfect thing to say, which again makes me wonder just how much I'll be able to resist him. "Do you want to be my friend, Handsome Jake?"

"I think we've already established that."

I smile. "Not a friend with benefits, or a baseball bunny. A friend, a real one, the kind you're comfortable grabbing dinner or a beer with — though I won't be drinking it — talking about your bad day with. Sharing exciting news with, even though you're not sleeping together."

He looks at me for a minute, those brown eyes serious and steady, and I can tell he's really thinking about it. Most people would have just rattled off an agreement, but not Jake. When I ask him something, he understands there's more to it, that I'm not looking for the easy answer, but the real one. Finally, he inclines his head. "Yeah, I do."

I sigh, and if it sounds a little like relief, neither of us acknowledges it. "I want to be your friend, too. I think I just realized how much I want that."

He doesn't say anything, just stands and tugs me toward him and then his arms are around me and my head is on his shoulder, and for a second I just let him hold me. It's not scary or heavy with implications or expectations. It's just right. He's hugging me like he cares, like I matter, and I don't feel so alone.

"I don't know about the other stuff," I tell him, as we pull away and he just shakes his head.

"Blue, it's no secret that I want you, but I also want this. So, let's have this while we can, and when we move to something more, we can rely on the foundation we've built to help us through."

"*If* we move to something more," I correct him. "I told you, I'm still not sure."

He just grins and reaches around me to open the door. "Just remember, you weren't sure about being my friend but you're the one who just asked me. That's what we call a prologue in literature."

"Wow, you really are a nerd."

"Name calling, is it? Just for that I won't tell you where I found your keys this morning."

"The freezer again?"

He shakes his head. "Basket underneath your desk… you know, the one with your knitting needles. That's quite a sweater you're making, Blue. At least, I think it's a sweater. Kinda hard to tell."

My lips are trembling on a smile and when he continues to stare at me, I let go and laugh, closing my eyes. "It's supposed to be a sweater," I confirm and he just smiles wider. "An admittedly ambitious project, since I barely know how to knit a scarf. No one was supposed to know about it."

"Since we're friends now, I won't tell anyone. But I do call dibs on being the first to see it."

I nod. "Deal." And then I take the hand he offers, and together we walk back to where my friends are waiting.

Chapter Fifteen

Jake

"Do you ever take a day off, Blue? You know, sit back, enjoy, over-indulge?"

"You wouldn't be asking me that if you'd known me even a year ago."

She shifts from one side to the other in her warrior pose (yeah, I know the name of it now), and I do the same. We're in some grassy park area with some other early morning crazies, overlooking the river and stretching after our run. In my head I've come up with ten alternate, and highly appealing, ways to spend a rainy morning with Cora, none of which includes a five mile run followed by douche-worthy stretching in some park. Though, I suppose if this were a scene in a movie, it would probably be a romantic one.

The fog just rising above the water, the lights of the buildings twinkling through the heavy mist, the early morning silence that hasn't yet been interrupted by commuters. I can see it clearly: the onscreen lovers would be talking while they stretched, and then one or both of them would shift just so and they'd come face-to-face and, before the audience knew what was happening, they'd be engaging in some sort of wrestling match that was just a ploy on the hero's part to get the heroine pressed up against him in all of the right places.

A fucking ingenious ploy.

And then they'd kiss and wander back the way they came, none the worse for wear, the intent of their departure clear enough they may as well say to the camera, *Yeah, we started this, now we're going to finish it.*

None of that romance exists here, and that's not just because I'm holding back and waiting for Blue to make the next move. The barge chugging down the river is loud, the mist is thick and consuming, and only half of my attention is on the idiot poses she's leading me through. The other half is on the homeless man sleeping under the bench twenty feet away. He hasn't moved in the almost thirty minutes we've been here since finishing our run, and I can't tell if it's because he's asleep, too cold to move, or dead. I'm watching for any sign of life or movement from him so I don't have to go make sure it isn't the latter before we take off.

The mist has made everything squishy and muddy, so as appealing as my fantasy of throwing Blue to the ground and wrestling with her in her skin tight running pants and Padres ball cap is, if I push her to the ground, playful or not, she's going to take my balls from me. Since I'm rather attached to that portion of my anatomy, I block out those thoughts as much as possible and go back to the conversation I'm trying to carry on with her.

"I'm not talking about drinking and sex — though, if you really think you're missing out on who you used to be, I'll get drunk and let you take advantage of me. Isn't role play part of therapy?"

Her laugh is a little shocked, and I can't help the surge I get every time I get her to give me a real one.

"That's generous of you, but I'll pass, thanks."

"Offer stands, in case you ever need it."

"You're such the giver, Handsome Jake."

This time I grin fast and meet her eyes. "No complaints before. Which is why," I continue before she can retort, "I'm thinking we should go do something fun today. Isn't it one of your days off from work?"

She nods and switches to her next pose, which I follow half-heartedly. The homeless man has moved, so now that I'm not fearing his death, I'm on alert to make sure he doesn't try and bring us to ours. "Then let me take you on an adventure."

She finishes up with the pose that has her standing straight up, eyes and arms to the sky so her body is one long, lean, line, and I'm momentarily struck speechless as I watch her. Something about the way she moves, sexy and efficient and so goddamn confident, has the ability to drain every other thought from my head, leaving me with only one: her. We've been living together for almost two months now, and in that time we've turned several corners.

We're friends, and roommates. We do all of the things normal people living together do, like share the grocery shopping, complain about loss of hot water and who's controlling the TV remote. She prefers to have music on when she's home, I like video games and SportsCenter. She likes fashion magazines, I like books. She likes pop and dance music with a trendy feel, I like old school hip hop, with some outlaw country and new indie rock thrown in to balance it all out.

(Though I did get caught with some classic Brittany Spears on a playlist the other day, and had to handle it while she laughed for over an hour.)

She's been more forthcoming in our relationship as of late, asking questions as well as answering them, and though I haven't asked any more hard ones yet, I know our relationship has progressed. Without being able to explain why, I know she trusts me, as much as she trusts anyone, and because of that I'm craving the next step, a step I know she yearns to take but doesn't because she's afraid. That's the part I'm hung up on, and the part that's making me keep my promise to try and think of her first.

I know she's had relationships in the past, including the ex-husband, and it seems they've jaded her. Jaded I can handle. It's the fear that's holding me back. I don't know why she was in rehab, other than she casually mentions it every now and then, but I suspect that the reason she holds back has more to do with that than her previous relationships. I'm trying to be patient because Ryan's words come back to me every now and then and, whatever Cora's been through, I don't ever want her to be afraid of me. This means I need to step up my game and show her I can be trusted all the way.

"What do you have in mind for this adventure?" she asks, as we walk back toward our apartment.

I swing my arm over her shoulders and smile. "It's a surprise. Dress warm, though, I feel like being outside."

~

I take her to the zoo because it's somewhere new for her too, even though she grew up here. I pause momentarily after we park, suddenly realizing that she might not like the idea of visiting caged animals. When I say this, her brow furrows and she asks why.

"You know, happy animals, happy meat, all of that stuff you talked about the first night I moved in."

She smiles and shakes her head. "I'm not that much of a do-gooder, yet, Handsome Jake. I don't eat meat from abused animals because it's just plain bad for me and I want to be healthy. My conscience doesn't extend too much beyond that. Mia's the natural philanthropist in the family, not me."

I smile and take her hand, leading her to the gate. It's crowded, despite the midweek visit and the misting rain, and for a couple of hours we wander among the throng of people through exhibits, laughing and admiring the animals and reptiles, though she shook like a leaf when we entered a part of Africa and saw the python. If I accidentally sought out some more reptilian habitats after she curled into me and held on for dear life, well, who could blame me?

She makes me pose in front of the warty pigs, and I snap a few photos of her in front of the giraffes. When her fingers are stiff and her hands are like blocks of ice, and even our rain gear isn't working to keep us dry anymore, we call it good and I take her to grab a sandwich at Lardo's. On the way home, she dozes off, her head resting on the seat, her face toward me. I park in my spot and lean back to watch her, wondering how the hell I'm ever going to get over her.

Which is a weird thought to have because I've never had her, but in the few months that I've known her something in me has shifted, changed, become lighter. The anger, the despair, and the grief that I carried around the last six months have lessened, until some days I forget that they were ever there. There's irritation, and plenty of annoyance, but at the end of the day, I walk home to Blue and all I feel is happy, even hopeful. That's a scary fucking thing, but it's also right. I can't explain it any further than that.

We're friends, and she might laugh at me if she ever knew that I value her friendship as much as I value the idea of more. It's the truth, though. Being with Cora shows me exactly what I wanted from my relationship with Lise, and even assumed we had. That's a lie, though, because Lise wasn't in love with me, and though I cared for her, I now know I wasn't in love with her either. Looking at Cora, I won't verbalize what I feel, but there are words floating around in my head, in my heart, that tell me that whatever she is to me, it's more than anyone else has ever been.

When her eyes flutter open, it takes her a moment to orient and in that time I take the step, pushing into her space, the fingers of my left hand tracing her jaw line and her cheek, up into her hair and around to cup her neck. She doesn't pull back, just keeps her eyes wide and steady on mine. When my lips brush hers, once, twice, her fingers dig into the fabric of my shirt and she angles her head just a little. That's all the encouragement I need.

My tongue traces her lips, followed by my teeth and, when she gasps, I take advantage and dip inside her mouth, tracing her tongue with my own, drowning in the flavor that is only Cora. Her hands are in my T-shirt still, gripping it so tightly I'm surprised it doesn't rip. And her lips, Christ, her lips are driving me insane as they slide together with mine. When she sucks my bottom lip into her mouth, I think I might die.

Instead, I fight with her seatbelt until it's off and then my hands streak to her waist and under her shirt until I feel her skin, burning to the touch, as if she's a furnace, ready to combust from the inside. My lips leave her mouth long enough to trail down her neck and to her collarbone, absorbing the flavor of her there. Her breath is shallow and when she grips my hair and yanks, I give in and fuse our mouths back together.

We kiss until we're breathless and our lips are raw. When I pull away, the windows are fogged, but all I can look at is Cora, with her swollen lips and wide eyes, as if she can't believe what we just did. I'm a little shaken myself, the aftershocks coursing through me until I'm mortally afraid I might tremble.

At some point, I pulled her halfway out of her seat so we're pressed together chest to chest, one of my hands at her back, under her shirt, the other gripping a fair amount of her very firm ass. I don't let her go, even when I see the fog clear from her eyes to be replaced with a kind of budding panic. She's not terrified yet, but in about thirty seconds she's going to be. Time to do some damage control.

"You don't regret this."

Her brow wings up and though it wasn't what I had planned on saying, I go with it, much more comfortable with her annoyance than her fear. "Is that right?"

I nod. "That's right. Whatever you're telling yourself is wrong with what we just did, stop."

The eyebrow notches higher. "Keep telling me what to do and *you're* going to regret it."

I remember back to December when we were dancing at the wedding and she was flirting a dangerous line, admitting that she never submits. At this moment, I feel like going head to head with her and showing her I don't either, that I always win when I play and that I have no intention of breaking that streak now.

"We have something here, Blue, you can't deny it."

"Yeah, we do have something here, a friendship and a lease, which is why we need to be smart."

"Smart doesn't mean acting like this was a mistake. We've been headed here since that first night Cora and, now that we've finally made it, I won't back off."

Now she shoves out of my hold and I let her, both of us sitting back in our seats. "I won't be told what to do, Jake, not even by you. I've done that once, and I can't do it again."

I don't let myself get sidetracked by that comment, but I shove it to the back of my brain to ask her about it later. "I'm not telling you what to do, I'm asking you to try. Just try, Blue," I say and stop her denial before it comes. "Did you have fun today?"

She hesitates and I can tell that she's considering lying. Why this makes me more attracted to her is anyone's guess. After a second, she sighs and nods. "Yeah, I did."

"Then let's have more fun, and this time let's kiss while we do it. Kissing makes everything better."

I expect a resounding hell no. In the very least, some knee jerk resistance, but instead all I get is a thoughtful stare. Holding my breath I wait, and after a minute she smiles, and I feel it all the way to my core. "Well, it was a pretty great kiss."

"Please, that was just a warm up. Wait until I hit my stride."

She laughs and I grab her, planting my lips on hers again, holding her against me, knowing, even while she doesn't, that she's mine now and I'm hers.

Chapter Sixteen

Cora

I spend every Monday from ten a.m. to one p.m. giving my mother her weekly salon treatment, just like the one she drove herself to for the last twenty-five years. Only I do it in the home she still shares with my father, the one she's made herself a prisoner inside. She doesn't leave the house anymore, despite the fact that the doctors have said that in moderation, exercise and entertainment are necessary parts of battling back some of the time her disease is trying to steal from her. They say that getting out, as long as it's with someone safe, someone who can help her, is good, but she won't.

According to my father, she stopped leaving the house the day she left it ten months ago and forgot where she was going and why. She ended up at the grocery store, a place she hadn't been in years since our housekeeper has always done all of the shopping, and after an hour spent in the parking lot, sitting in her idling car while she tried to get her bearings, a stranger had knocked on the door and she had to give in and let them help her. That was the first time she acknowledged that what the doctors were telling her was true, and it was the last time she went further than the backyard.

She now lives one hundred percent of her time inside of the

beautiful and sprawling estate that she and my father purchased almost twenty years ago, wandering the halls and the grounds, doing what she calls "correspondence" and verbally sparring with Sassy, her full time caregiver. Sassy is younger than my mother but older than me, with beautiful Italian skin and thick hair that she keeps pulled back off her face. She calls me *Cara* (a name I originally thought was a mispronunciation of my own until she noticed my frown one day and told me it was an Italian term of endearment), chats nonstop during my visits no matter how silent her ward is and ignores my mother's anger, serving her like a longtime friend and patting her on the shoulder after an outburst and exclaiming, "Oh Suzie, go on," an act which has my mother lashing out even more.

The first time I came over almost three months ago, I was horrified at their rapport, but now, as I'm here more regularly, I'm beginning to understand that Sassy, while a stranger to my mother, is also the only person she really engages with, even if it is to snipe at her. I don't think my mother has visitors, not just because she would keep them out, but because she never inspired the kind of loyalty visiting a sick friend would require.

She had acquaintances and allies in her social world, not friends.

Which reminds me of my night out with Liam and A.J., when I realized that other than Mia, I was truly alone when it came to friends and shared memories. Which also then reminds me of the fact that Jake's my friend, in a weird, we kiss like teenagers one minute and laugh like besties the next kind of way. Whatever our relationship is, I can admit in my head that Jake is good for me as I've become increasingly aware over the last eight months or so that I am my mother's daughter, no matter how much I try to ignore it or change it.

Living with Jake is an experience. Whether it's a good or bad experience, I'm still not sure (though, truth be told, there are certain parts of me that are already one hundred percent on board with this experience. They would also like to one hundred percent take it to the next level. I'm ignoring them as best I can). He just makes me jumpy — everything he does, from his questions, to his patience, his absolute awareness of the effect he has on me and his goddamn likeable personality. It's all so much when I've spent the last little while working to make certain that I create a life, and a person, I can be happy with. Maybe even proud of. Someone who isn't dependent on other people to make her feel good.

I called Mia again the other day to talk to her because she knows who I am, who I've been, and what I want, and I needed to talk to someone. Her answer was less helpful than I wanted, as it all boiled down to being careful and trusting myself, and also trusting Jake. That was the point she was stuck on. Whoever Jake was, whatever he was, I could trust him.

And I believe her. I just don't know if I can trust myself.

After our trip to the zoo last week, I don't think it's going to matter though, as he was abundantly clear he won't be backing off anytime soon, and I'd be a liar if I said I wanted him to. So, I took a small piece of Mia's advice and trusted myself, enough that we ended up making out in the rain on our way inside from the car, and then eating tofu stir fry (not his favorite meal, which he was more than happy to say even though he finished twice my portion in half the amount of time) and then watching a movie — which was code for make out and try to get to second base. I blocked him, but not before my clothing was significantly rumpled and my lips more than swollen.

By the time we'd gone to our separate rooms, I had to admit the night had been fun. More than fun, it had been amazing. Even at bedtime, when I expected him to push and come into my room with me, he pushed me up against my door, kissed me like a madman and then stepped back, brushing my arm lightly with his fingers before turning and stepping through his door and closing it behind him.

I want badly to be unaffected by him, to be levelheaded and in control of what we're doing, but since it's obvious that's not the case, I'm treading slowly. Last night he made dinner, and though it was a little on the manly side with French fries and cheeseburgers, he did make concessions that I know were for me. The fries were sweet potato, and the burgers were from an organic meat market that I've never heard of, but he made sure to leave the paper wrapping out so I could inspect it.

We ate while watching *The Voice* and it was really nice.

Now, he's off doing what he does during the day — training, working out, studying — and I'm just finishing up my mother's nails. We haven't spoken in the almost two hours I've been here. Not a word. Sassy let me in, directed me up to "Mrs. Whitley's private room" (the first master, which overlooks the grounds) and then disappeared somewhere. The fact that I wanted to chase after her when she walked out shows me that no matter how strong I think I am, there are still things that scare me.

After my initial panic at the thought of being alone with my mother subsided, I went in and set up as I normally did. My mother walked in looking smaller and thinner than normal in a pale blue bathrobe that she kept tied tightly around her, gripping the collar at her neck every now and then while I was foiling her hair.

Now, her foils are off, her hair freshly washed and dried with curlers sitting in it, and I'm almost done with her last coat of polish, a pale pink, barely discernable from her original nail color. I don't even have to ask when I start — it's the color she's always worn, as light as one goes on the color spectrum while my almost-black is full throttle the other way, just like we've always been.

I can hear small echoes from downstairs and outside, the closing of a door, the starting of a lawnmower somewhere far off. I swipe the brush over her nail, staring at just below her freshly trimmed cuticles and making one perfect sweep before raising the brush off her nail and doing it again until the whole nail is covered. She's watching me paint, her eyes never lifting, her hands never moving. If I didn't know she was human, I would think I was practicing on a mannequin.

The silence between us is endless, and without our usual buffer of Sassy, it's stifling and when I feel myself retreating, thinking of that familiar pull that comes with people — a bar, a club, a bedroom — my hands shake and I can't bear it a second longer.

"I used to want to be like you. When I was little. I would watch the ladies who came in to get you ready for an event, the way they would pamper you while you sat there, approving of things with a small nod of your head, discouraging others with just a raise of your brow. I would sit on the floor by this very vanity and think, *that's what I want when I grow up*, to have people pamper me."

I don't know where the words come from, but I do know that speaking is better than focusing on the familiar feeling of sinking, and that somehow the words I didn't even know I needed to say are keeping me from standing and walking out and making a choice I know I don't want to make, so I let them come and hope I'm strong enough to deal with them in the end.

"You were so strong the way you went after things, never taking less than what you expected, never backing down." I switch hands, not looking at her as I study the delicate fingers in mine, so small, fragile even, as if they belonged to a small child instead of a woman. "I remember being little and watching you and Daddy go out, watching the way he would look at you and I thought, *I want someone to look at me like that one day, I want them to love me like he loves her.* He used to light up when you walked into a room; everything in him changed, I swear, as if the sight of you gave his heart a reason to beat. But after a while, it didn't matter how much his smile was for you, because you could barely see it with everything else you focused on. I think maybe that's why I never bothered telling you — you didn't hear him when he said it, didn't see him when he showed it, and you never gave the words back to him. Ever."

My hand trembles slightly and I set hers down, putting the brush back into its polish and twisting it closed, never meeting her eyes, the pressure in my chest forcing the words out. "I was sixteen the first time you called me a whore. I don't remember what I did to make you mad, but I'm sure it was on purpose. It seems like everything I did was to make you mad — or maybe it was just to make you notice me. Either way, I can't remember what it was, but I remember you slapping me as I stood there, and then you told me I deserved to be lonely, that I was nothing but a disrespectful, spiteful, hateful daughter who had caused you pain your entire life. Maybe that was the day I realized love wasn't enough, especially when the one person you wanted to love you told you that you were nothing like she wanted you to be."

I stare at her fingers, focusing on those hands that had once struck me after I sassed her, the same ones that had once balled into fists and pounded the chest of my father as he soothed her during a tantrum. Now they do nothing, give no reaction, and that's worse.

When I finally look up, she's staring at me with those vacant eyes, still perfectly lined and lashed, the shadow I blended on the lids only moments ago standing out, highlighting the blue/green eye color that we share. But as I look back, I only see the glitter on the outside and the emptiness on the in; I only see what I physically put there myself and I wonder if I'm going to look in the mirror one day and see that empty hole that she's retreated into, or if I'll grow out instead of shrink in.

A few years ago, Mia told me she was watching her mother disappear. Aunt Margaret was growing smaller with every harsh word, missed dinner, and cold shoulder her husband gave her. Thinking of that I wonder if my mother's eyes are vacant because of me; was it my cold shoulder, my desire to shock her, my need to replace her and be anything but her that caused her to become so small? Or was it her desire to change me, ignore me, be better than me?

Did I ruin my mother, or did our inability to grow outside of ourselves cause both of us to shrink into the people we are now? Did we ruin ourselves, or did we somehow do this to each other?

That question haunts me as I pack up my tools and leave, it stays with me even through my workout. My mother never answered me, never spoke, and I wonder if she ever will again. I'm still wondering when Jake gets home and comes to sit next to me on the couch. I know I should have been in my room, gone for a walk, been anywhere but here when he arrived because the mood I'm in isn't a healthy one, or a nice one. After an afternoon of feeling shitty over something I can't quite explain, I want to draw blood from someone else, just to see if I can.

He leans in to kiss me, but stops when I lean back.

He raises a brow. "Problem?"

Too many to name, let alone understand. "I think Ryan plays in Corvallis soon. I was going to go down, meet Mia there and hang for a while. I didn't know if you wanted to come and watch him."

I see the blow hit him, and though I want to reach out and make contact, I don't. The non-conversation with my mother has left me raw and annoyed, angry at Jake and everything he stands for. Suddenly, I need very much to see if he's human, if he can bleed like I can.

"I understand if you don't want to see your teammates, since you aren't playing anymore."

Direct hit. I see his eyes darken, his body tense as he shifts away, but rather than the relief I was hoping for, guilt settles like a nasty ball low in my stomach. I block it and watch him, seeing the expression in his eyes that was lacking in my mother's as I spoke to her, the pain, the irritation and the wonder. But he doesn't slap back, and though a part of me is disappointed, I stay still and stare at him.

After a moment, he nods. "Yeah, I know when the game is, so why don't I call and get us tickets that are better than general admission? You can talk to the team afterward."

I nod, my mood shifting as rapidly to worry as it did to anger. I know I'm on dangerous ground here, getting ready to spiral. My counselors warned us about this, the emotional upheaval that can come from any event, big or small, and shake our whole foundation no matter how long you've been clean. I can see mine coming, but I can't seem to stop it.

"Do you think you'll go back and try?" I ask and he stares out the window blankly for a second. "Do you think it will be the same?"

"I don't know," he finally answers and stands to grab a beer from the fridge. I follow him and lean against the opposite counter, watching as he takes a long gulp. "The doc says I'm healing, and though I still can't imagine that I'll ever be back to where I was, I feel better today than I did last week, and every day I hold a baseball it feels more and more like it's supposed to be in my hand."

"And then what? When you recover? Do you try out somewhere, do you enter the draft?"

"My agent seems to think if I can prove my speed's still the same, and if I'm ready by draft time, I'll be picked up. If not, it's free agent and open try outs."

"And if those go well, and you make it, what next?"

"I pray to God my arm keeps up and I work to survive."

I frown. "It's not war, it's just baseball."

His laugh is sarcastic, and more than a little defeated. "The minors are their own kind of war, Blue. Minimal pay and long bus rides, bad food and hundreds of kids chasing the same dream that reality has told them can only be given to a select few, if not less. The majors aren't a reality, not for anybody, and when you've given it your shot and failed, you have to face coming home and trying to be someone else after over a decade of only knowing one thing. You have to learn to integrate into society as a human, not a ball player, and you have to do it while knowing you've already failed once, while facing the people around you who know the same thing."

He takes a long pull from his beer. I watch his throat work as he swallows, and I wonder somehow if he's swallowing the bitterness that firsthand experience with this kind of disappointment can bring. "It's a heavy thing for a man to come home with a shattered dream and no fucking idea how to find another one."

I think about my mother and whether or not she ever had a dream, a desire for something more than being the most popular, the prettiest, the most desired. And then I realize that in my own way that's where my dream was headed. All I wanted was to be someone everyone else knew and loved, someone who proved her wrong.

"What's going on, Blue? Why the questions tonight?"

I shrug, unwilling to explain, searching for the anger I felt earlier as I try to climb out of the despair that's surrounding me now. "Isn't that the game we play? Ask each other things so we can find out each other's weaknesses?"

"No, it's not, and it never has been. Why are you doing this?"

His jaw is tense like his words, and I feel my own shoulders tighten. He's done nothing wrong, nothing but offer me friendship and the beginning of a relationship that's sweeter and more real than anything I've ever had, and here I am, trying to cut him down because I can't seem to matter to anyone else in my life. I'm testing him, like I tested my mother today, only he calls me on it, clearly more affected by me than she ever was or will be.

"Never mind. I shouldn't have asked." I go to stand and leave but his words stop me.

"Who are you, Blue?"

He's still standing on the other side of the kitchen, but I feel his words as if he's right next to me.

"Nobody," I say calmly and watch the fire inside of him that he's been holding back all night ignite.

"Bullshit." His words whip out even though his stance stays the same. "That's a cop out, Cora, because you're too afraid to answer. You started this tonight, so let's do it. You wanted to know me? Wanted to see if I was real, was that it? See if you could make me hurt?

Well, you can. Now it's my turn. Who are you?"

I *hate* that, hate that he can see what I'm thinking when I feel like I barely know him, hate that he doesn't always have to ask to understand me. Even more, I hate that he isn't afraid to ask questions or say things that most people would never be comfortable verbalizing.

When I don't respond, he sets his beer down on the counter and steps toward me. "Let's try a different one. Why were you in rehab?"

"Lots of reasons."

My gaze is direct, my eyes shooting fire, my lips tight as I stand stock still, limiting my response to him. I know he won't let me go, but I also know that he expects a reaction, that he's working for one, just like I was.

"Name one."

"No."

"Are you an alcoholic, Blue?"

I laugh bitterly. "Sure."

"What does that mean?"

"That abusing alcohol was only one of my many flaws. Not all rehab is for alcohol, Jake, some of it's for addiction, some of it's for abuse, some of it's just because you need therapy."

"What was yours for?"

I'm used to his brashness, his inability to understand boundaries or just plain ignorance when it comes to personal space and feelings. If Jake wants the answer to something, he's not going to sneak around, he's going to ask the question, even if that question is hard. It's something I admire about him, not that I'll ever tell him that, especially now when I'm trying to avoid answering the question he's asked.

"That's personal."

"So's this," he says before I can move past him.

Chapter Seventeen

Jake

I knew the minute I walked in that she was in a mood and, when she started asking questions, it became clear just what kind. Something happened to Cora today and she's out for blood, out to prove that I'm just another person she can shrug off, out to hurt me and see if I'll walk away. Well, fuck that.

She can scrape me raw and I'll take it, but I'll also get what I want while she's doing it because no matter how much I've had to walk away from in the past year, the thought of walking away from her, from this, threatens to end me so I refuse to acknowledge it as a possibility. She took her gloves off and threw the first punch; I don't know what's worse, the fact that she did it or that she expected me to just take it without fighting back. Either way, I'm not backing down because whatever she thinks, I'm not like the other people in her life who have always let her run away — I'm sick of having my feelings thrown in my face, and now's as good a time as any to show her exactly who she's dealing with.

I cup her shoulders in my hands and she stiffens. We're still in the kitchen, but I've blocked her path so she's forced to look at me. When she does, her eyes are as devastated as they are angry. "I don't want to be touched right now."

I ignore her and feel a perverse sense of satisfaction when she tries to struggle away. I've never once in my life used physical force with a woman, but something about this moment makes me want to prove to her that I'm stronger, and I'm not leaving, no matter what she does.

"Blue, did someone hurt you?" The words stick in my throat and even the thought of what they mean brings bile to my throat. So help me God, if she says yes, I won't stop until I find out who it was, and when I do there's nowhere he can go where he'll be safe.

Her sigh is resigned — a purposefully bored sound, calculated to make me back off at the same time that it cuts me down and makes me feel like a nuisance. I ignore her, staring until she rolls her eyes.

"Let me save you the time and ask the rest of the questions you have lined up in your head so you don't have to: Why did I choose alcohol and then men? What is my relationship with father like? What is my relationship with my mother like? What are my friends like? My ex-husband? Are they the reason I chose alcohol?"

She's trying to be tough, throwing questions at me and challenging me to keep going. As much as I want to stop, to just bring her close and hold her, I won't, because I have a need to see this through, not for her or for me but for us. Somewhere deep down I think she knows that.

"Well?" I say and her eyes slit.

"Not all abuse is physical, Jake, and it's not always from someone else. I abused me," she says before I can ask what she means.

"I didn't care what I did with my life, or who I used or let use me along the way. I gave out my body like it was a piece of birthday cake and I drank until it was easy to believe everything I did felt good. Did I walk around drinking in the middle of the day, dependent on the substance to wake up and function? No, because my dependence wasn't on alcohol, it was on men."

Godfuckingdammit.

I want to rage, to yell and break something. I also want to bring her close and apologize for asking, for making her go through this, but I know we aren't done. I hate the thought of Cora and other guys — not because I expected her to be sitting quietly on the sidelines of her life waiting for me to come along, but because I expected her to want better for herself. She's telling me that she let other men have her because it was easier than living in the real world with her problems, and that's not fucking okay.

"Did they hurt you? Did someone hurt you?" I ask again and she shakes her head.

"No more than I hurt them." Her voice is no longer biting and strong, it's dull, weak, sad. "If you're asking was I forced, then no, never was I forced, never was I drugged, never was I young and innocent and naïve and taken advantage of. My choices were — *are* — all my own. I chose men because I realized at a young age they were the one thing I could easily have that my mother couldn't, and it made me happy to know that I had something she envied rather than just despised."

I don't know who's more shocked by the words, her or me, but it feels like even the air is still as the last sentiments from what she said echo around us.

I'm barely breathing as she stares at me, her eyes no longer challenging, though I don't think she knows that. Somewhere in that last twenty seconds she went from bold to sad, heartbreakingly sad, and even though I'm holding onto her, I know she's not with me. Her ghosts have her now and she's succumbing to them, falling further and further away from me.

Suddenly, I realize just how far I've pushed her. In my quest to know her, to have her, to challenge her to be honest and to keep her until she's healed me, I've pushed her here, to this place filled with demons and ghosts and memories that make her regret. Because I need to know her, all of her, because what I want from her is a hell of a lot more than what she's ever had with or given to anyone else. Or at least I tell myself that's the reason.

But really, right now as I stand here holding her and watching her, I know the real reason I've pushed her to open herself up and show me some piece of who she is without the mask is because I need her, and I want her to need me too. Whatever it is about her that saves me, makes me forget everything I left behind, everything I've lost until all I can think about is what I might still get to have, I can't let it go.

Even now, as I hurt her to get it.

I struggle to rein it in, to bring myself under control and think of her for a minute, to put aside my mounting desire not just for her, but for everything she is, and think of what my need is doing to her.

"Cora, are you okay?"

It's a fucking stupid question because even if she was a stranger I could see that she's not okay. My hands tighten on her shoulders for an instant and she doesn't move. Her eyes are devastated and I know she's battling not to lose it, not to let go in front of me. Another pain stabs me as I realize that she trusts me enough to kiss me, to possibly go to bed with me, but she doesn't trust me enough to hold onto me, and I don't blame her.

"I'm sorry I asked, sorry I pushed." I release her shoulders to take her hands and bring them to my mouth, pressing my lips to them not because I want to persuade her, but because I need to soothe her, make a connection, let her feel me and know I'm here. To let her know that I can be gentle and thoughtful, not just selfish and demanding.

Whether it's because of my contact or because of her strength, she comes back, her hands flexing once in my grip before her shoulders straighten and her eyes find mine. They're blazing, like a swirling, tumultuous ocean right before the storm swallows its sailors whole. She might have saved me from drowning a few months ago, but I think right now my siren would like nothing more than to watch me be dragged off land and thrown into the cold abyss.

I try one last time. "Blue — Cora."

She shakes her head and takes her hands back, pushing away from me as she steps slowly over and away. I see the effort it takes, the sheer willpower she uses to bring herself fully upright, with her shoulders straight and her head high. She stripped herself bare and I let her. Worse, I didn't really give her a choice because I wanted to prove that I was in control.

"You might not know it Jake, but sometimes giving up who you always thought you wanted to be is safer than staying on that path of destruction, the one that you know deep down is going to be one heartache after another. Even if it feels like failing to let everyone know they were right about you, that you weren't enough. Sometimes, you just have to fucking start over."

She walks away and I let her because at the moment I'm the weakest kind of man there is. I'm the one who needs more from someone than I even have to give them. I have nothing for her, and yet, all I want to do is ask her to be with me, to help me, to make me feel like a person again, not a shell, not a hollowed out, useless shell who has nothing for anyone.

The feelings of inadequacy and helplessness are overpowering, and I want to pound my fists into something, to someone, almost as much as I want to go find Cora and grab onto her and hold her, to tell her that whatever she thinks of herself, she's wrong. To tell her that I'm an asshole and I'm sorry.

I know what she was doing with that story — she was warning me, telling me that she's someone I don't want, someone damaged and worthless. But she's wrong. Just as she was wrong to think I'd walk away when she admitted that there've been others. I don't fucking care whose been here before, though I'd like to find her fucking ex-husband and the rest of the bastards she let into her bed and beat them faceless because the idea of them ignites a blazing fire in my blood, one that wants to wreak havoc on anyone and everyone whose ever hurt her.

Including myself.

That thought deflates me and my anger dissipates as quickly as it came. I stare at the closed door to the room she just walked into and wonder if I'm just another person on her list who's never been there for her.

Am I someone who's using her, or can I find something inside of me to show her just how much I want to give her, even if it's a long shot?

Chapter Eighteen

Cora

Every now and then I think back to my childhood and realize that things which appeared so black and white at the time aren't quite as simple. I always hated my mother's friends — the ladies with the perfectly tailored suits, or the ones with the outrageously expensive clothes that were cut too high or too low for someone their age. Then I realized that my mother didn't really have friends, just small groups that she associated with depending on her mood and theirs.

When my mother wanted to feel like a part of the elite, she associated with women from old money — the women whose husbands or families had founded a piece of the city, whose names were on buildings and streets. Those women who dressed in blazers and pumps and drove their Mercedes sedans to luncheons and committees and city council meetings.

And then there were the times she wanted to feel young, to feel wild and free and beautiful. It was then that she sought out her younger friends — the ones who had snagged a big fish or come into money recently. The ones who spent their days tooling around in Audi convertibles or Mercedes SUVs, hopping from a session with their personal trainer to a massage, followed by salon appointments and manicure sessions. Each day was rounded off with a trip to the local hotspot to pick at a salad and start happy hour.

These two groups ran my mother's life until she got sick and dropped off the proverbial social map. Now, my mother has no visitors, which is why I'm currently walking up to knock on her front door and see her on a day that is not Monday. I'm here to try and be her friend, whatever that means.

After my argument with Jake the other night, Mia texted me. I still think he somehow made that happen, but since I've stopped talking to him, I can't quite be sure. I didn't answer her call because I wasn't ready to hear her voice, knowing if I did I would break. Instead, she accepted that unwritten boundary and we texted, and when I told her enough of what had happened, from my day with my mother to my hurtful comments to Jake later on, to Jake's reaction and subsequent questions, she told me the one thing I know is true: we push people away because we fear that they're eventually going to leave, and we want to be the ones to take a stand and step away first.

I know Mia understands this, has even lived it to a point, just as I know part of the reason she told me was because of my relationship with Jake, and the other part was to remind me of my relationship with my mother. She's pushed me away her whole life, just like I've done the same to her. Mia's comment made me realize that it's the same fear inside both of us that's causing us to push.

Taking that new knowledge, I'm at my mother's taking the first step.

No one checks on my mother if there isn't a purpose — not

Sassy, not my father, not me. Sassy loves her, I can tell in the easy way she deals with her, the absolute care she takes making sure my mother gets proper nutrition and exercise, both mental and physical, but it's also her job. My father sits and talks with her every night, sometimes reading to her, sometimes brushing her hair or just holding her, as if she's become his child and not his lover. And me... I do her hair, her nails, give her back the beauty that's always been so important. Three days ago I tried to give her back some memories, but like usual I ruined it because I was more concerned about my feelings than hers.

Not today, though. Today, I've decided to drop by just to be social, to talk to her and let her know that I want to be with her, not because she needs something or because I do, just *because*. I failed last time because I made it about the past. Now, I realize I need to make our relationship about what it can be, not what it once was or wasn't. I have zero idea what step this translates into in therapeutic terms, but it's one I know I need to conquer if I'm going to continue moving forward.

The housekeeper who answers the door is new, because when my mother got sick she asked my father to get all new staff, people who wouldn't know who she had been and be sad every time she forgot something they didn't. I smile when the woman remembers me from earlier in the week, thanking her when she points me in the direction of my mother's rooms.

"Miss Sassy is out doing some shopping since it's her afternoon off. Mr. Whitley will be home shortly. Would you like to stay for dinner?"

I shake my head no, thanking her as I head up the stairs and into my mother's rooms. When I step inside, I don't see her, but I can hear someone in the closet, so I walk across the large space to the French doors and peek through them. She's in there, wearing a bustier that's become too large for her bony frame, and a garter belt already hooked to a pair of sheer stockings. Her hair is falling out of rollers she must have tried to put in herself, her face is pale and unmade, and she's racing around tearing clothing from hangers before holding it up, muttering something and throwing it to the ground before moving on. Her movements are hurried, panicked, and her mutters are growing increasingly louder as she rejects silk pant suits, dresses, blouses, skirts.

When her eyes fix on me, I'm paralyzed, immobile as I struggle to comprehend the woman in front of me. Before I can stutter out an excuse and leave, she snatches her tattered and over-worn blue robe up and marches across the plush carpet toward me.

"Finally. I've been waiting for you for over an hour." She sweeps by me, out of the closet and I stay where I am, watching her head toward her vanity, shocked at the vision in front of me that looks and sounds so much like I remember. Her eyes meet mine in the mirror and she snaps again. "Well? Where are your tools? Don't tell me you forgot. Never mind, you can use mine. I don't have time to wait while you go and get yours."

My legs feel numb as I walk over and stand behind her, taking the brush and curling iron that she's motioned to. She doesn't recognize me. I've never seen my mother have an episode, though I've read extensively on them, scoured the Internet and the Alzheimer's and dementia website for any information they could offer. The reality is that no one understands what triggers specific memory lapses, aggressive behaviors or black moments. The time of day, environment and physical discomfort are all things that can be a factor, but not always. Right now, I have no idea where my mother is or what she needs, so rather than ask her, I grab the curling iron and wind it through a strand of loose hair, uncurling the haphazard rollers with my free hand. For a few minutes, I unroll and twist, gaining a rhythm that's familiar while my mother sits with a straight back and talks non-stop about what she needs me to do to get her ready for her benefit tonight.

A benefit to aide children in public schools in the greater Portland area, who were victims of budget cuts, raising money to keep music programs alive. A benefit that she headed almost seven years ago, when I was fifteen and still subject to her whims. I attended, but ended up getting drunk and making out with a member of the wait staff in the coat closet. He got fired and I got slapped by my mother before she dissolved into a fit of tears and had to be carried away by my father.

I got myself home later, but the details of how are a little fuzzy.

I listen to her ramble for almost ten minutes without saying anything, and when her hair is done, I move to her vanity to hand her the mirror as I would any client and let her admire it from every angle. She nods her approval, and I shift to her vanity to search through her cosmetics and begin on her face. I've rubbed on foundation and eye highlighter, curled her lashes and I'm lining her eyes with a charcoal pencil that will surely look too heavy with her thin face when my father walks in.

I see him stop, his eyes wide, and then his face is happy, as if what he's seeing is normal. Before I can think of how to warn him, he says my name and I feel the world tilt under us all.

"Cora?" my mother repeats. Only this time, her voice isn't the authoritative, fundraising queen that it was a moment ago, it's smaller, unsure, and I know that we've somehow failed. That I've somehow failed. "James, where's your tux? We have to go soon."

My mother stands, but I can see her hands clenching at the neck of her robe — the dingy, threadbare robe that's been her security blanket these past months and looks almost as worn as she does under the make-up. She looks to me and then my father, whose eyes are sad as he walks toward her.

"Suze," he says and I hear it in his voice, the pain, the sadness. The fucking heartache.

She steps out of his reach when he gets close enough, her hands still clenched at the throat of her robe, only now they're clenching and unclenching. Her face that had been flushed with irritation only moments earlier is now pale with fear and grief. Jesus, the grief coming off all of us is so heavy I feel like I can reach out and touch it.

"No," she says but he doesn't move.

"Suze," he tries again, but she's shaking her head, the curls I put there springing back and forth.

And then she's falling into his arms and her sobs are echoing around us. My dad gathers her close, stroking her hair and murmuring to her in a gesture so familiar it could be anytime from the former years. She's sobbing and clinging, he's holding onto her, always holding her up, and when his eyes meet mine over her head, they're filled with helplessness. Instinct has me reaching out to lay a hand on her back, saying her name as I do.

"Mom."

Wrong. Fucking. Move.

When I look back, I'm sure I'll see that the anger would have come no matter what, that I'll remember that aggression is common in Alzheimer patients, but right now, when she whips around to glare at me, all I can see is hate.

"Don't touch me. Don't you dare touch me, you who comes into my home uninvited and unwanted. Why, so you can laugh? So you can remind me of what I'm not? So you can rub my face in the fact that I'm crazy?"

I'm so stunned I can't speak for a second, and when I do, it comes out in a stuttered rush. "No, no, of course not. I would never laugh at you — I just want to help."

"Well you can't," she screeches, her voice cracking and her breath heaving. "No one can. Oh, God, no one can. Leave."

"Mom," I start and she whirls to me again, her hand raised as if to strike. We both stand there, neither of us moving, and I can see the memory in her eyes, and the fear, though I wouldn't have blamed her for doing it. She trembles, once, twice, her body giving in and crumpling before my father sweeps her up and cradles her.

"Go away, goddammit. I don't want you here. I don't want anyone here."

I look to my father but he's not looking at me, he's only looking at her as he walks her toward the bed, pulling back the covers and laying her down before he lays with her, wrapping her close and holding her. He murmurs more words, never even glancing in my direction, and it's worse than the physical blow my mother wanted to deliver, this ability he has to shut me out.

I'm on the outside looking in and, even though it shouldn't, it hurts that neither of them acknowledge me, not even him to tell me that it's not my fault. It's childish and still, I can't help but wish he could have at least looked at me and shown me that he understands why I came, why I tried to make her happy. But he doesn't, not because he doesn't care, but because he doesn't think about it, or about me. He never really has, and though I don't want to blame him for it, I do. Goddammit, I do, and somehow that makes me feel even guiltier.

Wiping my cheeks, I take a deep breath before I do what she wants and I walk away.

~

I know going home isn't really a good idea, not in my condition, so I park near the salon and try window-shopping. When nothing catches my eye, I walk along the river and stare at the few boats brave enough to be out in this weather. I watch the little kids run and splash in their colorful boots and jackets, and the runners who ignore everything as they push themselves to go faster and farther. I could go again, scrounge up some gear from my car and run out whatever it is I'm feeling, push it all down until my lungs are burning and my brain is too tired to think of anything but my aching muscles.

I could call Mia again, tell her what happened. I know she'd talk me through it, as would my sponsor, Kari. Really, I should go and find a meeting, listen to people share and lose myself in the comfort of those who are like me — weak, and trying to be better. Anything that will take my mind off things and help me cool down, so that when I do go home I'm in control. Especially since Jake and I haven't really spoken in the three days, not since I tried pushing him away and he pushed back.

It's definitely smarter to avoid him and anymore emotional warfare until I get myself under control.

Even as I think these things I find myself rounding the corner to our building, pressing through the front door and swinging toward the stairs and taking them two at a time. I key in the door and fling it open, my breath heaving, my brain just registering that I walked ten blocks through the rain and am now dripping wet as I stand in our door frame, staring at Jake as he clacks away at his controller, playing some fucking video game that's all about annihilating people.

Letting the door slam shut with a crack of wood, I stand where I am, adrenaline pumping through my blood and causing my skin to hum while I wait for Jake to turn and look at me. He does, and I see that stupid headset attached to his ear that tells me he's playing his game against some other Internet nerd and talking shit.

For a second, I put aside my need for combat and look at him with sheer curiosity. As sexy as this man is, he's also a closet dork. The

English major, poetry reading, video game playing, cat owner. It's a good thing he has abs and a face to die for, otherwise, he'd definitely still be carting around his v-card.

As that thought passes through, it's immediately replaced by another one that's infinitely more appealing than continuing to sink in the overwhelming feelings of self-disgust and failure and — goddammit — hurt. I'm hurt and I have no right to be — if anything, I'm to blame. I spent the first half of my life wondering why I was never good enough for her, and the rest I've spent doing things to shock and hurt her, to garner some sort of reaction from her to remind her that I'm alive. Now that she's forgetting, I'm more terrified than ever because I've finally recognized that I want a relationship, that I'm ready to work for a relationship, one it appears we'll never have because she's too sick and I'm too scared.

I can feel the familiar pull of a party tugging at me, beckoning me to those dark waters where I can float in a mindless and numbing place of blurred faces and loud where I don't really feel anything. Scared, I push those thoughts aside and square my shoulders.

I just need to change my focus and, looking in front of me, I have a target. I eye Jake and embrace the zip of desire that courses through me and breaks up the ice, smiling at him even as a warning bell goes off in my head telling me that I'm making a mistake, that doing this won't solve anything, it will only be worse when I'm done.

I ignore it because, for the first time in a while, I feel like being reckless, and beyond that I just feel like *feeling*. Anything, everything, something other than disappointment, hurt, fear.

And I don't want to think. That's the kicker, the part my brain knows is wrong, the part I'm ignoring. Right or wrong, I need to feel wanted, desired, not like a burden, and I know just who can give me what I need.

Taking the zipper of my jacket in my hand, I lower it slowly, allowing the teeth to scrape and release one at a time, the sound echoing in the all but silent apartment.

Jake is like a stone on the couch, his gaze trained on me, completely silent. His fingers are still and I'm pretty sure the screen is telling him his player's a goner. We haven't really talked in three days, not since I walked away from him. We've played the run around game and I'm done. Done waiting, done pushing him away, done trying to be different. I want what he can give me, and I know he wants what I can give him. That's enough for now. It has to be.

My eyes on his, I release the zipper all of the way and let the jacket fall off my shoulders and slip to the ground in a wet heap. I take a step toward him, tugging off my half-calf Frye boots and setting them a few feet from my coat. I'm wearing a black shift dress, the standard color for work. It has no buttons or zippers, just falls in a straight line to mid-thigh after clinging to all the right places.

I reach for it as I step in front of him, crossing my arms in front of me and grabbing the hem, tugging it up and over my head in one swift move until it falls to the floor and I'm left standing there in nothing more than two lacy black scraps of material and my fading tan.

His chest is rising and falling, the harsh sound of his breathing mixing with the partially muted sounds of gunshots and explosions. I take those last steps as if I'm walking through water, slow and tantalizing, letting him take in the view. Leaning forward, I smile when he stops breathing altogether, his body flinching when I reach out and take the headset off, tossing it aside. I do the same with his controller, letting my body fill his vision, letting him see everything.

"Blue," he croaks out and I smile, sliding over him, straddling him so I'm balanced with my knees on either side of his hips, my center pressed to his, our chests brushing.

His hands come to my hips and I arch into him, bringing a breath from both of us. I avoid his eyes as I lean forward, my lips going to his neck, his ear, under his jaw. He's tense beneath me, unresponsive, and though I lean back and quirk a brow, my whole body feels a chill.

"Something wrong?" I lean down to bring him closer, but he leans back, holding me in place with his hands rather than bringing me nearer.

"What are you doing, Cora?"

My pulse spikes at the sound of his voice saying my name, still breathy, but something else lurks beneath it, something like worry. I force my stiff lips into a smile and sweep a look at him under my lashes.

"I would have thought someone as experienced as you would be able to figure that out, Handsome Jake."

I run my hands up the front of the Carhartt T-shirt that he's layered over a gray long sleeve and try to ignore the cold that's seeping back into me, making my movements stiff. "Don't you see anything you like?"

His hands catch mine before they can wrap around his neck. "Look at me, Cora."

My body trembles once, but it's not a shiver of desire like I wish it was. Something else is happening inside of me, something else like panic is growing and making me shake. I ignore his request, rolling my eyes and feigning indifference while I sit back and prepare to get up.

"Well, I have to say with everything I've heard and seen, I expected better. That's okay, big guy, no hard feelings."

The words are bitter in my mouth and my skin is clammy with cold and fear; the feeling of rejection is so harsh I want to run away. Instead, I stretch lazily, arching my back even as he still holds my hands and, avoiding his eyes, I go to pull away and stand.

He holds me in place, refusing to let me go when I try. "Look at me, Cora."

His voice is soft, lethally so, and the weight inside of me gets heavier. "Don't worry about it, Handsome Jake, I can find entertainment with someone else. I know it can be a lot of pressure."

Before the words are even out, I'm being shifted, rolled, my back hitting the couch before his body covers mine and presses into it fully. I have no time to think, to protect myself against the feelings that sweep through me and then he has my hands in his again, pressed to the couch above my head as his eyes bore holes into mine.

"Did you really think I'd let you do this?"

His voice is low, strained, like he's physically in pain as he grinds out the words. I don't answer, can't, really, as my body is at war with my head. I want to break down and curl around him, into him, to let him hold me and tell me that I'm not a failure, that it's not my fault, that I didn't push her to this point.

I want him to tell me he cares about me, that he feels something for me. That I matter. I want him to tell me everything I can't tell myself, and I want to believe him.

When I don't answer, he leans even closer, our lips inches from touching, his brown eyes almost black with emotion as they rake over every feature of my face. "I won't be someone disposable you use to make problems go away, and I won't be someone else who uses you. I want you, Blue," he says and my body freezes. "But I want it all, not just a portion. Do you hear me, Cora? I won't let you use my feelings against me because you're hurting and too fucking afraid to tell me why."

And then his weight is gone and he's pushing off the couch, leaving me bare and alone as he walks away. A second later, I hear the front door open and close and I stay where I am in the quiet of the apartment, my body rigid and cold as I lay where he left me.

One minute, two, I keep laying there, the silence deafening around me, my breath catching, my heart speeding up until I curl onto my side and bring my knees to my chest so I can keep the ache from spreading, keep myself from falling down into the darkness that will shatter my already brittle bones.

He cares about me; it's obvious in what he said and what he didn't let me do. What's not obvious is why that fact makes me want to prove to him I'm not worth it.

Chapter Nineteen

Jake

I left the apartment two hours ago and I've been walking in the rain since then. I wanted to stay, to hold Blue (or shake her) and force her to tell me what was wrong. But I didn't, because as much as I wanted her to tell me what was wrong, I also wanted to take what she was offering and bury myself inside of her until neither of us could think.

Sue me, I'm not a fucking saint.

It's been three days since she tried to push me to the edge before walking out on me, and in that time we haven't said more than a few words to each other, though I've thought of nothing but her and how to make things right. Then, suddenly she's there and I almost forgot how to breathe when I saw her grab the hem of her dress and peel it off, revealing all of that smooth, flawless skin, those gentle curves, and long, lean legs. The black lace that cupped her gorgeous breasts had the saliva evaporating in my mouth and everything in me going to iron.

I wanted nothing more than to yank her under me and plunder her until both of us forgot the pain that seemed to sneak up and take our lives away from us. And I almost did, was getting ready to, until I noticed how rigidly she was holding herself as she slid into my lap, how distant her expression was. How lost she looked.

My siren was breaking, and I wasn't about to let her use what I want from her as a way to shelter herself from reality. *I* want to be real to her, and in order to get what I want, she's going to have to let me in. Since the last time I pushed her only made things worse, I walked away this time, hoping that distance would help both of us come to terms with exactly what we want from each other.

But tonight isn't the night for that, it's not the night to push her or force her to give me the connection I'm looking for, so instead of slamming back into the house and demanding answers, I've walked in this godforsaken rain until I cooled down, and I'm now walking home with a go-cup of soup and some grainy bread from the organic café she loves so much on Broadway.

I don't know if it's a bribe, a peace offering, or an *I'm sorry*, but I needed to do something for her, to show her in any way that I can that I want her to be happy, safe, and not suffering under the weight of her demons before she's mine. I know she'll be mine at some point, but even wanting her as much as I do, I need her to be whole when she is. I can't risk taking her until then.

The only thought worse than never having Cora is having half of her.

She's at the desk that sits in front of the window and faces the main street when I walk in, which surprises me a little. I thought she'd be hiding out in her room again, and was fully prepared to go and beg her to listen to my apology. Since my plan has already taken a turn, I stand where I am, holding the brown paper bag with her food in it and staring at her, wondering what to do now. Her laptop is open and running, and it looks like she's reading some sort of online article. She stops to look at me and I'm relieved that her face is calm, clear, and not a mess from tears. And then I wonder if Blue's ever let herself cry.

She's always walking away, shutting down, closing herself off. My understanding (albeit from Google because isn't that where most of our curiosity is quenched?) is that she does that to maintain control — that her past of reckless behavior and impulsive reactions is something she's battling still, and she does it by maintaining this kind of ruthless control. A lot of addicts end up walking away — it keeps them from relapsing (it also keeps them from committing, according to Wikipedia, but I'm trying to ignore that). Any weakness Blue has she covers up, until tonight, and still, she was only giving a response that would cover up the real emotions running through her.

"I brought you some dinner," I tell her because I can't stand here staring at her another minute. "Some vegetable barley soup and bread. They're from that hippie café you like so much, so you don't have to worry that some vegetable lost his life unjustly or anything like that."

My insides loosen the slightest bit when a smile touches at her lips. I head into the kitchen area, glancing over my shoulder when I hear her pad in behind me. She's wearing those yoga pants she's so crazy about, the ones that fit her like a second skin and make her legs look longer than I thought possible. She's paired them with what she would term a casual shirt I'm sure, with its broad gray and white stripes and loose neck that has it almost falling off one of her shoulders. It stops just past her hips and almost covers her hands, making her look almost innocent the way it hangs on her.

Her feet are bare, her toes tipped a deep red, and her hair's pulled off of her face in a loose bun with strands spilling out. Her face looks freshly washed and free of any enhancements, and for a second I wonder if she's always been this beautiful, and if she knows just what kind of punch she packs when she's not even trying.

"Are you hungry?" I ask and turn away to set everything on the counter. If I keep looking at her, I might just go back on my word and take her, no matter where her head's at.

"I'm sorry." She clears her throat and steps further into the kitchen, placing her hand on my arm to show me that she means it. I know that it's a big step for her, since really the only time we touch is when I reach for her; even when we're making out on the couch like sex depraved maniacs, I'm the one who makes the move first. I try not to tense now and take it as anything more than the apology that came with it.

"You were right in everything you said — and not just today. You were right the last time about what I was doing, and you were right to stop me tonight. I was using you, both times, and that's inexcusable."

I watch her, staying silent until I'm sure she's said everything she needs to say. She's in control, back to being the cool and levelheaded Cora, but now that I know her better, I can see how much it costs her to hold her head high at times, how much energy it takes to stand up straight when it's obvious she's tired and hurting.

Again, I want to push her, to ask her what's wrong, what would make her think sleeping with me, with anyone, would fix what she's feeling. And then I remember how many girls made the trek from a party to my bed in the past year, my feelings for them never going beyond that initial physical desire that was soon appeased, only to leave me feeling the same sense of aching emptiness I had before they'd touched me. For a while, the hour of oblivion spent inside of someone else seemed worth it, but now I know the truth: the darkness always comes back, no matter how many times we think we can avoid it by ignoring it. We have to work to live in the light, and even then there's no guarantee of forever. So I don't ask Cora why she'd do this, not only because a part of me understands, but because I want to show her that sometimes things can just be easy. And forgiven.

"I think I'll get over having you strip down and plaster yourself to me. As torture goes, I guess I could withstand it again, you know, just in case you were ever thinking of punishing me."

It takes a minute, but then her smile blooms and it's almost real. She gives a small laugh and I do what seems natural and pull her in for a hug. There's nothing sexual about it, no pressure, just the need I have to give her comfort.

She surprises me when she doesn't even hesitate before wrapping her arms around my waist and holding on. She burrows her face into my shoulder and I tighten my hold, again wondering if Blue's ever let herself just let loose and cry, scream, rage. Not about something or someone, just for herself.

After a minute she pulls back and looks up at me, her eyes

serious. "Thank you. For not letting me… for not letting me," she finishes. "I was having a bad day and for a minute, it just seemed like if I could forget about it, it wouldn't be so bad when I came back to reality."

I know that's a lot for her, a lot of honesty, a lot of sharing, and I know if I push now she's just raw enough she'll give me everything. And still, it won't be because she wanted to. I can't get past that, so I smile and press my lips to her forehead.

"I'm here for you, Blue. Eventually I'm going to ask some questions," I say and she smiles.

"You have questions? I can't imagine."

I return her grin and press a small kiss to her lips that's more friendly than anything and step back. "I can't promise to never ask again, but I can promise to try and be patient until you're ready."

"I can't figure you out," she says after a minute and I bring her close again, hugging her tight before releasing her.

"I'm not that complicated, trust me. Here's your soup. It should still be hot."

She doesn't reach for it, rather, she stares at me for the span of a few heartbeats and then she nods, as if accepting a request I never made.

"My mom has early onset Alzheimer's — or dementia; I forget which one, though I guess they amount to the same thing. She's forgetting things, and it's getting worse." She presses her lips together for a second, preparing for what's coming next. "I go by on Mondays and do her salon treatment for her, though she never asks me to, never thanks me, never really speaks to me. It's been almost three months and this last Monday I couldn't stand the silence anymore, so I began talking, reminiscing I guess, but it turns out all of my memories with her are bad ones, ones where I went out of my way to shock her, and she responded by slapping me, or calling me names. I don't know if I expected her to give me a reaction still, but it doesn't matter because she didn't. Nothing changed when I spoke to her, almost like she didn't even register that I was with her and it hurt me enough that when I came home I took it out on you."

I nod but keep silent, because I know her story's not done yet.

"For some reason, I went by today in a kind of spontaneous gesture, like a friend would do, just dropping by to say hi. I think I wanted to prove to both of us that I'm different than who I used to be, that I'm making an effort, one that proves we can actually have a relationship if we're willing. I guess I went for the same reason that I still go on Mondays even though she doesn't really want me there. Just the thought that by taking care of her, of giving her that small thing that she's always cared about, I'm helping her, giving her some good memories to fight for, if that's even possible."

She shakes her head and offers a wry smile, a smile that says she's laughing at herself but doesn't find humor in anything that happened. "But instead, I fucked up, like I always do, thought only of what I needed and she paid for it."

"What do you mean?"

"She forgot me today, forgot everyone, really, and when she came to she was a wreck and it was my fault. I dropped by on a day

I'm not usually there, and it was her caretaker's afternoon off. My dad wasn't home yet and when I got to her rooms, my mom was rushing around half dressed, searching for a dress for the benefit dinner she was hosting. When she saw me, she yelled at me, ordered me to start her hair and I realized she had no idea who I was, or who she was, really. Not anymore."

She looks at me now and her shoulders are slumped. "She was in a different time, and when my dad came home and she was startled back, she broke, and when I tried to offer my comfort to her, they both turned me away and I let them, because protecting her from me has become habit for all of us."

None of this information is one hundred percent new to me. From the few conversations we've had about her family, I've drawn a picture of what Cora's childhood and young adult life have been like so far. She and her mother don't get along and never have, because neither of them felt good enough for the other (though that's not how Cora's put it). Cora's mom felt threatened because she saw how beautiful her daughter was and resented it and the fact that Cora wouldn't become the Barbie doll she wanted her to, and Cora felt abused, humiliated, *less*, because all she wanted was love from a woman who seemed hell bent on giving only criticism. Neither knew how to break the mold they'd lived in for so long, and now the choice to mend those fences has been taken from both of them.

I want to reach out and take her hand, to bring her against me and give her the contact that shows her how much I care, that she's not alone. But I don't, because if there's one thing I've learned about Cora, it's that she needs to stand on her own first, to trust that she really is strong enough to survive. Balling my hands into fists, I shove them into my pockets and lean back against the counter.

"I'm so sorry, Blue."

She doesn't acknowledge this, just stares out the window to the street and continues. "It's weird because for the first time in our relationship, I didn't fight back. I just stood there watching her fall apart, and I did nothing because all I could think about was that the woman I've wanted to overcome my entire life is finally going to forget me and I suddenly don't want her to."

Now she turns so she can look me in the eye. "Do you want to know the worst part?" I nod my head. "She's losing her mind, piece by piece, day by day, struggling with bouts of sheer darkness when she finally comes back, and all I can think about is the fact that I didn't have enough time to show her I could be the daughter she always wanted. Even as she's struggling to place my face, and I can see the panic clawing at her because she can't remember, not right away, all I can do is think about how I wish I had more time to show her I was someone different, someone she might have actually cared for."

There are times in life when people never shed a tear and you watch them shatter in front of you. That's Blue right now — her eyes are dark and hollow, her shoulders hunched protectively. I wonder if there's a way to reach her, or if I should let her be. When her eyes meet mine my decision is made, and I stand up straight before scooping her close. Her hands find the front of my shirt and hold on as she burrows into me.

I wrap her close, as close as I can, my arms circling all the way around so they almost touch the opposite shoulder. I don't think about the angle on my elbow, or the ache that's spreading through my chest at the realization of just how hurt my siren is. For a second, all I do is bring her into me and hope that I can be the anchor to hold her here, to keep her from floating away, just like she did for me the first time I saw her.

"Why can't I just let her go? We've always hated each other. Why does it matter that she's leaving me, when the truth is I left her first?"

I've been good with words my entire life — that's why I chose my major. I remember them, love the sound of them, love hearing the cadence each new voice can bring to them. Yet, standing here I don't have words, none that will do this situation justice. She's overrun with guilt and fear and hurt and I can't tell her not to feel them, because I know she has to. There's no living life without all of those things — it's knowing when to set them down that separates the weak from the strong, the survivors from everyone else.

Despite what she's been through, or maybe because of it, I know Blue's a survivor and I know that eventually, when she gets past the overwhelming pain and shock she's feeling now, she'll find a way to move on and make her relationship with her mother as right as it can be before the end. Until then, it's my job to make sure she remembers how to fight, for herself and everything she wants.

Leaning back, I say her name. When she looks up, I wait until her eyes clear enough to actually focus on me. "If you want your mom to stop blaming you, if you want her to accept you and believe in you, you have to do it first. Stop thinking you're always wrong, Blue, and stop waiting for people to be disappointed."

There's fear in her eyes as she stares up at me, and I worry that she's going to finally let loose and cry. My belly clutches and I breathe deeply. She's looking at me out of wide, devastated eyes, eyes that have been ingrained in my memory since that first night when I couldn't look away from her. For perhaps the first time since we met, though, there's true vulnerability. There's no anger, no shock, no annoyance or resistance — for once her eyes are open and clear and in them I can see more than I ever imagined.

"Why do you get it?" She's still staring at me, her hands gripping the front of my shirt as she shakes her head. "We barely know each other and I haven't been particularly nice to you, but you always manage to understand what I'm feeling before I do. No one's ever done that before."

I'm treading on dangerous ground right now. I'm so needy for her my body physically aches. Warring with my desire for her is my intense need to protect her, from me and everyone else, including herself. Carefully, I reach out and skim a finger down her cheek, my eyes watchful and alert to everything hers give me.

"I'm starting to understand you, Blue. And more than that, I care about you." I swallow with a throat that's gone suddenly dry. No time like the present to put it all out there. "I care a lot, Cora."

The words are quiet, but they change the air around us even still. She steps closer until we're molded together from chest to toes and looks up. She swallows and then her tongue darts out to wet her lips and my already aching body bursts into flame. "I don't know why, or how, but I — I care, too. More than I ever have. More than I thought I ever could."

I can't hold back from her, not now. I know it's not the time, that it shouldn't be now after she's told me everything she has, but I can't step away from her, can't make myself stop because whatever's happened, this is real. Right now, her and me and everything we're building between us, it's fucking real and I need her more than I need air.

Leaning down, I stop a breath from her lips and look into her eyes. I need to know, to be sure, and I need her to tell me because I've lost the ability to walk away. She's all I can see, all I can feel, and every second that passes I need her more.

"Yes," she says, and again, bolder, "Yes," and that's all it takes. My lips are on hers and my hands are at her hips, urging her closer until I shift and boost her up. When she wraps her legs around me, I wrap my arms tight around her and head toward the hallway.

Chapter Twenty

Cora

I used to dive into a potential bedmate the way a swimmer dives into the water — quick, clean, effortlessly really, after following a very specific routine. With Jake, every move I have is obliterated until everything I feel is all I can think about. I have no moves, no protocol, no brain power to do anything but feel his words and see from his face that he means them.

Which is why I'm wrapped around him and meeting his lips with my own, rocking my center against his and praying to God he gets us wherever we're going fast. After years of being cold, the fire smoldering between us is consuming, and he's the only one who can make it better. I hear a door kicked open, a thud, and a curse from him. I pull back a little look around his room.

"Why not mine?" I ask. He grins and throws me onto the bed where I land in a heap of covers.

"Because I want you in mine." And then his body is covering mine and I don't know or care where we are as long as he never stops kissing me. His hands are sure, slow and thorough as they peel away my clothes and explore my skin, and just when I'm ready to beg, he shifts away and stands, walking over to snap on the standup lamp in the corner before he returns to the foot of the bed, his eyes blazing into me.

"I want to see you," he says and I lay still, too mesmerized to speak or look anywhere but at him. Even with a tan, my skin is shades lighter than his, and I watch in euphoric rapture as he picks up my foot, skimming his hands down the length of my leg and back before pressing a small kiss to the inside of my arch.

"These legs have fascinated me since the first time I saw you."

"You can barely remember the first night you saw me, let alone what my legs looked like."

He shakes his head and places another kiss just above the last. "Not true. I didn't want to remember you because you stunned me the first time I saw you." Shivers ripple through my whole body as I lie here watching him watching me, my heart beating so hard I wonder I can even hear him over it.

"Your skin is so smooth, the muscles beneath so strong. And then I saw your eyes and I knew even from across the room that I had to be near you. I won't hurt you," he says and my breath catches in my throat.

My eyes burn and my vision blurs with unshed tears because I know he's reassuring me that what we are together is different than what we've ever been with others. I'm not a virgin — the pain he's talking about won't be physical, and I wonder how I think I can know him and still be surprised by his tenderness, his thoughtfulness. His ability to know what I need, even when I don't.

"I want to see you," I tell him as he makes his way back up my body.

"Then you better get started." There's a smile in his voice as he skims my breast with his lips and I suck in a breath at the sensation. I don't move instantly, too steeped in what he's doing with his tongue to function, and then I feel his teeth on my nipple and my eyes snap open to meet his laughing ones. "If you keep closing your eyes, you're going to miss it."

I grin and shift so I can grip his T-shirt, yanking impatiently and reaching for the bared flesh when he pushes to his knees and tugs it the rest of the way off. His skin is warm and I feel it all the way to my core when he reaches for me again and our bare chests brush against one another.

A year ago, I had wondered if a small part of me had died inside and the connection I once craved through physical contact had forever altered my ability to feel anything anymore. Now, feel is all I can do.

Every time he touches me a fire ignites and my body bends to its desire. It's as if Jake has reached inside and warmed all of those frozen places, bringing my passions back to life and nurturing them, and me, as I come alive with them.

What was once a fast and frenzied escapade with only the end pleasure in mind is now a moment made up of touch and taste, a time to discover one another in ways I've never known. He leaves no place of me untouched, unfulfilled, as he takes his lips on a tour of my body, reaching my hip bones, the inside of my thigh, the back of my knee and up again. I want to roll him and give him the same treatment, to make him feel the drowning pleasure and desire that I feel, but at this moment I can barely lift my arms. His tongue joins his fingers, pressing inside and curling up, and my body throws itself from the cliff, my back arching and my hips bucking until he uses his other hand to press them down and ride through the wave with me in place.

I'm shivering, my body absorbing the last aftershocks of my orgasm when he makes his way back up and kisses me. The pressure that was relieved just seconds ago begins to build again when his tongue twirls with mine and his thigh presses between my legs, igniting my sensitive flesh. His lips leave mine when I gasp, and then he shifts and I hear the crinkling of a cellophane packet before I feel him shift back.

"Look at me, Blue."

I do and what I see is impossible. It's as if I'm all he sees, all he wants to see, all he needs, and then he braces his weight on his forearms and kisses me long and hard as he begins to move, gently rocking back and forth, easing his way inside until he fills me all the way. The sensations that envelop me are too many to name.

I hear him suck in a breath and he pauses for a moment, our eyes locking, our bodies frozen. He feels it. I can see it in his face, feel it in the pulsing of his body all around and inside of mine. Whatever we are, this has inflamed our connection and smart or not, I can't turn back. When he begins to move again with long and torturously slow strokes, I think I might die of pleasure. One hand reaches down and curls around my leg, pushing it higher as his movements become more forceful, more uncontrolled. My breath catches, my lungs freeze, and all I can do is hold on as he takes me to a place I've never been.

~

"Tell me this wasn't a mistake."

We're lying wrapped together, my head on his shoulder, both of his arms around me and mine draped over his waist. His fingers are sifting through my hair and I'm more content than I ever remember being. What we just did... I've had sex before. Sex with Jake is something else, something more. Something I'll never forget. Which worries me, and prompted me to ask for his reassurance. I've never needed reassurance before. It appears that this rendezvous, whatever it is, is new for me all around.

"Were you here with me twenty minutes ago? Because I can assure you, if you were you would *not* need me to tell you that this wasn't a mistake."

He rolls and I'm under him, our eyes locked. "No?" He shakes his head. "Then what was it?"

"Amazing," he says and I smile, because he's right. Scary? Yes. New? Yes. Amazing? Oh, God, *yes*.

Then his face gets serious and I reach my finger up to trace the line of his brow. "I don't want you to think I'm like everyone else, Cora, or that you're like the other girls I've been with. This? Us? It's nothing like that."

I nod, and though I don't want to have this conversation, I know I started it because we need to have it. "I want to trust you, Jake, trust this, but I have to be careful, too. I told you once that I used to be a girl who believed everything because it was easier to convince myself it was true than it was to really look at why I was so needy for the words in the first place. I don't ever want to be that girl again."

"I get that, just as I get how scary this is for you. But you need to know one thing." He waits until I look at him, and his eyes are blazing and serious as they bore into me. "I've slept with other women — some more than once, some once, some I remember, some I don't. I've had one serious relationship that I thought might be forever, and then I lost everything and I didn't think forever mattered anymore." Now he rests his weight on his right elbow and brings his left hand up to cup my cheek. "Blue, one glance at you all those months ago showed me that I might not be able to see forever, but I definitely want to see tomorrow if you're there."

My heart rolls over, it doesn't have a choice. Part of it's from fear, but the other part is from something greater, something a lot like hope, which is pretty fucking scary. For a minute I try to decide if I can block the words and how they make me feel, and then I realize that even if I could I don't want to. I won't lie to myself that much, not anymore, and I don't want to lie to him, either. Everything he's said, I want, and so I tuck the words close, knowing I'll take them out and remember them over and over again later.

But now, I take that last step and bring my lips back to his, pushing closer until I'm rolling him and shifting so we're chest to chest with my legs resting on either side of his hips and my hair curtaining around us. I hear him groan and I smile before taking my lips on a journey over his face, down his neck and onto his chest, lower, absorbing the scent that is Jake, something tangy mixed with the smell and salt of the sea that seeps into my body as I taste him everywhere I can. When I move lower and take him into my mouth, his hips buck and I hear a groan rip from his throat.

His breathing is ragged, his chest heaving and he says my name, his hands fisting on the bed beside me, but I ignore him until we're both breathless again, both ready to explode. Sliding up his body, I straddle him and take his lips again, reveling in the desire I can feel coming from him. One of his hands grips my hip while the other tangles in my hair, fisting there while he yanks me closer and fuses his mouth to mine. He's not a gentle kisser right now, not the lover worried about finesse and smooth moves and I respond more because of it. I want him uncontrolled — I want everything that he feels to show in every way that he touches me.

"Now," he says and I just grin and continue to torture us both. "Cora, Jesus, now." He reaches over to the nightstand beside the bed, knocking something to the floor before I hear him rip open a condom before he sheaths himself. And then both of his hands are at my hips and he's shifting me, sitting up in one fluid move so my legs are around his waist and he's pushing inside, claiming me, making me his until we're moving together in a rhythm all our own.

When I come apart, his lips are there and he swallows my cries, throwing himself over the edge with me.

Chapter Twenty-One

Jake

"Tell me about your family. You've already said you don't have a mom, but you've mentioned your dad a few times. Tell me about him."

Cora's question brings me out of my reverie of the street scene beneath me. It's been forty-eight hours since we went to bed together, forty-eight hours since I felt what it's truly like to be consumed by someone, and I've relished every minute of it. We've talked, laughed, loved, messed around, all of those things you do when you're first with someone. Only this time it's different, because we're living together, and because for the first time I understand what it means to be powerless. She holds the power here, whether or not she knows it.

Now, we're both done with our work days (a work day she was late for thanks to yours truly and my skills in the shower), and we're sitting on our small balcony enjoying the dying early spring sunshine and an after-workout drink. I don't know how to answer the question she's asked, so I shrug and settle down deeper into the glider, my feet kicked out in front of me and crossed at the ankles as I rock us back and forth. She's sitting next to me, a water bottle in one hand while her other taps out a light rhythm on the seat. Her hair is pulled back from her face to spill in a long line down her back and her shoulders are bare in her running tank top. Her legs are crossed under her Indian style, and I take a minute to appreciate that her small running shorts are made even smaller when she sits like this.

It's crazy how beautiful she is, how much I can just look at her and get lost in everything she is and let it all go until the only thing I think about is her. I've known this girl just over four months and already she's done what even baseball couldn't, and she's taught me to simply live where I am right now, without looking forward or backward.

This thought shakes me a little, enough that I give her a grin I'm not really feeling and ease away from whatever emotion is creeping its way toward me. However deep my feelings, however much I want her to know that what we have is special, I'm not ready to acknowledge just how much I feel for her. Not yet. When she raises her brow, I shrug.

"There's not much to tell. He raised me, fed me, taught me about baseball. When I graduated, I went south and he stayed in Montana. We talk every month or so, I tell him where I am and how things are going, he tells me to call again soon, and we hang up."

"What does he do?"

"Not a whole lot of anything."

She sighs and I know I'm making this difficult on her, but shit, I don't want to have this conversation. Everything between us is great — better than great, and I don't want to ruin any moment we have together with talk about something I can't change. But she asked, and we've talked about her parents, which reminds me why this conversation we're having now isn't out of the blue. Feeling like an asshole because I can remember her breaking when she told me about her own parents a few days ago — something I pushed her to do, goddammit — I gulp down a little bit of my beer and think of how to begin.

"Like I said, I never knew my mom. People told me she walked out on us before I was even a month old, so it's always just been me and Dad. He was a good guy — *is* a good guy. He taught me everything I know about baseball since he was a pitcher, too. Signed straight out of high school, moved his way up to Triple A pretty quick, made a name for himself."

"And then what?"

"And then, he did what the majority of ball players do while trying to make it to the big leagues and got stuck. Just couldn't get out, couldn't get his big break, became a spot filler. When my mom got pregnant, he decided that it was happening that year or he was done. The money isn't great in the minors, and the travel schedule is murder. When I was born and she took off, his decision was made for him."

I take another drink, knowing I need to finish and wishing there were a way to avoid it. Since there's not, and I've grown accustomed to uncomfortable things in the past few months, I bite the bullet and lay it all out there. "Now, he's a part time mechanic and a full time alcoholic. He's been on the wagon three times," I say, though she doesn't ask. "And all three times he's fallen off with a pretty heavy crash. He works during the day when he's sober enough, or the demand for money is great enough, and he drinks his nights away, suffers for it in the morning, and is a mildly content person. I let him be because it's easier to see him like that than to watch him be devastated each time he tries to quit and fails."

I wonder for a second if I should have admitted to her that he's an alcoholic, one that doesn't appear to have the ability to quit. I sit in the quiet and worry that she's going to tell me I'm a bad son, that in excusing his drinking, I'm only taking the easy way out for myself. They're all things I've said to myself, but now faced with Blue and the knowledge that she *did* pull herself out of the pit, I wonder how much more shame I can feel. She has the same weakness he does, yet in Cora I see nothing but determination to be something other than a label, and in my father... well, I don't see anything, because I try not to look too hard.

"Did he ever see you play in college?" she asks after a minute and I come back from my thoughts to shake my head.

"Nope, but he taught me to play, so I figure that ought to be enough."

"Is it?"

It's the first time she's asked what I would consider a truly personal question. Asking about my dad, my family, even baseball, that's all basic inquiry for people who are doing the dance we are — getting to know someone because they've *become* someone to you. But that question is personal, one that requires a feeling rather than a story.

I shake my head, my fingers tightening briefly on the bottle they hold before easing off. "No, it wasn't. But then, his life never really gave him what he needed, either, so I can't really blame him."

She nods like she understands, but doesn't say anything for a minute. I'm awed at how quiet she can be, how still, when I know inside she's processing, thinking, always adjusting her attitude, responses, feelings until she's satisfied with them. It makes me want the quiet too, but there's also a part of me that wants to find out what her response is like when she doesn't process it, doesn't filter it.

Sitting here with her, I'm suddenly very aware of the fact that I want to find out who Cora is when she's unfiltered. Like she was in the bedroom the other night, a dark haired siren above me, her own hands in her hair as she rocked us both to madness until I could see and feel nothing but her. When we're together like that, when I'm touching her, inside of her, I know I have Cora, the one who can't hold her responses back, who doesn't have time to think and process her response. I touch her and she becomes mine. Now, I want that outside of the bedroom too.

"What's wrong with us that we don't want to save everyone around us?" she asks and I raise my brow.

"What do you mean?"

"Me with my mother, you with your father. Countless kids have fucked up families and the majority of them work day and night to be the adult, the savior, the one who keeps everyone together. I thought it was just me, but listening to you say that you're okay with your dad how he is, even if it's destroying his life, I understand because that's how I am with my mom. She's losing her mind a little more each day and I go and paint her nails once a week, and I really only started doing that because it was part of my recovery program, a step I needed to complete. I'm not looking to become a nurse or her personal savior. I'm doing what I want, just like before she got sick. Even when she had her health, I let her do what she wanted, even when it was harmful, even when I hated her and wanted her to be someone else. I never tried to stop her, save her, understand her. I still don't. Half the time I'm with her neither of us says anything."

She finally looks at me and I can see that though her voice isn't sad, there's sadness lurking just beneath the surface. I want to gather her close and tell her I'd save her if I could, but that's a lie because I already know I need her more than she needs me, and in a way, she's already saved me. Instead, I keep my voice casual with the hope it will lighten whatever fear she's carrying around.

"Not everyone's made to be a hero, Blue, or we'd all be off fighting wars or diseases or fires, and then most of us would probably just end up dead."

"Jesus, that's an awful outlook."

I shrug and tip my bottle back. "The trouble with being a hero is that there's always someone who needs to be saved and, eventually, you just get sucked dry until you can't fight anymore and you fail. You and me, we know this already, so we don't try and jump in when it's obvious that if someone wanted to, they could save themselves."

Or that it's too late. I don't say this, but I know from a glance that it went through her mind too.

"I'm not sure if you believe that, but I think you want to."

I slant my eyes to her and see that she's angled toward me now, her head cocked slightly as she studies me. For whatever reason, her stare has me opening my mouth again. "I tried to save my dad once, but he didn't want my help and it made me realize that being disappointed sucks, so instead of being disappointed I accept who he is and we both live our lives in relative peace."

"And you battle his demons for him each and every time you get on the mound."

There's a little clutch in the bottom of my belly when she says it, partly because I don't want to acknowledge anything that has to do with what I used to be, and partly because for the first time I feel like someone gets it. I ignore it, focusing instead on the scent of her that's wrapping around me and filling me, taking me to that place that makes me want to believe in anything as long as she's there. "I used to. Now we both battle our own demons."

We're locked on one another, our drinks forgotten and gazes unblinking as the air between us becomes palpable. "Blue," I say and lean toward her. She doesn't hesitate to meet me halfway, and soon I hear her water bottle thud to the ground, my beer bottle clanking after it. Neither of us pauses. Instead, she shifts until her knees are bent and on either side of my hips and her hands are in my hair. And her lips, Jesus, her lips are pressed to mine as our tongues tangle together and I can't breathe without inhaling her.

"How can it be like this?" she asks as we break apart and my lips go to her neck. "How can it be better each time?"

"Because it matters," I say and stand, keeping a firm grip on her as I walk toward the slider, shouldering the door open as her legs lock around my back and her lips find my ear. *Christ.* I stumble when Yogi darts in front of me, silently swearing to extract revenge from him later, but Blue only laughs as she tightens her legs and continues nibbling on my neck. In an impressive show of multitasking, she wiggles out of her tank top until there's only a thin, electric pink athletic bra between me and that gorgeous rack of hers.

I stop and stare at her, noting the flush of her cheeks and the challenge in her eyes. "We're not making it to a bed," I tell her.

"Why do you think I got such a big couch?"

"God, you're perfect." And then I'm sinking down over her, searching a condom out of the pocket of my jeans before we're a tangle of limbs and mouths, each racing toward the peak again and again until we fall into an exhausted heap.

Sometime later, I'm on my back with Blue sprawled across the top of me, her head nuzzled into the nook between my ear and shoulder, her arms tucked between our bodies. Her breathing is deep, but every now and then she arches slightly under the stroke of my hand over her back.

"You were wrong earlier," I say. I keep my hand moving over her back, and though she doesn't respond, I know she's listening so I continue. "You are a hero, Blue — every day you get up and battle your demons, every time you go and see your mother even though it would be easier to let her forget, or to let her blame you for not seeing her; those are the actions of someone strong, someone heroic, and your mom knows it. Just because she doesn't know how to react to it doesn't mean you should quit."

She doesn't say anything, but I don't expect her to. After a second, I feel her lips at my throat and her arms snake out and around my neck before she settles more securely so we're now holding each other. Kissing the top of her head, I hold her close as the sun sets and the night falls around us.

Chapter Twenty-Two

Cora

When I knock on the door to my parent's house on Monday, my father shocks me when he opens the door during a time that he's normally at work. We stand there, staring awkwardly at one another until he clears his throat and steps back.

"I'm glad to see you, Cora. I didn't, uh, know if you'd be returning after last week."

I step past him and stand inside of the entryway as he closes the door. I watch him for a second, floating back in time as I recognize he's in what he considers his casual-wear of crisply pleated khakis and a polo shirt, this one a light blue. He's wearing a belt and the matching loafers, and his hair is parted and combed in his original gentlemen's cut. If my father wasn't in a three piece suit when I was growing up, he was in this outfit right here. Even Christmas morning, he wore a rendition of this with a sweater thrown over the polo.

I can see my reflection from the large foyer mirror behind him — my camouflaged half shirt paired with high waist black jeans and black stiletto sandals and a leather jacket — and I wonder how I've never noticed that I'm so much more my mother than my father. He's the steady one, the tidy architect who keeps himself as professional at home as he does at the office, never losing his temper, never overreacting, just always there. He's cleaned up so many messes over the years, some made by me, some by her, some by both of us, and I suddenly wonder if he's tired of it. But then I remember the other day when he walked in and saw us together, the joy on his face before he realized exactly what was going on, and I know that he'd do anything to see her happy again. He loves her, almost blindly, and though I know he cares for me, I've never pushed for more because it's always been obvious that she needs him more. I wonder if he knows just how much I need him too, or even if I knew just how much his affection mattered before this moment.

"Cora," he says and I flick my gaze to him. "I said, I didn't know if you'd be back."

"Neither did I," I tell him and watch him nod in understanding. "I know she hates me, Dad."

He shakes his head, a small sigh escaping him. "She doesn't hate you, Cora, she just doesn't know how to deal with you. She never has," he admits and slides his hands into his pockets. "Now, she doesn't know how to deal with any of it."

I watch him handle the grief that washes over him, and I understand. We both love the same woman who can't love us back, not like we need, but where I spent my early years revolting against her and trying to make her mad enough to show me she cared, he's spent their entire marriage holding her up and giving her whatever she needed in order to be happy. Only now, he can't give her what she wants, because he can't fix what's happened to her, and neither can I.

Maybe it's time we both start recognizing that.

"I know you love her," I say and his eyes find mine. "Believe it or not, I love her too, or I want to. I don't really know how, like her I guess, but I do know I'm trying. You have to try too, Dad." He goes to say something but I shake my head. Right now, there are words that I need to say and that he needs to hear. "You can't just let her stay in this house, silently hating the world and everyone in it. You have to try to make her go out, talk to someone, anyone, and try to live, because this isn't helping her and it's not helping us. Sometimes the only way to help someone is to tell them what they don't want to hear," I say, thinking back to Rafe, and then to Mia, to the Scientist and now to Jake, the people who wouldn't let me wallow in my shit and anger and resentment because they cared too much to let me.

"I know," he says after a second and I nod once then turn to walk to the stairs, but when I reach them, I rest my hand on the banister and turn back.

"I've been here for three months and you haven't called me once to go to dinner. I guess it's because I haven't called you either, and I don't know why except that I was afraid you wouldn't want to see me."

His eyes widen and his mouth opens, but it takes him a minute to form words. "Of course I want to see you, Cora. You're my daughter."

"And she's your wife. Neither of us are easy to be around, but I'm trying. I need you to try too. Stop being so scared of me, of her, of what you think might happen if you rock the boat, and stop thinking that leaving things as they are is what's best. Things need to change, for all of us, or we should just give up now."

I'm halfway up the stairs when he says my name. I stop and neither of us speaks for a second. "I have to go out of town for business. Two weeks, maybe three. Can we have dinner when I get back? Maybe at Ricardos, like we used to?"

My throat closes and I nod my head without looking at him, finishing my assent and heading toward my mother's quarters. Sassy meets me at the door to her suite and one look at my face has her opening her arms wide and taking me in. I don't wrap my arms around her, but I do close my eyes and rest my head on her shoulder.

"*Cara*, I heard about last week. I'm sorry, I should have known it was coming. She was agitated all the day before from a phone call."

I shake my head back and forth and talk into her shoulder. "I guess it needed to happen. At least she finally spoke to me," I say with an attempt at humor, but neither of us laugh.

Instead, Sassy pulls back and cups my face. "You're a good daughter, Cora."

I close my eyes again before taking a deep, cleansing breath and opening them. "I wasn't always, Sassy, but I'm trying. And I'm going to keep trying, whether she likes it or not. I'm not ready to give up," I say, thinking of my father.

She raises her brow at me and then steps back to let me in. I straighten my shoulders and stride through, walking straight to the vanity where I begin to set up. I watch my mother come in wearing her robe, which lets me know that she was expecting me and, without looking up, I speak.

"I'm going to put a toner on your hair because it doesn't need new color. Your brows need to be done, and so do your nails. I'll give you a facial after your brows and the mask can sit while I do your nails and toes." I look up now and meet her hollow gaze straight on, ignoring her blank stare and hunched shoulders. "And I'm going to talk to you while I'm here, because I know you can hear me. I don't care if you respond, but you should know I'm just going to keep talking, because I want you to get to know me and I really want to get to know you."

One arm moves from its clenched position at her waist so she can reach up and grip the lapels of her robe and squeeze them together. "I don't want to talk to you. What's the point? It's not like I'm going to remember it anyway."

Irate with her for being so goddamn stubborn, sad because I understand more than she knows, I walk over to her and watch her eyes widen and flood with shock, an emotion so opposite from the blank indifference that I want to crow in triumph, but I don't. Instead, I stop so I'm standing right in front of her, looking down and waiting until she sees exactly what I'm about to say.

"We're the point, Mother. Right now is the point." Gentling my tone because I can see panic starting to sneak in with the shock, I reach out and lay my hand on her shoulder. "I'm sorry for last time, but I'm not sorry I'm here, and I'm not leaving, Mom, so let me talk to you. Let me try," I finish and I see her eyes fill with something else.

She swallows several times and I wait, almost missing the way her head nods lightly. And then we're walking toward her vanity and I can see Sassy's grin a mile wide in the mirror. I respond with a determined one of my own before throwing a cape over my mother's robe and getting out my bottles. My hands tremble but I ignore them, determined to see this through.

"So, Mia's wedding. Are you ready to hear about it? Aunt Shannon, you know, the tall ginger from Uncle Thomas's side? She fell down drunk and took a table with her. I thought Auntie Mags was going to combust she was so mad."

I stop talking and fussing when her hand reaches over her shoulder and grips mine, so hesitantly, but there nonetheless. I stare at it, and then into the mirror, where our eyes meet again and hers aren't empty anymore. They're full of things I don't understand but things I feel.

"I—" She clears her throat and I see her eyes twitch to Sassy, who stays where she is and nods. "I don't like forgetting," she finally says and I stop breathing completely. "But there are some things I don't like remembering, either. I hate that the most — that I don't get to pick and choose what I forget and what I don't, like the disease is taunting me with how much power it has over me. I don't always deal well with things," she finishes, and her chest is moving up and down so rapidly I wonder if she's going to hyperventilate. She doesn't, and I don't, we just stare at each other until I finally nod.

"Yeah, well, don't go to therapy, it's all about remembering." I hope I haven't gone too far, and feel a little rewarded when a small, almost-there-smile forms on her lips. Out of the corner of my eye, I see Sassy nod approval before settling back into her magazine.

Taking my mother's thin hair in my hand, I begin to brush it and continue on with my story.

~

I text Mia when I'm done, just to let her know I'm doing better. I want to call her, but I know she's getting ready to graduate and Ryan's baseball schedule is in full swing, and regardless of what she says, I know they deserve uninterrupted time. She texts me back almost immediately and I smile, grateful that she understands why a conversation – albeit one-sided – is such a big deal. Mia's own family suffers from silence the way mine does, though it's gotten better in recent years thanks to Mia's relentless pursuit to keep them together. Unlike me, Mia is the middle of five children, and instead of revolting when her parents outlined her life, she stood up and demanded they accept her as the person she wanted to be. Now, she's living her real dream, finishing a degree for a career that she believes in, married to a man who has never wanted anything the way he wants her, and I want nothing more than to be as happy as she is.

When I get home, Jake's on the couch reading. I stop to shed my heels and lay my bag and jacket on the chair, studying him while his eyes follow me instead of the words on the page in front of him. Whatever he's reading, it's bent and scratched, an actual paperback book that I forgot they made since the invention of the tablet. At this angle I can see the inside of his left arm, his pitching arm, and the words scrolled there in black ink that's barely legible unless you're close enough to study them as I have been lately. *Still I Rise.* It's from a poem by a woman whose name I can't remember, but one that spoke to him the first time he read it because it was about staying upright, always standing, no matter who tried to shove you down.

We were laying there in bed a few nights ago, our hands sliding over each other's skin, my head on his shoulder as it always is when we wrap together, and I traced the words with my finger, wondering if ever someone had spoken to my heart like he did. I asked him about the words and he recited the poem to me from memory, his voice pitching and lowering, steady on the words as he released them into the room to curl around me.

Remembering that moment now, I know that no matter what happens in our futures, whether we ever get to be like that again or not, he's held me up and helped me rise so that today I could walk into my mother's house and have her start to forgive me.

I don't say anything, I just stare while he stares right back until I walk straight to him, sinking down in his lap when he opens his arms, curling into him as he wraps me up and holds me against his chest. He's quiet for a minute, stroking his fingers through my hair, waiting for me to explain.

"I'm going to dinner with my dad."

He continues stroking. "That's good."

"And I told him he had to stop treating my mom like an invalid; that he had to stop letting her die and start fighting with her so she learns to fight back."

I feel his lips form a smile on the crown of my head. "And then I went and told my mom I was going to talk to her, whether she wanted me to or not. She didn't respond right away, but then, there was this moment when she did, and it hit me that she feels like I do." I have to pause and swallow to clear the emotions blocking my throat. "She's sorry. She didn't say it, but after today, I know it, and it's not just for last time. She's sorry like I am, for all of it, everything we did, what we didn't do. She's sorry, and I think she wants to love me."

That's when I break, the thudding of my heart too much to hold in, the pressure in my chest too great to control. I sob like I haven't since I was a little girl, everything inside of me breaking and pouring out and over. Only, Jake's there to hold me together, scooping me closer until he's holding me more securely, rubbing his hands up my arms and down, murmuring things in my ear so I know he's there.

I think of my mother and all of the time we've lost, and I cry and cry and cry and he never lets me go.

~

We don't talk about it, but something in our relationship has shifted again.

For the past two weeks Jake and I have shared the same bed, spending hours each night exploring one another before falling into an exhausted sleep of slick skin and tangled limbs. In the morning, we wake and do it all over again before starting the rest of the day. Our routine hasn't changed much, I still get up and work out and sometimes he joins me, sometimes he doesn't, saving his energy for his own workout later in the day. I go to work or my parents', he studies and then goes to his training session in the latter half of the day, and at some point we both meet back up at home and argue over what we're doing for dinner. The idea that we wouldn't have dinner together never even crosses our minds.

There have been times over the last couple of weeks that I've stepped back and wondered if what I'm doing is safe, or if it's a disaster waiting for the time and opportunity to devastate me. I never come to a conclusion on that thought, partly because I'm too happy to pick it apart for long, and partly because I'm trying not to think into the future, only of now. I know Jake feels the same.

Both of our lives were ruled by one thing before this: the desire to make someone of ourselves. Not just something, but *someone*, a name people would remember when for so long the people who mattered barely knew who we were.

Where I ruined my own life, Jake's choice was made for him and we both ended up broken and wondering how we were going to pick up the pieces. I'd be lying if I said he didn't make me feel more like myself than I have in a long time, that somehow who he is and who he allows me to be has shifted all of the pieces I reconstructed until I look in the mirror and actually see the girl staring back. Since that knowledge scares me, I ignore it and focus on the fact that whatever we're doing, I'm having fun. That has to be enough for now.

"Girl, fun can never be overrated. It's about damn time you recognized that."

A.J. and I are standing in the back of the salon while I mix color and she flips through her phone while she waits for her next appointment to begin.

"And from what I saw when I walked in on him giving you

some of this *fun* out back the other day, I can guarantee a boy like that knows endless tricks to keep a woman entertained."

"Walked in? You mean, purposely sought us out after I told you I would be back in five minutes?" She grins and shrugs. "And I thought *you* knew how to keep women entertained," I say with a raise of my brow.

"I do, that's how I recognize it in someone else. With the look you've been carrying around the past few days, I'd bet that boy has some moves that would make me proud."

They definitely make me something, though I'm not sure if it's proud or just really grateful. I don't say this, mostly because I know that once you give A.J. an inch, she won't back down until you've given her everything. Instead, I smile smugly and put away the rest of the color tubes before stirring the mixture.

I listen with half an ear as A.J. chatters on about her newest lady, the place they went for dinner a few nights ago and how bad the live music was. When Liam comes in to mix his own batch of color, A.J. is flipping through our newest color additions, trying to choose a new one for herself.

"What about this?" she asks and holds out a caramel highlight next to her black and red hair.

"Too innocent," Liam and I say at the same time and she laughs.

"Why are you changing?" I ask her and she shakes her head.

"Girl, how can you even ask that? Changing hair color is what we do for a living."

I point to my own mahogany locks that she just updated for me. "And yet, I haven't changed my color in months."

"Point made," she says with a raise of her brow.

"What's that mean?"

I look to Liam and he holds out his hands. I look back to A.J. and she smiles. "It means your hair is vanilla because you want people to think you are, too, but we," she points back and forth between she and Liam, "know better — as I'm betting your man does now that you're sharing a bed. You wear boring hair to hide the fact that you're not boring. What we still don't know is why."

It annoys me that she's right, that a while ago I decided that I couldn't be the platinum blonde that I once was because I was a different person. I chose brown because it was safe, almost sedate. I never add highlights or lowlights or an ombre, just an all-over rich color that borders on dark chocolate. Looking at A.J. and Liam, I know they understand that.

I don't take risks with my hair because I'm afraid to take risks with my life. Yet, hasn't the last little bit of time with Jake proved I'm more a blend of who I once was and who I turned myself into? The fact that I can now look at that person I was and not be repulsed by her, that I can remember parts of her with some affection and understanding, shows me that Jake's opened more doors than I thought, and that I've locked too many.

So thinking, I smile and tap the color she's holding. "Then get ready. I need some updating, and I want you two to do it."

I turn and head back to my chair and I hear her laugh follow me   the   entire   way.

Chapter Twenty-Three

Jake

I'm at the stove cooking when Cora gets home. I don't even turn down the music (because, really, you don't turn down Run DMC), just shout at her over my shoulder and go back to grilling the fish I know she likes so much.

My mood is high, higher than it's been in a really long time and I'm riding the fucking wave. I threw today. Not hard, and definitely not up to the caliber of what I once considered throwing, but I fucking threw the ball. From the mound. At fifty percent. And I hit my target. Best of all, it was pain free.

The fact that I wanted to call Blue the minute I did it didn't even concern me. I'm too far in to pretend anymore, and though I'm not quite ready to express my undying love for her (mostly because I'm not sure either of us is ready), I chose to cook a celebration dinner that was about her because that's how I feel. Everything is about her, everything is because of her. Today was only one day throwing, but this happiness inside of me has been there a lot longer, and it started with her.

I hear her heeled footsteps trek across the floor and then nothing, so I know she's slipping out of those heels, an act that has me turning around to watch because my new privileges include watching her dress in the morning, and fuck if there's anything sexier than watching her wrap the package I've had my hands all over the night before. Knowing I'm going to get to watch her undress everything twelve hours later is a turn on I never expected.

Only, when I spot her, she's still wearing her heels and her skin-tight black jeans and light denim button down she paired them with today, and I'm no longer staring at her legs, I'm staring at her.

Her hair is lighter, but not, like she took the ends and dipped them into liquid gold, blending and drawing it out until her normal chocolate locks fade to a gentler, more caramel brown. The contrast is stunning and for the first time since we met, I feel like I'm seeing the true Cora.

Those secrets she always wears are still there, but this time rather than hiding them I feel like she's challenging me to unearth them. When I just continue to stare, she cocks a hip and leans against the counter and I feel myself go rock hard. I've had this girl at least twice a day, every day for the last fourteen days, and it's still not enough.

"I think you might be burning your fish," she says and it takes me a minute to comprehend her words. With a curse, I turn and grab the spatula, flipping the two filets and smirking over my shoulder as I grab the second pan and shake the arugula.

"I like your hair."

She smiles a female smile full of power and secrets and walks to the fridge, still wearing those shoes that make me want to drop to my knees and thank the man who invented them. Grabbing me a beer, she gets herself a mini bottle of Pellegrino and brings both over to the stove.

"I'm glad. I have to say, it was nice to have someone to make an entrance for. Are we celebrating?" she asks and points to dinner. I nod and take the beer from her, lowering the heat under the pans for the last few minutes of cook time. "Anything in particular?"

"Let's get this out of the way first," I say and grab her around the waist. She doesn't resist; rather, her body flows easily into mine and the rhythm we've developed together. My hand anchors in her shirt at the small of her back, forcing her to press even closer, an act to which she responds, gripping my shirt in the same spot, arching her back until we're driving each other nuts.

"I didn't think you could be any more beautiful," I tell her between small kisses. "I was wrong." And then deeper, deeper until we're both breathing hard and I have to pull back or risk dinner while I pull her to the ground and finish what I just started.

We stand, breath heaving, staring at one another. Her grin comes first, and then mine, and before I can stop myself I lean in and give her a friendly kiss, one that says something different than the devouring I just handed her.

"Why don't you set the table, then we can eat and you can tell me what inspired this change?"

She nods and, after a beat, leans in to kiss me. Neither of us acknowledges that this is the first time she's done something so simple when it's been unprompted, but I'm smiling as she grabs two plates and walks out.

~

Dinner is edible, more than, which is pleasing, and for a bit we sit and eat, both of us going through the wind down of our day that's become as routine as sharing a meal. The step we took earlier in the month cemented what we were already building toward, that this relationship is just that, and I can't describe how it feels to know this awaits me at the end of the day.

When our plates are clean and the table cleared and Blue has her fancy coffee from the foreign machine that sits unused if she's not home, I grab another beer and her hand and pull her to the couch.

"Spill it. What's with the new hair?"

She shrugs and settles into the corner while I sprawl on the cushion next to her, throwing my arm over the back. "I don't really know. I wasn't planning on it, but then I got to work and A.J. and I were talking and I realized that I'd left my hair that color for too long. Like I was trying to convince myself I'm one dimensional, but I'm not." She sips from her coffee. "I guess that sounds stupid."

I sip from my beer and shake my head. "Actually, it sounds dead on. You went through something and changed who you were, but that doesn't mean that you can forget her. Or that you should," I say and watch her nod slowly.

"I think I came to that realization at some point in the last week," she murmurs and I slide my eyes to hers. For a beat they hold and in them I see everything I feel. I nod and then she smiles, slow and easy, and I want nothing more than to freeze this moment and live inside of it forever.

"Now you," she says. "Even in your appreciation, you didn't know my hair was changing so I know dinner wasn't for that. Spill it. Why were you ready to celebrate?"

"I threw today." I barely get the words out before she's cheering, grabbing my hand and almost spilling both of our drinks as she lifts them up in victory.

"Oh my gosh, Jake, this is huge. I should be cooking you dinner, what are you doing spoiling me when it's your day? We should have had steak. And French fries."

I laugh and pull her into my lap, cutting her off as I press my lips to hers. I'm so fucking happy it's unreal, and when she wraps her arms around my neck and drives her fingers into my hair, I know it's bigger than the milestone I hit today. It's her, she's my happy, my sunshine, everything that's pulled me from the dark and saved me the past few months.

"You're the first person I wanted to call and tell," I say as she leans back and smiles at me. "But then I thought this was too big for the phone and wanted to wait until you got home. Your hair distracted me."

"Well, I'm not sorry about that, but this is big, Handsome Jake, and it deserves major attention. We have to celebrate. Let's go dancing."

"Dancing?"

She nods, already scrambling up. "Yeah, dancing. Let's get done up and go out, find some music and some people and celebrate the fact that you just threw a fucking baseball."

I stand and follow her as she starts walking toward our bedroom, shedding her shoes as she does, starting on her denim shirt next, and then the shirt beneath it. When I get to the bedroom, she's naked except for a red lace bra and the jeans she's skinnying out of to reveal matching panties and I can no longer think.

"Does that sound like a good idea?"

I nod, aware that I'm no longer hearing her but would agree to anything so long as I could watch her peel out of her clothes for the rest of my life. When she stills, I look up at her and she raises a brow. "Are you even listening to me?"

I shake my head and she laughs. Then I grab her and toss her on the bed, craving her in a way that no other thing in my life comes close to mimicking.

~

Two hours later, I'm showered, dressed, and having a beer in the kitchen while Yogi eats his dinner and I wait for Blue to finish primping. She called her two friends from the salon to meet us, explaining to me that I needed male companionship and Liam was actually a big baseball fan. Since I didn't care as long as Cora's there, I nodded and came out to wait.

My phone rings and I take it out, frowning when I see my dad's name light up the screen. Swiping my finger across it, I set my beer down.

"Hey, Old Man, how's it goin'?"

"Old man, is it?" His voice is scratchy but sounds mostly steady, which means he hasn't had enough to drink today to make this conversation painful. Exhaling a tense breath, I smile and pick my beer back up again.

"Well, I guess if thirty's the new twenty, forty can be the new thirty, which means at forty-five you're not that old."

"Smartass," he says, and I can hear the affection. "What are you doing? Still living in that hippie city and chasing the pretty girl?"

I called my dad the first month I was here to let him know about my move, and then about Cora. I didn't give details, but I suddenly wish I had so I could have him give me advice — another odd desire as I haven't asked anything from my dad since I was fifteen and it was clear he could barely cope with his own life. But right now, able or not, I need fucking clarification. Whatever I'm doing with Cora has changed me, but who I am hasn't changed, as if that makes any sense. She feels like my center, but today I was reminded that my center is baseball, and it may be mine again soon. Which means leaving Cora.

When my dad repeats his question, I come back and laugh, swallowing down the rest of my beer in one gulp to clear my throat of the fear that's suddenly sitting there. "Yeah, still living in Portland, still chasing the pretty girl, but she lets me catch her now and then to reward me."

He grumbles something on the other end and, because Cora

steps out at the same time, I don't hear him clearly. She smiles as she sashays forward, fully aware of the picture she makes in the skintight, shiny black pants that fit like a second skin and end in skinny black heels with silver studs and a million straps that crisscross up to her ankles and let her red toes peak out. Her shirt is black lace and sleeveless. It should be modest in the way it fits her to her hips, leaving only her toned arms bare, except it's not because I can see everything beneath it, right down to the straight black piece of fabric that's confining her breasts while still offering a tempting view of that lace covered cleavage. Jesus.

Her lips are pinker, her eyes darker, and everything in me is hard as a rock. My dad's still jabbering and I tear my eyes away from her mouth to meet her eyes while I listen.

"How's the elbow?"

I nod and then realize he can't see me. "Good," I croak out and Cora smiles, stepping closer until her perfume, an exotic scent that's barely there until you're close enough sneaks out and wraps around me.

"Hey, I'll call you tomorrow, okay? I'm just about to head out."

"Take care of your arm. Throw 'em hard, Jake."

I soften slightly at the sentiment — the same one he's always given me as a goodbye or good luck. "Always do," I respond and click off.

"Who was that?" Cora asks and I shake my head.

"I don't know. Wow. You look… wow."

Her smile is all female confidence and satisfaction. "You're pretty wow yourself." Then she holds out her hand, no hesitation, no uncertainty, and I lace my fingers with hers. "Let's go celebrate you, Handsome Jake."

Chapter Twenty-Four

Cora

The club is loud and packed when A.J. pours herself onto one of the abandoned stools at our table. I sat a moment ago, having left the dance floor in search of something to cool my throat and my skin. Jake can dance, like, really move in more than the usual awkward white boy grab-her-hips-and-gyrate-back-and-forth way.

I'm embarrassed to admit that he's definitely the one keeping us afloat on the floor, as all I seem capable of doing is holding onto him. Now, he's headed toward the bar to get a mineral water and lemon for me and another beer for himself, and I'm sitting with A.J. while Liam spits some serious game with a redhead in the corner. When the girl bites her lip and flips her hair for the fifth time, I can practically see the triumph on his face. I never would have pegged Liam as a player, but watching him work I'm certain this is a regular activity for him.

I look around at the other people crowding the bar and the dance floor, the dark corners that house couples, the balcony where still more people stand and flirt, watch the dance floor and wait for their turn, and I realize that after more than a year away from this scene, I haven't missed it. Being with Jake on the dance floor was nice

— more than nice when I pressed up against him and he moved in a way that showed me his skills reached far beyond the bedroom or the ball field — and it made me realize that what used to be something that filled me, gave me energy and purpose, now only means something because he's here with me. It's not the club that has me happy and relaxed, almost content. It's Jake.

"Looks like I'll be getting myself home," A.J. says with a motion toward Liam and I laugh, tuning back in, grateful for her interruption from the path my thoughts were taking. Giving in, I prop my feet on the stool across from me. My studded Alexander McQueen peep-toe booties sparkle back at me, and I wince when I think of the walk home in them. Sexy? Yes. Comfortable after two hours of dancing and walking in them? Not exactly.

"We'll get you there," I tell A.J. when she mirrors my pose. "Besides, I thought Chloe was meeting you here."

"We broke up," she says and I stop admiring my feet long enough to shoot her a look.

"When?"

"A couple of days ago when it became clear that however into me she was, it wasn't enough for her to be open and honest with the people in her life." A.J. shrugs her shoulder and clicks on her phone, scrolling through some texts, looking busy to mask what I think is the hurt in her voice. "I don't hide who or what I am, and since that's what she needed from me, I decided to take a walk."

"That black and white?" I ask and her eyes stop scanning her screen long enough to shoot to me.

"Yeah, Snow White, that black and white. You're either with someone or you're not. Hiding them isn't the way to show them you want to be with them."

"Was she hiding or was she trying to figure it out? You said it yourself, you're her first serious girlfriend, the first person she's done more than go to dinner with. However ready she might be, she's also probably pretty scared. Doesn't she deserve some slack?"

I don't know why I'm defending Chloe, especially since I've only met her a handful of times, each one in passing at the salon. All I can see is that A.J. walked away from someone that made her happy because she was hurt. I've been in counseling long enough to know that walking away from things, from people, can be just as dangerous for a person as staying. There's a precious balance we have to work to maintain, the one that allows us to be more open, more accepting, more willing to try, and the one that tells us when enough is a enough, when it's time to walk away and save ourselves anymore unnecessary hurt. For whatever reason, the way A.J. looks is telling me walking away isn't necessarily the best decision for her or Chloe right now.

"What do you know about being scared, Snow White?"

It's a challenge, and one she's earned, so I lean back and cross my ankles. "I wanted everyone to love me and no one to know me, A.J., and as a result I got married and divorced before my twenty-first birthday, stopped talking to my parents, and ended up in rehab. I'm over a year sober now, and because I didn't walk away, didn't let anger and fear rule me, that hottie walking toward us is sleeping in my bed regularly. And more, he's with me right now, dancing and celebrating a night that's important to him, and he's friends with my friends. That's something I was too afraid to have a couple of years ago, because I was afraid the hurt would be too much in the end."

"How do you know it's going to end?"

I want to say I don't, that what we have has shown me that it doesn't have to, that what I feel with him is so strong, so different than I ever imagined real love could be that I know it actually has a chance, but I can't. Since the beginning, I've known why Jake was here, what he was working toward. Our futures don't line up, so all we can take is right now.

"Sometimes you can see the end before it even starts," I tell her. "And still, what we get in those brief moments together is enough to make the ending worth it."

She stares at me, keeps staring even as Jake sets down my water and stands beside my chair, sipping his beer.

Then she shakes her head. "Goddamn, Snow White, anytime you want to change teams you let me know."

"And me," Jake says and we all laugh.

A.J. rakes her multicolor nails through the side of her hair that's long. "It's been a long time since I was ashamed of who I was, and I didn't like it then. I like it even less now, especially since someone who matters is the one making me feel this way. It wasn't so bad when it was a stranger, but now, when it's the person I want to feel for me the way I feel for her? It hurts a lot and I can't fucking stand it."

I think back to when it was my mother making me feel like less, when all I wanted was for her to tell me just once that I mattered or that I looked nice, that she noticed me, maybe even she loved me. And now I think about all of the regrets I have because of how I responded to her carelessness, how many times I didn't tell her I loved her or needed her or respected her, and I realize the bad things can't be the only things that matters. Sometimes, you have to move forward, and know that the pain may be there and you can survive it.

"Are your feelings for her going away just because you walked?" She shakes her head. "Are you feeling any better about yourself?" She hesitates and then shakes her head again. "Then maybe you should call her, try introducing her to a small group of people first, see how it goes. And be patient," I tell her, looking at Jake. "It helps when you're scared to know that someone's willing to wait it out and just be there, no matter how often you tell them to go away."

I watch her walk away to call Chloe a minute later and then Jake turns my chair so my legs fall and he's standing right in front of me. When he brackets his hands on the back of it and leans down so our eyes are level, I smile and reach out, tracing my fingertip across his brow, over and down his straight nose to his lips. He's wearing one of the few button downs he owns, this one a dark blue denim, paired with his khaki colored cords, cuffed and resting on the top of his lace up brown boots that aren't vintage and trendy, but worn and well lived in. His shirt sleeves are rolled up to the elbow and I trace his tattoo while he looks down at me, mesmerized as always with the words that he chose to make a part of himself.

"You're going to do it, Handsome Jake." I linger on the last letter and then look up at him, inches away from those beautiful brown eyes. "You're going to get your dream back. You're going to rise from this, too."

I know he's had a life that doesn't hand out second chances, one where he worked to carve out a place for himself, even a girl, but she left him, just like his mother. He's never said it, but he doesn't have to. I see him, better than I've ever seen anyone else, and I remember what he said that night on the golf course when he told me that she just didn't love him, and then after when he told me that his mother left because she wanted something better. He's a riser, someone who's walked from the ashes and made a man of himself, and this time is no different.

He doesn't say anything, but his hands tense and his forehead drops to mine and for a second we stay like that, both finally acknowledging that whatever we've started has a shelf life. We both came here to escape a memory, but where this is the final destination in my journey, Jake is only in the middle of his, and the other half leads him back to where he came from, just like me.

He's going to go back, to finish becoming who he's meant to be, and when he does I'll stay here with the memory of him and how he pulled me from the in-between and into life and held onto me until I was strong enough to remember who I was and make her a part of who I am.

And I'll never forget what it felt like to know that for a while, I loved, and it was real.

Chapter Twenty-Five

Jake

I was ten the first time I threw a solid pitch with something more in mind than getting it over the plate. Montana isn't the hotspot for baseball — not the way it is in the south and southeast, but I found a team at eight and by twelve we played all year round. I rotated between outfield and the mound, two of the limited positions a lefty can play, and I was soon known for my curveball and my speed — throwing, not foot. As I got bigger, my velocity got better, to the point that I never doubted I'd get a chance after high school.

The day I left for college, my dad stepped out onto the barely-there front stoop of the double wide we lived in and leaned a shoulder against the metal side of the trailer, watching as I threw my two duffels into the back of my beat up '87 Land Rover that he'd rebuilt and given to me when I turned sixteen. We didn't have a bad relationship, it just wasn't a verbal one. Maybe it's because we were two men living in a kind-of-house with no female to soften the rough edges on either of us, or maybe it's because I wanted what he once thought was his, and he wanted to forget that time; either way, we never talked much and that day was no different.

Only, I wanted to talk to him, wanted to hear his voice and his encouragement, anything to tell me that I wasn't going to fail, that I wasn't chasing a dream that was going to end in a fiery pit of depression like it had for him. I didn't get that, even when I shoved my hands in my pockets and walked back to where he was standing.

"I guess that's it," I said and he nodded.

"Don't forget to stop somewhere in Utah. Seventeen hours plus is too long for one day."

I nodded, scuffing my feet in the dirt that was speckled with weeds, wishing just once that the words I'd always been able to use would come to me when I was faced with my father. As usual, they didn't, and we both stood there in silence, the sounds from the other residents of the trailer park booming around us. Sighing, I looked up and held out my hand, waiting for him to take it. The words were still stuck in my throat, the need to say them physically painful, but I didn't. Whatever I needed, he needed things too, and silence was one of them.

He grasped my hand and, after a second, surprised us both by hauling me forward and pounding on my back with his left. "Don't listen to anybody but your catcher, and remember the best pitch to throw is the one you can do the most accurate, the most often. Throw 'em hard, Jake."

Then he let me go and turned to walk inside, the metal screen door slapping closed behind him and echoing like a gunshot. I stood and stared at it, even when I heard the television click on and the sounds of an old western pour out of the windows. It wasn't reassurance in the traditional sense, but it was more than we'd said about baseball in a long time, and more than enough for me to read into it and know he was proud of me. He couldn't say it, couldn't push past whatever stood in his way and kept him from being truly whole, but he could acknowledge me as the pitcher I was, and it was enough.

That memory floated back to me today as I took the mound for the first time in eight months with the intent to *release* the ball, really release it, like a pitcher, like the ball player he had made me all those years ago. My arm didn't revolt, my elbow didn't tingle or weaken. It all held together and finally, I was back to the place I never thought I'd be.

I'm throwing from the mound every day now. My fastball is at seventy-five percent, and next week I get to start throwing breaking balls from a flat surface. Although my arm feels strong, there's still this sense of awkwardness, a learning curve to adjust to the foreign ligament that's now holding my bones together and allowing my arm to throw. The doctors assure me that this is normal, and most players feel like this until up to twenty months after their surgery. I'm only eight months out of surgery, and though there have been setbacks (my inability to focus at the beginning, my move from Arizona to Portland) I'm back on track. If everything continues as is, I'll be able to practice in game-like conditions soon, which means scrimmages and a batter, moving on the mound and taking calls from my catcher. It also means the future that I had put to the side all those months ago is now staring me right in the face.

Only now another future is there with it, one that includes Blue.

The lines of Hughes's *A Dream Deferred* run through my head and I wonder if sacrificing one dream for another is smart, or even possible. I'm terrified of leaving her, terrified that she's become just as big as the dream that came before her, but I'm also terrified of being like my father and sinking in the overwhelming feeling of failure. She knows this, because she asked me one night and I couldn't lie.

"Are you afraid of anything, Handsome Jake?"

We were sitting on the couch, her feet on my lap, a fashion magazine resting on her chest while I played Call of Duty. Like the other times that she asked me a question, it was out of the blue and took me by surprise. My initial answer was *no*, but then she gave me that look, the one that said she knew I was brushing her off, so I paused my game and sighed.

"Why does it matter?"

She shrugged but then she said the one thing that we both knew I couldn't refuse. "Because you matter and I want to be there for you. Is it the idea of never playing again?"

"That's one of them," I admitted.

"What's the other?"

Swallowing, I looked at her. "Ending my career like this, like my dad did, broken and used up, sad and angry. I promised myself a long time ago that wherever baseball took me, for however long I got to play, when the end came it wouldn't be a bitter one, it would be one where I looked back and thanked the baseball gods for the time they looked out for me, one where I could be grateful for the chances I had rather than resentful for the ones I didn't." I clenched my fist and looked down. "And then I tore my UCL, ended my career, and broke my promise all at the same time."

She was silent a second, like she so often is, and then she was sitting up, curling her legs under her as she pushed up enough to turn my face toward hers and look into my eyes. "You're not done, Handsome Jake. You're just taking a break."

I couldn't help the small smile that formed. "Oh yeah?"

"Yeah." And then she kissed me and I kissed her back, because whether or not she knew it, she made me believe that anything was possible in that moment.

Now, I'm walking toward her salon after my workout, just getting off the phone with my agent, whose been talking to the ASU coach, both of whom happen to agree with Cora. The draft is in two months, and if my progress continues like it has been I'll be entering… which also means going back to my team soon and engaging in those game-like situations to finish out my rehab.

Why this feels like giving up on Blue is confusing to me. We both know I've been rehabbing for one specific thing, yet I can't help but think I'm letting her down, walking away, doing what everyone else has done that I swore I wouldn't. I stop outside of the salon and look at her through the window as she finishes her check out process at the register. I'm almost a half an hour late, which means she had a walk-in or an appointment that ran over. Either way, I stay where I am and stare at her while she clicks away with the mouse and A.J. comes up from behind her, her approach clearly startling to Blue as she jumps and looks over her shoulder with a laugh and a glare.

The spunky brunette with the badass style and a sensitive heart just laughs and smacks her lips on the side of Cora's cheek. An ache forms in my chest as I watch her another few moments, noting that Liam eventually wanders over to add his opinion on whatever they're talking about. Cora laughs, A.J. scowls, Liam shrugs his shoulders in an *I call it like I see it* gesture.

She's opened in the last few months, bloomed and become more of the person I think she once was before she thought she had to shed those memories and start over. Four months ago she was a girl with a mission, but I'm not sure if she even knew that she was running. Running back to face her demons, running away from those she'd already shed. My siren, so fragile when she lets herself believe, and just tough enough to survive disbelief. Every day I'm with her she imbeds herself deeper and deeper inside of me until it's difficult to think of being anywhere she isn't.

After last week, the intensity of my feelings has doubled and so has my need for her. When she reached out and traced my tattoo at the club, her slim fingers dancing over the letters as if memorizing them onto her own skin, it almost brought me to my knees. And then she said what she did, told me I was taking back my dream, and for a second all I could think of was her and making her mine, of being hers and finding a new dream, one that ended with the two of us together.

I didn't say it because I won't put that on her, won't place on her the strain and stress that my own father's dream placed on the woman who once loved him enough to want to build a family with him. Whoever she was, he wasn't there, and when he came home he didn't have any idea who he was, let alone what she needed. Then she left and he's spent the rest of his life trying to erase the memory of her and his other failures from his brain. I won't do that to Cora.

Which means I only have a few weeks left with her, almost a month if I'm lucky, and I need to give her everything I can, so she never doubts what she means to me, or who she is inside of me.

She steps out the door, a sky blue bag big enough to fit a bowling ball inside over her shoulder, her legs showing their impressive tone and length in a pair of fitted black shorts that end just above mid-thigh. She's paired her sexy shorts with a simple black T-shirt sporting a chest pocket in the same blue as her bag, and some sort of wedge sandal in black and cork that wrap around her ankle and show her cute blue toenails. Needing to touch, I reach my hand out to her waist and bring her close, pleased when she sinks her fingers into my hair and drags them through.

"Hi.

"Hi back. How was training today?"

I shake my head and begin to walk, my arms still around her so she's forced to hold onto me and trust me to keep her safe as I guide her backwards. "Nope, we're not going to talk about training, or work, or anything real for the next twelve hours."

"We're not?"

I shake my head. "We're just going to be you and me, right here, right now."

If she senses my urgency or the reason for this need, she doesn't say anything. Instead, she studies me for a minute before nodding, and then she times it so that she shifts and lifts in a reverse sit up motion while my momentum propels me forward, allowing her to easily wrap her legs around my waist without so much as a mere hesitation in my stride. Tightening her legs around me, she brushes her fingers through my hair again and looks down at me.

"Sounds perfect."

And it is. I carry her all of the way home and laugh at the looks people give us, stopping to pose for a picture from some romantic soul. We make dinner and eat it on our miniscule balcony overlooking the parade of people below us on the sidewalk. We talk about movies and music, she explains the hilarious text conversation she had with Nina that had something to do with another engineering nerd, a school social, and a mixed piece of communication that ended with a broken heart and an irritated Nina. When the sun sets and the shadows take over, I take her hand and link our fingers, leaving our dishes from dinner on the small table as I lead her inside.

She comes willingly as I lead her into the bedroom — the one we've somehow morphed from hers to *ours* with carelessly discarded clothes and forgotten pocket items on the dresser and night table. Several of my paperbacks sit on the table next to the bed, her earrings on top of them. My boots are kicked against the closet door, a lacy red bra next to them.

Turning her to face me, I put my back to the window so the dying light pours over her skin while I look at her. Her eyes are wide and her chest is moving up and down but she doesn't blink, doesn't shake or back away from me. She waits while I look, my fingers still threaded through hers and my other hand reaching for the band in her hair, tugging until those gold tipped locks break free and spill around her shoulders.

I still don't say anything, just stand and drink her in with my eyes, my memory reminding me of the scent, taste, feel of each curve I skim over until my fingers are no longer content to stand on the sidelines. Releasing her hand, I bring it to my mouth and place a small kiss on her palm, then the inside of her wrist, tracing the sensitive skin there that's spiced with scent, something floral with dark undertones, that contradiction of secrets and serenity I noticed in her the first night I saw her five and a half months ago.

Now, she's trusted me with her secrets and I cherish that knowledge even as my lips cruise to the inside of her elbow to worship the sensitive skin there.

"Jake," she says, her voice whisper soft and breathless. I shake my head, cruising up to her shoulder and the curve of her neck, the shell of her ear, before I take the lobe into my mouth and scrape my teeth along it.

Her fingers grip the front of my shirt, twisting into the thin jersey material as she struggles to hold on while I assault her senses. My lips cruise to hers, sipping at them, teasing the seam as my fingers skim up her sides and under the silky soft fabric of her T-shirt, taking it with me as I continue up to her breasts, pausing at their sides as Blue raises her arms over her head, allowing me to continue until the shirt is in a heap on the floor. One look at her breasts contained in the barely-there light blue lace cups of her bra and my restraint threatens to snap, a tether strung tight and almost to its breaking point as I strap down the need that wants to claw free and *take*.

I'm not ready for that, and neither is she. What we're doing here is different than just sex, even great sex. It's more; it's the words we're afraid to say, the feelings that burn bright and hot between us and have no other vehicle for expression. So I don't do what my body begs and throw her over the bed to pound my release into her. I battle the raging pulse below my waist and continue to assault her over her clothes, cupping those full breasts and massaging them, using my tongue to drive into her mouth and set a rhythm that shows her exactly what I want.

Time and again I run my hands over her, innocent touches trimmed with bold ones, always pulling back before either of us gets too close to the edge, stripping her down until she wears nothing but the matching panties to that bra. When it seems like she might break apart just from a touch, I please us both and dip my head to lick my tongue into the valley between her breasts, laying her back as I do, curving my right arm under her hips and holding us up with my left as I hitch her toward the center of the bed and lay down on her side, one thigh pressed against her heat while my lips assault the sensitive flesh of her chest.

I'm a solid rod of iron when I push past the thin barrier of her panties and slip my fingers inside her to bring her over the edge, my mouth drinking down her cries even as I push her up and over again. As she lays there, sated and vibrating, I stand to shed my clothing, grabbing a condom from the drawer in the nightstand before returning to her. I don't suit up right away, instead waiting until she's come back to me, working my lips over her breasts and then her stomach, slipping her out of those panties and cruising my lips over the inside of her thighs and in, covering her with my mouth so she cries out and arches against me, shattering once more as I use my tongue on her.

Shifting to my back, I roll the latex on and then shift back over her, sweeping my fingers over the hair that's fallen to her cheek, stroking the skin of her jaw, her neck, her lips, until her eyes meet mine. And then, watching her while she watches me, I slide inside with one push, flexing my hips and ripping a cry from both of us before the animal inside unleashes and claims her as no one ever has, or will again.

Chapter Twenty-Six

Cora

I'm standing at the kitchen sink wearing Jake's Yankees T-shirt that's thin and worn at the shoulders and faded on the front. Some might call it vintage — I think it's actually reached the stage where *old* is the only description applicable. And still, the stretched neck of the graying white fabric with faded blue sleeves rests against my skin softer than any silk I've ever worn, mostly because it's his and wearing it feels like being next to him.

Which I was, ten minutes ago, right before I got out of the bed I'd been in for almost thirteen hours to get water and ease the dryness in my throat that's partly a result of the non-stop touching and exploration of each other's bodies we spent the night engaging in, with only minimal breaks for sleep and recuperation, and partly from the way it felt to lie there watching Jake as he finally succumbed to sleep, sprawled on his stomach, his left arm thrown over my hip, his right shoved under his pillow with the sheet twisted carelessly below his waist to reveal all of his glorious brown skin.

Sleep is the only time he's completely still, the only time I can watch him openly and not worry that he sees more than me. Lying on my side, content to feel the weight and warmth of his arm, I started with the outline of his profile, those sharp cheek bones and slashing dark brows, his thick mop of brown hair curled into a disheveled mess from my fingers alternately twisting into it and yanking at it last night. Down my eyes swept, over his broad shoulders that are roped with muscles, apparent even in this relaxed position, further to his tapered waist and the slope of his lower back to his backside that disappeared under the sheet.

It was that sight which had me getting out of bed, because it caused things to start stirring low in my belly, and however much I used to be a rock star who partied all night, I knew if I started something there was a distinct possibility I wouldn't be able to finish it. Jake had out-sexed me last night, plain and simple, and as much gratitude as those memories evoked while they swirled and spun in colorful detail through my mind, accompanied by the requisite tingle or two, I was more than a little sore and even more grateful that he wasn't awake this morning to watch me limp from bed, whimpering when I leaned down to grab his T-shirt from the folded but not yet put away laundry in the basket by the bedroom door.

Now, I'm downing my second glass of water over the kitchen sink in the morning light that's quickly turning to afternoon, and my head's clearing enough from the sexual fog to see what I couldn't when I walked out of the salon yesterday and into his arms. We've started our goodbye, and I can't stop it.

I think back to when he touched me last night, the first time and all others, how he transitioned from a careful, almost reverent lover to a brutal and demanding one, dragging responses from me that are terrifying on more levels than just the physical. I didn't want him to stop touching me, ever; even more terrifying, I couldn't have asked him to if I did. The power he has over me isn't physical — it's a connection of my soul that has woven him within its fabric, forever tying me to him and the person he's let me be. Alone, I was surviving, finding my feet and learning how to get through each day, but with Jake, I've learned to be happy. He woke me from my slumber and showed me that life can't be lived in the fear of yesterday, but has to be cherished for what I feel, what I can be, what I can offer today. And what everyone else offers.

He offered me freedom from the walls I was living behind, and I'll never forget that.

My skin prickles, that natural warning bell that tells me he's close, so I set my glass down and turn to face him, prepared, yet still shocked by the overwhelming swarm of desire that sweeps through me at the sight of him in low-strung sweats and nothing else, his long, lean frame a foot from me. I lean back against the counter and stare at him while he stares back, and then he's moving forward, pushing into my space as he did time and again last night and has every night since we met really, until my hands grip his shoulders and he lifts me, settling me on the counter where he stands in the space between my legs.

His hands stay at my hips and he inclines his head now that I'm slightly above him. I take my hands and run them through his hair, scraping my nails along his scalp and back, watching him the entire time.

"How was training?" I ask again, and this time his eyes flutter closed and he leans forward to rest his forehead against mine, his hands slipping from my hips so his arms can band fully around my waist.

"It was really good," he says, and I hear it, the words we won't say but are being forced to acknowledge as every day gets closer to the last. *It's almost done, it's almost time for me to go.* I nod and hold on tighter, knowing that soon enough I'll hold him for the last time.

~

The average addict relapses seven times before sobriety takes hold. This statistic is one I know well, not only because I'm a recovering addict, but because I've felt the pull of oblivion more than once since I left The House.

I'm an alcoholic, but really, I only use that label because it's the most straightforward and people need a label to understand other people, especially those people who are different. The reality is that most addicts are more than their substance of choice — alcohol is not my weakness, it's my escape, my crutch to lean on when I don't want to deal with everything else that's weighing down on me. My weakness is control, fear, self-loathing, my never-ending need for *more*. More attention, more things, more fun, more love.

I wasn't a lovable child. No one had to tell me that for me to know it's true. I was contrary from the moment I could speak, always saying no when someone else said yes, always pushing the envelope when everyone else accepted the limitations given. I didn't feel loved because I didn't accept it, and then when I realized I wanted it, no one knew how to give it to me, not even myself. So, instead I filled that void, that need, with substances and people. Lots and lots of people.

Anyone, everyone, so long as I didn't have to hear the silence that told me I was well and truly alone.

I knew by age seventeen that I had pushed my mother far enough she wasn't coming back. It took me until almost twenty-one to realize that every party I went to, every pill I swallowed or joint I smoked, and every morning after that I let her see me hung-over and used, I was challenging her to challenge me because even if she was done with me, I wasn't done with her. How could I blame my mother for not loving me when I understood why she couldn't? Why she shouldn't. I wasn't smart like Mia and Lily, her own sister's children, or beautiful and dynamic like her friends' daughters. I wasn't athletic or motivated or perfect... I wasn't anything, and that was the problem for both of us.

~

I called my sponsor the weekend after he picked me up from the salon. I know that as strong as I am now, what I feel for him is so big, so terrifyingly real and wonderful that when it's gone, I'm going to hurt. Since I don't want to fall into an old habit, I called Kari, the fifty-year-old single law clerk who had dragged me back from the edge more times than Mia and Nina could ever even think of doing in those first few months. Mostly because she was an alcoholic, so she herself understood the pull of addiction, even when repercussions for it were staring you right in the face, giving you a goddamn good reason you should walk away.

"There's not always a reason we want to relapse, Blondie," she once told me, using the nickname she first gave me back when I wore my hair as white as Gwen Stefani. "Sometimes, life's enough to make you want the escape. When you feel the urge, you call me and we talk, then you find a meeting and you sit there and let other stories remind you why you're stronger than your addiction."

"What about texting you?"

"I'm fifty, not fifteen, so we'll talk like humans and not those robots you young kids are turning into."

So, Kari and I talk, and even text sometimes, though she's never happy about it. We talk less now that I've hit my one year mark than we did in the beginning, but I know she's there and so I called, needing to tell her what I just figured out: Jake has to go and be who he was meant to be, and I have to let him, because however wonderful we are right now, there are things you have to face alone, without anything or anyone holding onto you.

I wouldn't hold Jake back, but I would hold on, and he needs someone who's going to let him go and fight that battle and win, so he never feels the shame of failure his father did. And he needs to do that without worrying about me and the fact that I might get bored or lonely or needy for him while he's gone for hundreds of days on end.

"Blondie, I think you need to find a meeting."

Kari's rough voice scrapes over the line and I bring myself back to the conversation. I'm standing outside of the salon, watching as pedestrians walk or bike by, bro-tanks and maxi dresses in full effect as April teases Oregon into bloom.

"That's why I called you."

"And I'm telling you that you've got too much shit going on to just call someone. You need to sit down and face some people, listen to them and maybe let yourself talk, and you don't need to just sit with someone, you need to sit with your people, people who understand what a trigger moment is."

I know all of this, which is why I called her instead of Mia. Sometimes, no matter how much people love you, it's the strangers who don't know you but who are *like* you that help the most. "I think you might be right."

"I know I am, that's why I'm your sponsor. Listen to me, Cora," she says and I know she's serious. "You've got some heavy shit going down. You can handle it, I know you can, but that doesn't mean you need to ignore the other things that are important, like your meetings and your recovery. It's only been eighteen months, Blondie, that's not that long. You need to take care of yourself, so you can take care of the rest of the people you love."

I sigh and close my eyes, understanding now why a sponsor is different than a friend, and why Kari's always been able to be both. She's like the Scientist with her no nonsense ways, her direct statements, and blunt attitude. She has a heart bigger than most and a shell that's tough to crack, and she's as different from my own mother as a person can possibly get. That's one of the reasons I chose her. At my first meeting I just sat and listened, did what the counselor at The House recommended and watched, listening to people share countless stories, relapses, heartaches, and then I saw and heard from Kari. She didn't cry when she spoke, and I could sense right away that her tears were private, something she wouldn't share, but something I sensed were just below the surface. Kari regretted who she had been, and the limits it put on the person she was, even now. She was happy, and she was strong, but Kari was alone. Alcohol was a crutch that had taken her husband and her chance at a family away from her. Her battle was in reminding herself that she deserved forgiveness, even if she couldn't give it to herself right away.

I was lost at that first meeting, but, looking at Kari, I felt like she could help me find myself. She was strong, it showed in the sturdy set of her shoulders and the way she held the eyes of everyone in the room rather than looking over, around, or down as so many did. She challenged all of us to complete our steps, and I wanted more.

I went to meetings for two weeks, not seeing her again until the last one at the end of that second week, and I decided right then that I wanted her to be the one to help me off the ledge when I needed it. A year and a half later, she's not only telling me how to survive, she's making sure I know I can, that I'm stronger than anything or anyone I've ever let hold me down, my fears included.

"You there, Blondie?"

I nod and then clear my throat. "Yeah, I'm here."

She sighs over the phone and I hear the heartache in it. "Life's a real bitch, hon, that's why we tried to tune it out. Now, you can't tune it out but you do have a chance to change what you hear. How's everything with your mom going?"

I think back to the past few times I've visited her. The conversation hasn't exactly flowed, but the silences are less tense and our rhythm feels more natural, less like a forced routine. And, oddly, she's picked out a new color for her nails every time. Whether I should or not, I'm taking that as a sign that she wants to be something different than she was too, something more.

"Of course she does," Kari says when I tell her this. "Blondie, listen to me. Just because we're adults doesn't mean we think everything we do is right. Shit, half the things we do are unplanned, and even the half we plan don't always turn out right. Your mama might not be able to say what she's feeling, but she's glad you're there and, from everything you've told me, she wants to make things right, just like you."

I release a breath. "Thanks, Kari. I'll find a meeting tomorrow, but this helped."

"That's why I'm here. Let me know when you find a meeting. And Blondie?"

"Yeah?"

"One day at a time, remember that. You just survive one day at a time."

"What about all those days ahead that you can't see, but that you know are waiting for you?"

"You treat them like you do any other pushy person and tell them to fuck off until you're ready."

The laughter is a relief as it rolls out of me. One day at a time. I can do that.

Chapter Twenty-Seven

Jake

Murph answers on the second ring, his voice cutting out as I hear the echoes of other voices around him.

"Handsome Jake? Is it really fucking you?"

I laugh and step out onto the balcony, angling my body so I can see the front door and Cora when she gets home. She had some things to do after work, like she has a few times since the morning we woke up and realized our time together was ending. I think she's going to AA meetings, but since I sense that it's private, I don't ask, I just make dinner and wait for her to get home.

Now, I'm standing here after my final workout with the trainer and I'm calling the guy I consider my best friend, because I'm getting my dream back, but in the process, it's breaking my fucking heart. Not that I'll tell him that — I'm hurt, not a woman.

"Just calling to tell you only a pussy hits a double and three RBIs against Cal State. I expected a homerun and some stolen bases, but here Twitter's telling me you're barely scoring these days. I hope Mia isn't too disappointed to realize you can't find home plate."

"Leave my wife outta this, Pitch, and say that from the mound next time. I bet I can still hit you."

"You might just get a chance sometime soon," I say and there's a pause.

"Hold on," he says and I hear a few muffled thuds and a curse before a door opens and closes. "Jake?"

"Who the hell else would it be?"

"Jesus Christ, you did it. You're coming back."

"That's actually why I'm calling. I finished my rehab today — at least, everything that I can do on my own. The rest needs to be done with a team, and with the trainers down there. Got a room I can use?" I ask and he laughs into the phone.

"Fucking A, just under ten months. I knew you could do it. Didn't I tell you?"

"Probably more like twelve when it's all said and done, but, yeah, you told me."

"Well, Jesus, when are you coming down here? Our schedule's in full swing, but Mia's here and your room's still open. We need to celebrate, have a welcome home party."

I nod and watch the front door. "Yeah, soon, I just have some things I need to take care of here first."

We're both silent a second and then I hear Murph blow out a breath. "Shit, I wondered if that would be the case. Does she know?"

I give in and shut my eyes, pressing the fingers of my free hand to them. "She knows I'm healing and that it's only a matter of time before I go."

"What did she say?"

I shake my head and open my eyes. "Nothing. Blue knows I

can't stay, just like I know I can't ask her to wait. Won't ask her to," I add.

"But does she know you want to stay? Jesus, Jake, have you told her how you feel? Because I can't even see you and I know after a ten second pause exactly how you feel about her."

Fucking Murph, reaching the dream that disappeared isn't enough, he thinks I deserve the girl too. For the last ten months, other than Cora he's been the only person to text me, to continually encourage me, even when I ignored him those first few months after I moved. And still, as much as I want to do as he says, I can't. "No, I haven't told her. And before you ask, no, I'm not going to tell her. Shit, I've taken enough from her, Ryan, I can't leave her with the pressure of my feelings too. We're both just getting back on our feet — it was selfish enough of me to force myself into her life and make her care about me. If I tell her how much I love her and then walk on her, what's it going to do to her?" I know what it's doing to me: killing me, slowly, with every thought I have of walking away.

"Why can't you just ask her to wait? Tell her you want to be with her but you need to try this too. It's not like you're leaving the country."

I shake my head, the image of my dad in various stages of depression and self-pity throughout my life popping up and running through my mind. I'd been honest the day I told Cora the minors were like war. Bad pay, a horrendous schedule, and no certainty of ever making it. Six months of traveling with maybe ten days off, hours a day at the field and a paycheck per year that's lower than the national poverty line. How do you bring someone into that with the hope that loving each other is enough?

"I can't, Ryan. Waiting works for some, like you and Mia. What you have, it was here before, and it'll be here after. Blue and me... I can't risk her, man, I can't risk losing her while I'm somewhere else, or worse, coming home broken and taking my failure out on her, hurting her because I couldn't be the man I wanted to be." I think of what it would do to me to know that Cora relapsed because of me, that she went back to being someone who couldn't see her own worth. Someone who couldn't look at me and see that she was loved. My chest contracts at the mere thought. I might have been able to risk myself, but not her, never her.

"My dad never got out of the funk, Murph, he never stepped up and did anything else when the minors killed him, never got over losing the dream. You saw me when I thought I was done — it was girls and booze, all day every day. What if I fail and it changes me, changes who I've become since I've been with her? What will that do to her if she's waiting for me and I come home a used up bastard, or worse, don't come home to her at all?"

My heart is beating too fast and I have to work to take slow breaths, in and out, while there's silence on the other end of the line. I know he sees my point or Murph would have already told me I was being an asshole, to get over myself and go get my girl. Part of me was hoping he would say it so I could do just that, be selfish and ask Cora to wait for me, to love me even though I'm not nearly good enough for her. To belong to me because she's made me a better version of myself than I ever thought possible. But he doesn't. Instead, he blows out a breath and agrees with me. Bastard.

"You're right, Jake. I wish you weren't but it's not fair to ask her to wait knowing what lies ahead, not when you're both so unsure of yourselves. And not when she's already had enough people use her and then forget about her."

My fingers tighten painfully on the phone and I want to rage at him that I'm not like any of those people, that I would cut my fucking arm off and never throw a baseball again before I used her, but I can't, because we both know that I followed her here because she did something that no one else could and made me care again. Before I even knew her, Blue snuck past my defenses and made me feel something and I've held onto that for long enough — falling in love with her doesn't change the fact that I saw something I needed and I took it, it just makes it that much fucking harder to walk away.

"Shit, Murph, why does it hurt this goddamn much?"

His silence tells me he's remembering his time without his own girl, that awkward in between high school and college time when no one has their shit figured out and even loving someone doesn't mean you can have them. "Because it's real. It doesn't matter if you were always going to walk away, Jake, you fell in love and it's like being hit by a line drive, right between the eyes. You don't always recover, and even if you do, that hit stays with you and echoes through you every now and then, so real you can feel it, and it hurts all over again."

His words are still playing in my head minutes later when Cora opens the door and steps through. I stay where I am, watching her as she drops her keys and purse on the bench just inside the door, then walks a few steps to the couch where she rests her hand and leans down to slip off one heeled sandal before switching feet and doing the other. When she straightens, I slide open the door and we lock eyes.

The air between us electrifies as it has every time we've been in the same room in the past few weeks. The urgency that has pushed us to be together as much as possible comes to a boil and spills over and, all of a sudden, the air is thick with not only need, but understanding, heartache, grief. A minute passes and then two, but neither of us moves as we stare at one another, our bodies fighting the magnetic pull that's urging us together as we acknowledge what's happening.

"When?" she finally asks and I step inside, closing the door behind me.

"Soon. Tomorrow."

She nods and I stay still, waiting to see what she wants. My heart is thumping against my chest so hard I can hear it in my ears, and my breath is backing up in my lungs. When she steps toward me, I have to fist my hands to keep them at my sides, still uncertain if she's going to touch me or slap me. But then she's cupping my face in her hands and meeting my eyes, a small smile on her lips as she raises to her toes and presses her mouth to mine.

"Then let's take tonight."

Chapter Twenty-Eight

Cora

Tomorrow.

His words vibrate down to my core and settle in the pit of my stomach. The dread, the pain, the hurt… we knew this was coming and still, the pain is worse than either of us could have predicted. But I won't have him regretting leaving, won't have him feeling sad to be chasing the dream that he's worked so hard to get back, just as I won't have him regretting coming here in the first place. Pain or not, I wouldn't change any of it.

When I see him go to speak, I shake my head, my smile firmly in place though my cheeks ache with the effort.

"Jake, there's nothing left to say, we both know that. This is your dream, something you thought you lost but can now have. It's everything you've ever worked for, everything you've ever wanted."

His eyes are devastated when they look at me and I know what he's thinking. *But what about us?* I stop him before he says something he'll feel forced to see through, something that I'll want to believe even though I know better. Who understands better than I that sometimes you have to make a choice.

"We never made any promises, Handsome Jake, and we both

know too well that life can change. People can change. I'm grateful I had you," I tell him and my breath catches in my throat, hitching until I have to stop and swallow. "You and I got what we needed from each other, let's not make it into something it was never meant to be."

He's processing my words and what they mean, for him, for me, for us. I know he understands that I'm telling him he needs to go, to make his future and be the person he was meant to be. It feels like the air has been sucked out of the room, making it difficult for me to draw breath, but I work on it, slowly breathing in and out as I watch him, memorizing every feature since this might be my last time.

It hurts to think that, right down to my bones, and it hurts to know that what we are is temporary because I let myself believe, for even a second, that we could have more. But more than the hurt is the fear that if I don't let him go, if I beg him to stay and try to make it work, what we have will be tainted by regret or blame. That eventually it will make both of us feel nothing more than mild contempt for the other person, and I won't risk that.

It's not a selfless act that has me letting him go; no, it's fear that if I try to keep him and balance our worlds together, we'll one day end up like the parents we both claim not to need, stuck in a relationship that eventually causes us to despise one another, or worse, causes one of us to need more than the other can give. I can take watching him leave now if it means we don't ever look at each other or back at what we were with regret, that we have this memory of what it felt like to be alive together.

I think I can survive as long as I know we have that.

Needing somehow to show him everything I can't say, I rise to my toes and press my lips to his. My fingers sink into his hair and bring him closer, molding us together as we make that much needed contact. For perhaps the first time since we've been together, I let everything I'm feeling translate into my touch. I don't hold myself back, don't try to slow myself down; instead, I take everything I need and give him everything I have, hoping that I can show him without saying the words exactly what he means to me. Words are too easy at times, too simple. What we have isn't simple; he's the first person to touch me and feel more than my body, the first person in my life to ever reach inside of me and see who I really am, the heart that beats inside of me, and he's the only person I've ever wanted to give it to, free of expectation.

Jake showed me that love isn't a balancing of scales, it's a gift, one that's given and accepted freely, one that makes looking at someone and saying goodbye easier because you know deep down it's the only thing that will allow them to truly be whole.

When he wraps me up and lifts me, so reminiscent of our first time together, I have to battle back the tears that spring to my eyes. I wind around him, my legs anchored around his hips, my arms around his neck as I take my lips on a journey of face and neck while he carries us into the room we've shared for months now.

Neither of us says anything as he stops at the side of the bed and I slide slowly down his body until my feet touch the floor. The time for words has passed, and now we're looking at each other, standing pressed together as the dying light pours through the open window and invites in the sounds and scents of the outside world. A world we made our own for just a little bit.

For a second, I'm transported back to those early days we were together when we would love playfully, when he would shush me and tell me the neighbors would hear and then do exactly what he had done the second before to make me cry out. It didn't matter if there were thousands of noises coming through the windows and surrounding us or nothing at all — for those brief periods of time, all we needed was each other and what we felt when we were together.

Hoping I can remind him of that now, I take my time undressing him, my fingertips brushing lightly over exposed skin, my lips exploring each new piece of flesh I uncover. His shirt falls behind him as I push it over his head and my lips immediately find the smooth skin of his chest, resting over his heart. I reach for the top button on his shorts and he grabs my hands, shaking his head even as his mouth comes down on mine.

He takes the power easily, his mouth demanding, his touch consuming as he strips me of my dress, laying me back on the bed as his lips go to work covering every inch of me. He's tender in his assault and so thorough, letting no part of me feel left out, covering me with his body as his fingers take their own journey from my breast to my stomach and more, the sensations so overwhelming I can barely breathe.

"Don't forget this." He speaks the words against my lips, his tone fierce and urgent, and I shake my head. Never. We can't have it all, but we have this, and it's special. No matter what happens, neither of us will forget. When his mouth closes over my breast and his fingers press into me, I'm thrown from the cliff, my back arching and my body breaking apart as he works me ruthlessly over the next peak as well.

Shattered, I lay there when he shifts away to get a condom, my lungs burning and my limbs weak, and then he's back, his forearms bearing his weight as he rests over me and waits for my eyes to meet his.

"Was it worth it?" he asks and I don't pretend to not understand. Were we worth it, the pain we both know is coming, the opening up of secrets and pieces of my life buried? Was everything we did over the past five months worth this moment?

I look into his eyes, my own free and clear of tears, my hands going to his face. "Yes."

His forehead drops to mine, his body shuddering for a heartbeat before he's moving, rocking inside of me and taking me to that place where it's only us. I hold onto him, bring his lips down to mine and take everything he has to give me one last time.

~

In the morning I wake alone, his ratty Yankees T-shirt and a note on the pillow beside me.

"…I might not be alive now, only for you…" You saved me from myself and gave me back my dream, I'll never forget that. Yogi wanted to stay. Check to cover the rest of the year is on the counter. Be happy, Blue, and remember you're not alone. xoxo

I stare at the piece of paper, something that most people would have sent in a text. Not Jake. *My Jake*, I think. The poetry reading, paperback holding, pen using, cat owner with brown eyes and a heart bigger than most. He wrote me a note to keep, something I can take out over and over to trace the words that will protect me against loneliness.

Curling into his pillow, I don't cry. I breathe him in and let his scent fill those places inside that are already lonely without him. Then I grab his note and get up to feed the cat.

Chapter Twenty-Nine

Jake

Mia's waiting for me when I finally arrive at my old Arizona apartment thirty hours after I left Blue sleeping. I don't know if it's the haggard scruff I carry from the almost fourteen hundred miles of driving with minimal sleep, or the fact that I hurt everywhere and it shows, but one look at me has her stepping back and reaching out a hand to bring me inside.

"I won't blame you if you take a swing at me."

"Ah, you're thinking of Cora — she's the fighter." She must see my face because the Angel's smile is sympathetic as she wraps her arms around my waist, resting her head on my chest for a beat. "She's stronger than we think, Jake. You both are." When she pulls back, she smiles up at me and I feel the tenuous bit of control I have start to tremble. "Come on, Ryan told me you were coming and, though I'm sure I'm not as appealing to hang out with as a bunch of sweaty guys, they're on the road at Stanford until Saturday night, so I'm all you've got. But I did buy you beer and some tacos to make up for such a quiet homecoming."

"Muph's a lucky guy, Angel."

Her grin is lightning quick and blinding when she throws it

over her shoulder at me, and for what feels like the millionth time, I think of my siren and her smile, the one that was so rare in the beginning, and made me feel like a fucking king every time I got her to give me one when we were together. And then I remember her smile that last time we were together, the small curving of her lips as she told me she wouldn't change anything about us even if she could. There's a gaping hole in my chest, something that tells me I've just left the best thing behind and when I see Mia watching me from the kitchen with knowing eyes, I understand that love, however new, however short lived, changes us more than any other experience. Hefting my bag, I block out the images of Blue and follow my best friend's girl into the kitchen.

~

"Have you talked to her?"

Mia looks up from the sink where she's rinsing dishes and I see her eyes narrow, assessing how much I can really take. Finally, she nods.

"This morning, and yesterday after Ryan texted me and told me you were moving back in. I'm going to see her this weekend."

Don't ask, don't ask, don't ask. Shit, just ask. "How is she?"

"About like you'd expect, I guess."

My smile is humorless as I tip my beer bottle back. "Not gonna make this easy on me, are you, Angel?"

"Can anything really make this easy, Handsome Jake?"

It's not the statement but the tone she delivers it in, not full of resentment and condemnation, but of understanding. That alone has me cracking enough to set my beer down and scrub my hands over my face.

"I just couldn't stay — and I couldn't ask her to wait. I wanted to, fuck did I want to, I just knew that asking could be a promise broken. Leaving her honestly, leaving without expectation and hope, letting her go instead of tying her to a possibility seemed more honest than anything else." I pick up my beer and swallow half the contents as Mia comes to sit on the stool the next to me. The apartment is the same, small kitchen with a breakfast bar and two stools that leads into the small living space, which leads to the hall and two bedrooms. But it's different — when Murph and I lived here there were beer cans on the table and baseball posters on the wall. The television was the only thing that was taken care of, and it was almost always hooked up to some kind of game console. Now, there's some flutey-type music with a contemporary feel playing over the sound system and the screen is blank. The carpet is clean and void of any stains and debris, and the kitchen smells and looks clean.

My mind flashes back to the apartment I left almost two days ago, the windows that filtered in light and sound, the comfortable furniture that had become a place for Cora and I to love each other in the afternoon. The kitchen where we made meals together, danced while we cleaned, stood while she cried on my shoulder, and where I admitted that we were close to an end.

Mia sits patiently while I gulp more beer, erasing the images even as I erase the emotion in my throat. She's pulled her knees to her chest on the small stool and has her chin resting on them, her eyes strong and steady as she watches me. She's similar to Cora in ways that show me they're more than good friends — certain expressions, her ability to sit completely still and listen. But Mia's demeanor isn't controlled so much as ingrained. Assessing things, figuring out the best approach and all possible outcomes is as a part of who is she is, something as natural as her eye color. Blue, she was my siren, the temptress who was controlling her body and her heart while she learned to control her choices and her life.

Until me. It isn't arrogance, it's plain understanding that until me, Cora was living with the hope to survive in peace, and then I came along and wouldn't take no, and eventually, her walls began to come down and together we came alive. Even as the memory comforts me, it makes me feel like a bastard. I walked away, but I'm starting to wonder if I ever should have walked toward her that first night.

"It was braver than you think to walk away, Jake."

Mia's words penetrate my thoughts, as if she knew where they were headed, and I look up from the counter to meet her eyes.

"Most people would think walking is the weak choice — that fighting for her is the brave thing to do, giving it all up to be with her so I can show her she's all that matters."

"Is she? All that matters, I mean."

I take a minute to think about it, remembering what it felt like to go home each night knowing she would be there, waking up in her bed in the morning, moving with her, inside her, loving her.

"She matters more than anything or anyone else ever has. More than I thought anything or anyone could," I admit, and Mia nods like she gets it. "But I can't say she's the only thing that matters because I want others things too. I guess that's why I left. I want to be a ball player, and I don't know how to do that and be with Cora, not the way she deserves."

Mia stays quiet, even after I stop and drink down the last of my beer. When I stand to drop the bottle in the recycling bin, she waits for me to come back before speaking.

"Did Ryan ever tell you about my family?"

I nod. "Some, but it was enough to understand that loving a guy like the Murph was probably scary as fuck for you at first."

"And then some," she adds with a smile that draws one of my own. "My parents don't know how to think of each other and of themselves at the same time, if that makes sense. Like both of them lost their identity when they got married and started a family, so they adopted roles that can only be defined as a member of that family. My father runs the family business, and his family when they need order and guidance, and my mother does everything she can to keep my father happy and our appearance perfect. It's not a hard way to grow up," she says when my eyes narrow, "just different. I have three brothers and a sister and we've all dealt with our own understanding of love differently. My older brother gave up his life for a girl, just as you said people think we should. He dropped his dreams, his family, his future, and followed her around because he thought this was the only way to show her he loved her, to think only of her."

"But…"

"But in the end, he realized he couldn't forget about himself and his life, not even for her. When Ryan and I started dating, I always held back because I figured if I thought of him too much I'd become my mother, never looking forward for my own life, only thinking about his. Even when I realized Ryan would never let me forget about myself and my dreams, I had to walk away from him and make sure I was ready and willing to fight for him *and* for me. I had to be ready to fight for us."

I sit and let the Angel's words sink in, filling in the gaps to her story with the tidbits I've learned from Ryan over the years.

"It's okay to walk away if you aren't sure how to stay, Jake."

And there it is, the one thing I needed to hear. Closing my eyes, I scrub my hands over them again. "Christ, Mia, what do I do? I pushed myself into her life, made her feel something for me, and then broke my own heart and possibly her hard earned stability when I walked out. Who does that?"

Mia reaches over and puts her hand on mine. "Sometimes, you have to understand what each of you need before you can be together. You need to do this, Jake, and Cora needed to let you. Both of you know that."

I think of the quote I left her, of Scarlett and Rhett and the love story they tried to make, the one they may still have had a shot at, who knows. And then I think of what Mia's said, of what Cora said all those weeks ago on the couch when she told me I wasn't done, just taking a break, and I know Mia's right. Walking away was necessary, for both of us, I just wish it didn't have to hurt quite this fucking much.

I tell the Angel this and she smiles, standing to wrap her arms around me one last time before stepping back. "You're a good person, Handsome Jake, or you wouldn't have been too scared to stay."

As Mia walks down the hall and closes her door, I wonder if she's right, or if the real reason I walked was because I loved Cora more than I've ever loved anything else, and if there's one pattern I've known in my life, it's that everything you love eventually goes away and leaves you with nothing.

Chapter Thirty

Cora

My mother's having a bad day. A really bad fucking day, and as a result, my head is about to pop off my shoulders. I take deep breaths as I continue breaking her hair into sections, silently reminding myself that she's dealing with a lot, and the fact that's she's talking to me at all should be enough. But when she criticizes the way I'm doing her hair for what feels like the millionth time, the same hair I've done every week for almost seven months now, I have to stop what I'm doing and step back in order to avoid throttling her and ruining the progress we've made.

In the past two months, the time since Jake left, we've really turned a corner, come to a type of truce I guess you could say. She isn't always talkative, but she listens when I talk, and in the last little bit, she's actually asked me a question or two throughout our few hours together. I've told her about Mia's college graduation that Ryan texted me a million pictures from since I couldn't make it with my busy work schedule — which is partly true. The other part is that I didn't try to make it as I know Jake is still there and seeing him now might just make me confess how much I need him and miss him. Since that's not what he needs, and since Mia knows that and came to see me two weeks before her graduation so we could celebrate her achievements together, I stayed home to spend more time with my mother and build a more solid client base at the salon, and Ryan sent me a thousand pictures of his beautiful wife as she crossed the stage with her undergraduate degree in sports and exercise science. I tell my mother all of this and show her the pictures, only omitting the part about Jake, though a part of me really wants to tell her, which is strange.

Even stranger is the urge I regularly feel to tell her what's going on in my life.

At Kari's insistence, I finally told my mother about my time in rehab, the counseling, and now my recurrence at AA meetings. As if Kari knew it would, this caused her to open up to me a bit more, rather than criticize me, like the admission that I had my own demons allowed her to let her guard down so I could see some of hers. I've started coming over twice a week, now, once to do her normal treatments, and another evening during the week to say hello and have dinner with her and my father.

It's surreal, those nights, sitting at the table in the dining room and having a meal with both of my parents, no one shouting, no one sitting in icy silence, no one walking out. I had to go for a run after the first time, the emotions swirling through me too large to name or comprehend. Even after several months and multiple dinners, along with a Fourth of July picnic in the backyard, I still feel the emotions swarm through me when we manage to sit and talk and eat like a family; it's even weirder to think that, and to finally understand the term. Family. Before, I had parents, people who had raised me and paid for my life, but we weren't a family, not like we are now. Now, we talk, we care, we even manage to laugh.

Which is probably why today, I'm done taking my mother's shit. She's sick, she's fragile, but she always has been. Just like she's always used criticism as a defense mechanism, and I've always taken her bait, exploding and then storming off, leaving her alone to stew and feel sorry for herself. Well, this time I'm not leaving, and I'm not taking any more of her complaints, either.

"Mom, enough."

"I just don't think you need to use so much—"

"Enough," I cut her off and turn her chair so she looks into my eyes. Hers are dark, not yet hollow, but I can see the blue transforming, the black overtaking, and for the first time in a while I'm reminded that my mother isn't just sad, but that she's ill. "What's going on? You've been mad all day. Are you feeling all right?"

"That's a stupid question. Why would I feel all right? I'm losing my mind, every day. Soon, I'm going to be shitting my pants and getting my food from a tube."

Her hands are clenching and unclenching at the throat of her robe again, and I can hear her uneven breathing. I'm shaking a little as I try to go backwards and think about what Sassy told me when I asked how to deal with an upcoming episode. I wanted to be prepared in case it ever happened again, but now I can't remember anything she told me as I stare at my mother while she grows more and more agitated.

"Mom, did something happen?"

"The same thing that happens every day. I lost my mind. Why can't he understand that? I can't go out, can't go somewhere. What will people think when I can't remember them? When I can't remember where I am let alone who I am?"

I stand watching her, my heart rate spiking as her hands continue to clench and unclench on the neck of her robe, her breath wheezing, her eyes wide with fatigue and anger and sadness.

"Are you talking about Dad?"

"How can he expect me to go anywhere? To dinner, he said, as if it's just that easy. Nothing's easy, and it never will be again. Why can't he see that? Why does he refuse to see that?"

I crouch down so our eyes are level and though I want to hug her as much as I want to yell at her, I do neither, I simply wait until her eyes meet mine. My voice is low and steady when I speak, nothing like the nerves swimming inside of me. "He loves you, more than any woman could ever hope or dream of. Dad loves you, Mom, and he wants to take you to dinner to remind you and everyone else that it doesn't matter what you remember and what you don't, he'll never forget you. Ever."

Her eyes fill with tears and fear, and I wonder if I misspoke.

"He should put me in a home and let me rot," she whimpers.

"No, he shouldn't and, goddammit, you should think of what it does to him when you say things like that."

She shakes her head, her motions weak and spastic, her breath still wheezing. Her eyes are a little darker now, her face odd and suddenly I'm afraid that there's something more than panic running through my mother.

"Mom, are you all right? Do you need me to call Sassy?"

"I don't need you to do anything, Cora, how many times do I have to tell you that?" I squint to hear her, my concern rocketing to panic. Her speech is slurring and she's now rubbing her right hand, but I can hardly focus on it because her eyes are blinking and there's a flutter on one side of her mouth, a side that barely moved when she spoke. Alarm bells are going off in my head, and when she goes to stand and stumbles, I start screaming, cradling her against me as we hit the floor, rocking her as I yell for help over and over.

Her body's shaking, but other than that she's still. When Sassy comes barreling into the room, she takes one look and starts barking out instructions and orders. Her phone is to her ear when she crouches down in front of us.

"What happened?" I shake my head, my eyes wide. She snaps her fingers in front of my face. "Cora, I need you to tell me, so I can help her. Pull it together."

I breathe, nod, and breathe again. "She was cranky, all morning just grumpy and complaining. I thought she was having an episode but when I turned her to face me, her speech got slurred and her face... it stopped moving."

"Stroke," Sassy says and then she's cupping my mother's face in her hands, speaking loud and slow. "Suzie, Suzie, I need you to look at me. Can you smile at me?" I can't see my mother's face but Sassy's talking into her phone and I hear her say no. "Did she fall?" It takes me a second to realize Sassy's talking to me, and when she asks again, I nod.

"She tried to stand, but couldn't. Her legs gave out or she lost her balance or something. I caught her before she hit the ground."

Sassy nods and speaks into the phone again. I can hear sirens now, but I don't move. I just sit there, holding my mother, my hand stroking over her hair as I wait. Although it feels like hours, it's maybe ten minutes from the time I cried out to the time that there are EMTs walking through with a stretcher and bags, taking her from me and asking all of the same questions that Sassy did. I answer them, never taking my eyes from my mother as they strap her to a stretcher and place a hand held breathing bag to her face.

I follow blindly as they take her down the stairs, grateful that Sassy is talking with them now. When we get to the back of the ambulance, I stop, foolishly scared. Sassy looks at me and I motion for her to go. "She needs you," I say, swallowing hard when I realize how true those words are. She needs Sassy, not me. "I'll call my dad and be right behind you."

She nods and squeezes my hand once before stepping into the ambulance with my mother. I watch as they drive out of the estate and down the lane, pulling my cell phone out and turning toward my car once they're out of sight. Clicking on my dad's name, I wonder how to tell him his wife just had a stroke.

~

I'm sitting with my mother in the hospital, rubbing hand cream on her palms, massaging them gently as I navigate the I.V. and attached tubes. There's a breathing mechanism in her nose and she has her eyes closed. I've been here since she fell yesterday, since Sassy called 911 and the ambulance took her away. I've been here since my father walked in like a ghost after speaking with the doctor, sinking into the chair with his head in his hands as his shoulders shook and silent tears trekked down his face.

And I've been here since my mother woke up and was sedated again when she panicked because she couldn't remember the fall, or the stroke, or anything that came next.

I put away the cream and take out my cuticle scissors and brush, completing my weekly routine in the silence of the hospital, Elton John crooning on my iPod speaker in the background (*Candle in the Wind* is her favorite, a true tribute to Diana, the most elegant of ladies my mother used to say). The doctors told me I could talk to her, that it might help to hear a familiar voice when she starts to wake, but I don't because I'm not sure what to say, or if she'll want to hear it, so I do what we've done for the past seven months and I manicure her nails, filing, smoothing, polishing until her fingers are beautiful and elegant again, tipped in the rose-colored pink she chose yesterday before we began. I had walked in, ready to start the day, ready to see if our slowly progressing relationship would allow for another small conversation and the polish was out and waiting, a nice blend between the dark colors I normally wear and the pale pink she always stays with.

Like me, it seemed she was trying to grow, to blend the best parts of who she once was with the person she wanted to be now, however limited her time — or I'm so desperate to believe we've moved forward that I'm reading into nail polish color like it's a fucking symbol, when it's nothing more than decoration.

"Look at you, still working. Suzie will have to pay your some overtime."

I smile at Sassy as she walks in and hands me a cup of tea, but only because I know she needs the reassurance as much as I do. She was amazing when she was barking out orders, saving my mother during all of those minutes that both the paramedics and doctors assured us were precious and imperative for healthy recovery. Now, though, she looks a little shaken under her usually calm appearance, and rather than rested and playful, her eyes are tired and worried.

"You were amazing, Sassy. All I could do was stare and shake and ask her what was wrong, but one look and you moved. I've never seen anything like it."

"It's my job, *Cara*. Strokes are common, and still, we can't stop them from coming. We can only hope to move fast enough to prevent too much permanent damage."

Permanent damage. The words want to slam into me, but I nod and sip the tea I don't really want. Words from one of my meetings only days ago play back in my head and I hold onto them, gathering strength from their memory and their meaning. *GOD, GRANT ME THE SERENITY TO ACCEPT THE THINGS I CANNOT CHANGE, COURAGE TO CHANGE THE THINGS I CAN, AND THE WISDOM TO KNOW THE DIFFERENCE.* I want to be able to control this – to take the blame, to somehow make this my fault rather than believe that someone's life can simply fall down around them for no reason other than bad luck or genetics. But I can't take the blame, and I can't fix her. I can only be here and hope for more time with her when she wakes up. So I sit with her, drinking tea with Sassy, and I pray that we're all strong enough for whatever comes next.

Sassy and I stay silent for a minute, staring at my mom, at her monitors, at her form that appears frailer by the minute. When I hear Sassy's breath catch the tiniest bit, I stand and wrap my arm around her shoulder. "You did all you could, Sassy. Even the doctor said your fast diagnosis and call saved her."

She shakes her head and hooks her arm around my waist. "I take care of her because I love her too. But I didn't save her, not today and not any other day. You did," she says and I look down at her. "You saved her when you came back and gave her yourself every week, even when she tried to push you away. It's love that saves us, *Cara*, because it gives us something even medicine can't."

"What's that?" I ask and she smiles, reaching a finger out to touch my chin.

"Acceptance."

I think of Jake and understand exactly what she's talking about. The ache for him is so deep I feel like it's a permanent part of who I am, and still it gets a little lighter when I think of him following his dream and becoming the man he's always wanted to be. Standing with my arm around Sassy, watching my mother lying in her bed, I realize that life isn't always fair and it isn't always kind, but Jake gave me a glimpse of both of those every time he loved me, playfully, passionately, quietly. Those memories show me exactly what my mother can't see, the reason my father wants to take her to dinner, the reason he's always chosen her, right or wrong. And then I understand that love doesn't always work the way it should, but when it does, it's really quite beautiful.

Chapter Thirty-One

Jake

I grew up poor, living in a rundown trailer, hand me downs and five dollar repurposed clothing the only things that graced my closet. I got to play baseball because I threw hard enough and well enough that a teammate's parents were always coming up with money for me to travel. When I got to ASU, I still remembered what it was like to be poor, I just wasn't poor anymore and it eventually became that I got used to eating well, living well, and having my rent paid.

After a month in the minors, I can't help but make the correlation between where I am now and my time before college, the bad food you eat because it's cheaper and filling and you don't have the time or money for anything more, not to mention anywhere to keep it. The few outfits you wash and carry with you are rolled into your duffel bag, the shady parts of town you find yourself in when you're on the road because the team can't afford anything more than the hourly rate hotel.

In college, my body was pushed and exercised and treated like that of a god. Trainers stretched and worked me, coaches spent one-on-one time with me every day, sometimes for an hour, sometimes for two or more, and my per diem or scholarship check covered enough that I had actual food, cooked in an actual kitchen, or at least purchased from a restaurant whose menu wasn't pasted on the wall above the kitchen with the most expensive thing being a six-dollar-burger.

The minors are like growing up in the trailer park — everything just gets dustier and grimier the longer you're there. The only difference with the minors is that even though we make a little over a thousand dollars a month, and some of us sleep two or three or four in a two room apartment, we're all still happy, because we're all still chasing rainbows and praying the pot of gold at the end really does exist. Hope's a fucking bitch when she latches on to you and refuses to let you go.

I've learned to adapt in my twenty-two years, and the past two months have been no different, as I've gone from being a pampered scholarship athlete, back to a grunt worker that's just trying to make a name for himself. I'm in Spokane, Washington, drafted by the Texas Rangers and now wearing the affiliate jersey for the Short A team, the Spokane Indians. Like the rest of the college players, my season will now only go June to September, while the rookie league and double and triple A leagues have been playing for months already.

Murph was drafted by the New York-Penn league and is playing somewhere in Maryland for the affiliate team to the Baltimore Os. We don't get to play against each other, but I follow his stats on his team's homepage and Twitter, and I assume his does the same as I get a text every now and then congratulating me on my strikeout count, which continues to rise.

Internet stalking appears to be the only thing second to baseball that I'm excelling at, as I've sunken low enough in my desire to see Blue that I've searched the media tirelessly, trying to find even the smallest glimpse of her. Like her ever disappearing keys, she's hard to find, as she doesn't have any of the regular Instagram, Facebook or Twitter accounts, but I did find relief after I found her salon's Instagram, and then her friend A.J.'s, both affording me tiny glances of Cora. For a starving man, those small glimpses were like appetizers, teasing the taste on my tongue but never offering me enough sustenance to alleviate the gnawing hunger I feel. It's been just shy of three months since I've seen her, and I've completely stopped trying to block the memory of her out like I did at the beginning.

After that night with Mia when I spilled everything, I stopped mentioning Cora and so did she. Whether she told Ryan to leave it alone or whether he sensed that was the best way to handle it I don't know, but he never asked about her and I never offered any information. From then, my life was baseball, and so I threw myself into training with the gusto of a man whose life depended on every pitch. When the draft came Murph and I waited together, as he and the boys were knocked out in the regional qualifiers and ended their season before June. He went higher than I did by quite a few rounds, which wasn't a shock as I wasn't really on the front of anyone's radar and had only simulated statistics to back up my performance, not seasonal ones. Murph was also awarded a signing bonus for going in the first round, whereas I was lucky to go at all.

But I went.

Sitting there, Murph on my left, Mia on the floor at his feet, I saw my phone ring at the same time that my name was called and for a second I couldn't move. Murph's none-too-gentle shove broke me out of my trance and I answered my agent, barely hearing a word. When it was all said and done, the first person I wanted to call was Blue, so I got shitfaced and passed out instead.

That was the first and last time I've been drunk, as once I started my training with the team I was too fucking tired to do more than go to training or a game and go home. Now, I'm in the second month of the season and I'm learning more than I ever thought possible. The Rangers' organization was taken over by the great Nolan Ryan and he's changing the way we view baseball from the bottom up. Unlike most teams, I pitch a live batting practice in between starts. I do a shit ton of short and long toss, and I run every day, since the captain of our ship is determined that we should have over a two hundred inning season, and so he's giving us the stamina to do so. Since my elbow feels better than ever, and my strikeout count is starting to earn me some credit, I'm not complaining.

It appears the only thing training isn't making better is the ache inside of me, the one that tells me something's missing, and it's nothing baseball is ever going to give me.

While I had actively avoided remembering anything about Cora and our time together after that first night in Arizona, it had taken only one night out with my teammates and countless offers from girls for me to crack and start searching the Internet one night.

I was four beers in and ready to call it a night when a redhead had set her sights on me. I've never been one to discriminate before — red, brown, blonde, purple, short, tall, skinny, curvy, small breasts, stacked — women were always appreciated for being women, never because of their hair color or one dimensional shape, yet, one look at the smoke show in front of me with pale skin, electric green eyes that could have been real or fake, and candy apple red hair that was most definitely enhanced, I couldn't work up an ounce of attraction.

Being a man, and therefore an idiot, I had engaged with her longer than was wise, to prove to myself and everyone else that I still had it, that I could still feel, that I wasn't going to be the guy who lost his shit because the love of his life wasn't his anymore. Only, then she moved faster than me and her lips were on mine and her hands were tugging at my hair and after the initial shock that had frozen me, I came back to life and felt nothing. No spark, no twitch below the waist, no interest beyond getting the fuck out of there.

And when I did remove myself and set the startled viper aside, I had walked back to my shitty hotel room and started my metaphoric cutting; I Googled Cora Whitley. I got a notice about deactivation of accounts, but the need was too great to give up, and so I searched deeper, clicking on the images link until pictures of different Cora Whitleys filled the screen. I had scrolled for a little longer, and then I found them.

Old photos came up, ones that had my breath catching as I scrolled through them, ones where her hair was nearly white, her eyes clouded and dark and... vacant. I studied each of these photos in detail, looking at her clothes, her skin, her face, her posture, and in all of them I saw nothing of the strength and determination I had found in my siren. Instead, I saw moments on end of sadness and discontent, and it was almost enough to break me. But then the shots stopped, and I knew it must be around the time when she had deactivated her accounts and went into building a new version of herself. At odds, still craving the sight of her, I had tried another avenue and Googled her friends. When I finally found A.J.'s Instagram with a current shot of Cora, it was like a vise around my chest was released and I was able to breathe easily for the first time.

Her hair was down, free to spill over her shoulders, and her skin was golden, so I knew she'd been in the sun, most likely running, from the way her legs looked in the form fitting mini dress she was rocking. But it wasn't just her gorgeous face and impressive legs that caught me — it was her expression. She was smiling at A.J., a sassy look as she worked at her station, cleaning up or setting up, but it wasn't quite the smile she'd had when I last saw her. It was less, bright but not full, and in seeing it I pressed my hand to the screen and wondered if maybe my siren ached as much as me.

Chapter Thirty-Two

Cora

"Vascular Dementia. What's that?"

I'm sitting with my father and the doctor as we discuss my mother's prognosis and all of the possible side-effects and outcomes of the stroke she suffered. My father is mute, as silent today as he was yesterday and has been since he sank into the chair and cried. I'm taking point with the doctor, throwing my father small glances every now and then to see if he's all right.

Understanding, Doctor Quo addresses me. "It's what your mother was originally diagnosed with. Two years ago during a routine physical exam, it was discovered there were lapses in your mother's memory. Further tests drew the conclusion that she had suffered what we call a TIA or mini stroke — a temporary clot that keeps oxygen from getting to certain parts of the brain. How many she suffered and over what period of time was never conclusively determined, but the best estimate was somewhere between five and eight in a one year period, which ultimately led to several larger ones in the past year."

I'm silent and my breathing is rapid because I had no idea. I knew my mother had memory problems, but all research I've done has been for early onset dementia and Alzheimer's because that's what my father made it sound like. He never mentioned strokes, never mentioned the fact that these strokes were the precursor to everything she's going through now. I listen as the doctor continues, the heavy feeling getting worse as he explains that stressful situations exacerbate the dementia and increase the possibility of a stroke because they spike the blood pressure and anxiety.

I think back over the past few months, all the way back to the day I turned fourteen and my mother found me rolling around on the couch with one of her country club waiters, after which I promptly did it again the next night because she'd thrown a tantrum and embarrassed me as she screamed at the man, who was really no more than a boy, to get out. Other moments in our relationship crash into me until I'm buried under bad memories and hateful choices, early ones which were made in the hopes of getting her attention and then later on, the choices that were made in order to prove I didn't need her attention or anything else she had to offer. All the way up to January, when I started visiting her once a week, demanding in my own way that she forgive me and let me try and make a relationship with her.

And then to yesterday, when I demanded that she listen to me, hear me when I told her that she wasn't a burden, that Dad loved her more than anything, that the only thing that hurt worse than her disease was her lack of desire to live, to love anymore. To the moment when I told her to think of him if she couldn't think of herself, to think of him and everything he would do and had done for her just to keep her with him. I demanded she let him take care of her, and I demanded she show she loved him as much as he loved her by trying to live again, and then her brain malfunctioned and she seized and fell and all I could do was demand she wake up and stay with me. Always fucking demanding.

The doctor finishes, handing me a pamphlet and some instructions for further check-ups and briefly explains what will happen as she wakes up, what they're doing now as they monitor her heart and brain waves, but I barely hear him as I stand and walk out, so lost in my own pain and grief and regret that I have to pause and sit down in the chairs a few feet outside of his door. When I feel someone sit next to me, I look up into the eyes of my father, eyes that are finally alive for the first time since we got here. He must understand what I'm thinking, must know exactly what's going through my head, because he grabs my hand and holds it, squeezing so tightly that I want to wince in pain. But I don't, I just stare at him and wonder if I can really take the blame for my mother lying in the next room, unconscious and hooked up to tubes.

"It's not your fault," he says and I just continue to stare, my heart raging, my breath heaving. "It's not your fault," he says again. "She wanted you here. She *needed* you here. We all did."

"Did you?" I ask him. "Or did I need more from her than she had to give, like always? Did I push her here, Dad? Did I do this to her?"

He shakes his head and brings me into his chest without hesitation for the first time in years, and somehow that makes the pain worse. "No, Cora, you didn't bring her here. You brought us back together, for just a little bit. And it's been wonderful."

Tears gather but I don't shed them. Instead, I let my father hug me and try to think of my prayer again, but the words don't come. Instead, all I can feel is grief, and it's consuming.

~

They call it a trigger moment because it's a loaded gun waiting to go off. It doesn't matter what it is — the national debt, a hang nail, a bad manicure, a really bad fucking day — anything can set an addict off and spiraling toward relapse, and though I've fought long and hard to not be a part of that group, when I leave the hospital after almost seventy-two hours by my mother's side watching her sleep and then wake up disoriented and devastated, I don't fucking care about being an addict or a recovering addict or a goddamn statistic. I care that it motherfucking hurts way down deep, an ache so strong and poignant that all I can think about is making it go away.

I stop by my apartment, but one step inside shows me that it's not the peaceful safe haven I want it to be. It's full of memories and feelings, full of things I don't want or need when I'm already so filled with everything else, so instead of changing and going for a run like I wanted to ten minutes ago, I do the only thing I can think of to stop feeling: I pull out my sexiest outfit, a short pencil skirt in black sequins and a barely-there top, and I shower and primp, deleting anything from my brain that goes beyond what I look like. Soon, the familiar buzz of going out is pumping through my veins, the feeling intense enough that I pause and grab my phone, texting A.J. and letting her know where I'll be. She texts me back, and then she calls when I don't answer her, but I ignore her.

Somewhere deep inside I know I'm asking her for help at the same time I'm pushing her away, but I can't concentrate on that or anything else right now. Instead, all I can do is focus on my lashes and my hair, my outfit that is anything but pure, and the feel of freedom that comes with checking out.

Chapter Thirty-Three

Jake

I've been home for an hour when and I get a text from an unknown number and am half tempted to just ignore it, thinking that Laken or Woo gave a girl my number just to fuck with me because I declined their invitation to go out again. Since it's the third rejected invitation this week, I know they're planning retribution, especially since some girl at the game shouted that she'd give us a deal if I promised to come with her. Major emphasis on *come*. I declined and my teammates were less than pleased, their stares of disbelief enough to tell me that my locker was in grave danger of being filled with something disgusting and impossible to clean.

If your teammates can't be bastards to you, who can?

I reach to delete the text and then I see the area code, the five-zero-three that signifies Oregon, and my heart leaps at the thought that it might be her, even though I have her number and that logically means her name would come up, not a random number. When I swipe my finger across the screen, I read the words once, rub my eyes and have to read them again.

Fucktard, her mom had a stroke. She's at a bar with me and Liam, and I just had to throw a glass of champagne over her head to keep her from drinking it… and then letting the asshat she was talking to take advantage of her. We're walking her home now, and she's on the phone with her sponsor. I couldn't get ahold of her cousin. Phone went straight to voicemail both times. Get off your ass and call her.

Another message bubble pops up as my heart careens to my throat.

Btw, this is A.J. Now fucking call her.

Before I can think of what to do, my phone's ringing in my hand. One swipe and I answer.

"Are you a fucking idiot?"

The voice on the other line is not the female one I imagined it would be, which means… Liam.

"Is she all right?"

"No, she's not fucking all right. She's a goddamn mess and here I am, punching fucking people and keeping her from sinking in her own shit when it should be you she's leaning on."

An ache spreads deep inside of me, filling that hollowed out cavern until I can barely breathe. Clenching my fists, I take a deep breath. "I didn't know about her mom, Liam. I didn't fucking know."

"No, but goddammit you should have," he says and I realize how right he is. "I called because I know she meant something to you man, and I thought she still might. Unless you want me to step in and be her man."

I see red, visions of Cora wrapped around someone else flashing in my brain and before I know it, my clenched fist is through the wall and my breath is heaving. I hear an echo of a laugh on the other end of the line.

"That's what I thought," he says with a sigh. "She's sinking, Jake, and she has been since you left. Don't get me wrong, she won't say anything about it, swears up one side and down the fucking other that you both knew from day one that it was only temporary between you, that neither of you was looking to get serious, but we all know that's bullshit. Whether or not you were looking, it was serious, Jake, and it did matter. So why the fuck are you radio silent when your woman needs to hear from you every day so she knows she has someone just for herself?"

I'm having a hard time keeping it together, mostly because every word he speaks rips my already battered heart once more, shredding it until it's all I can do to keep from crumpling over. I can see Blue saying all of those things, and I can see her trying to mean them, mostly because until a month ago they were things I had convinced myself of too. But things change, life gets real, and everything you did in the name of *what was best* seems like the stupidest fucking thing in the world.

"Tell me what happened," I grind out.

"I don't know everything, I just know that her mom had a stroke and, sometime in the last three days of being permanently at the hospital, Cora came to the conclusion that she's to blame, that somehow she pushed her mom too hard and everything bad that was happening to her was Cora's fault. She sent A.J. a text earlier tonight saying she was going out and then when we get to where she said she'd be, I find some fucking Armani lookalike she apparently went to high school with panting over her, calling for drinks, hovering over her shoulder and trying his hardest to reunite with your girl."

"Jesus," I breathe and the image in my head almost brings me to my knees. "Did something happen to her?"

"Other than the fact that A.J. ripped into her and threw the drink in her face instead of letting it go down her throat? Or the fact that even while she was pretending to enjoy the shithead's attention she looked miserable? No, I took care of him, A.J. took care of her, and now we're taking her to our place. We tried calling her cousin, but her phone's off."

"She's on her way home from Baltimore," I say absently, wondering if she even knows about Cora's mom or if Cora kept that from her so Mia wouldn't cancel her last trip to see Murph before she started back as a full time student. I run through my options, wondering where to start so I can get out of the house and into Portland by morning. Before I can let Liam know I'll be there, he speaks again.

"Go get your dream, Jake, but don't forget to call your fucking girl and tell her that you love her and that you're here for her. She deserves that much, and so do you."

I hang up on him without saying anything else and immediately swipe through my contacts until I find the number I'm looking for. Pausing long enough to tap out an emergency text, I then hit send and swipe to a different number, writing a new but similar message before sending it.

Clicking back to my contacts, I tap a different number and grab my backpack from beside the bed. "Laken — no, I didn't change my mind. I need a favor."

Chapter Thirty-Four

Cora

I wake in an unfamiliar bed and tense instantly when I feel someone next to me. Panic seizes me and for a minute I stop breathing, the pain of failure and disgust so large I think they might crush me. And then that someone speaks, and my heart stops.

"Relax, Snow White, your virtue is safe."

A.J.. Sweet Jesus, thank you.

Now that my heart's pumping again, albeit a bit unsteadily, I relax enough to take in my surroundings. The room I'm in is what I would consider true bohemian flare with a ton of clutter. There's a red sheer fabric over the window, giving the room a weird, ethereal glow. The majority of the wall space is taken over by some sort of painting or photograph or collage. There's an old style oval vanity in silver against one wall, its surface covered in earrings, makeup, hair tools and more. A sewing mannequin stands in one corner with several necklaces, scarves, hats, and other paraphernalia decorating it. Finally, I turn to the girl in bed with me and I take in her clear skin and bed head.

"You remember now?" she asks and I nod, though I desperately wish I didn't. Flashes of the crowded bar, my over enthusiastic flirting, the almost hook-up that was closely paired with the almost drink so I could go through with it. My anger toward A.J. and Liam after they saved me. Knowing the fact that I do remember those things, however awful, is something I owe to her, I swallow the bitter taste in my mouth and meet her eyes.

"Thank you."

I don't have any other words, nothing that will truly be able to tell her what it feels like to know I almost lost it, almost had to start over and work out of the hole that I'm now positive comes with that relapse.

She's lying on her stomach with her pillow smashed under her cheek and her arms tucked under her body, staring at me. Without her black eye liner and exotic makeup, she's still beautiful, but there's a much more innocent appearance to her. Then she speaks and I realize it's still the A.J. I know.

"Yeah, well, I figure there's enough going on in your life that you get a pass for being an idiot. And if I'm being honest, throwing a drink in your face holds its own kind of satisfaction."

I smile because she says it without sting, and because I can see the worry in her eyes. "I was a bitch to you yesterday. You could have just left me and let me ruin myself."

She eyes me for a second before inclining her head on her pillow slightly. "Yeah, I could have. But, seeing as how I've been a bitch a time or two, and you helped me a few months ago, I figured our friendship could withstand a little turmoil. We *are* friends, Snow White," she tells me, and for some reason it makes my throat want to close. "And regardless of bitchy outbursts, friends don't let friends ruin sobriety and everything else to sleep with a douche who in no way would have been good enough in bed to make her forget why she was sleeping with him in the first place. Since you admitted to never sleeping with him in high school, despite his abundant attempts, I think you already knew that."

This makes me laugh and I give in to press my fingers to my eyes. "Shit, A.J., I'm a mess."

"You're actually pretty fucking put together, Snow White, considering."

"Christ, how can you say that? I almost ruined a year and a half of sobriety and slept with someone I couldn't stand four years ago and barely remembered until last night, all because I'm angry." And sad. Goddammit I hate being sad.

"Yep, but you didn't, because even before I got there to give you an ass kicking, you'd already stopped yourself a few times, hesitated enough that it gave me time to get to you, slap you around and make you call your sponsor, who also verbally slapped your around, which I must admit shocked me. Aren't sponsors supposed to be supportive and coddling?"

I smile. "Kari's a breed of her own, that's why I like her." Blowing out a breath, I kick off the covers and smile down at the boxers and T-shirt I remember struggling into in a haze of tears and self-pity last night. They're Liam's, and when I hear a throat clear at the doorway, I look over to see him leaning a shoulder against the door jamb, a cup of coffee in his hand, an amused smile on his face.

"Now here's a familiar sight. Coffee, anyone?"

"I'd give you any sexual favor you wanted for it," A.J. responds and Liam laughs.

"I've got enough of those in reserve from others, thanks, so why don't we settle for you brushing your teeth and doing away with the dragon breath before you come into the kitchen. You, too, Cora," he says as he stands up straight. "That way you can have caffeine in you before I take my turn yelling at you for thinking the dipshit you were letting hit on you was worth any of your time or tears."

I flick my eyes up but he's already turned his back and walked away. A.J. must see my face because she laughs and flings off the covers. "Having friends can be a real bitch, huh?"

My mind flashes to Mia and guilt settles over me as I think of the fact that I haven't called her, haven't told her any of what's happened in a feeble attempt to let her live her life without my interference and constant need for help. "You're telling me. Why's he so mad?"

"Liam's a regular white knight. Doesn't like to see anyone hurt — especially when the person hurting them is themselves. After he laid into the guy you were doing the pre-sex dance with, he called your cousin and left a voicemail, and then he called Jake and laid into him, too. I don't think your hunk will be hearing normally for a while."

This stops me cold. Even the mere mention of his name has my body tingling, yearning, needing… everything. And that's why I had to let him go — I need too much and he deserves more than some rehabilitated leech who can't control her own emotions.

"He shouldn't have done that," I say as I throw back the covers and stand. "Mia has a life of her own, and Jake needs to be focusing on his career. Neither of them needs to be worrying about me."

"Wow, you're dumber than I thought."

I whip a glare her way as I search for my clothes. "Fuck you."

"I knew you'd ask eventually," she says glibly and I'm struck with the twin urges to laugh and scream. I hear her get out of bed while I'm searching out my shoes, and pause when I feel her hand on my shoulder. "Cora, listen to me and listen good. Sometimes, you have to let people know you need them — and more than that, that you want them. You gave me some advice once, now let me give that back to you. Your cousin loves you, which means she wants to help you. And Jake? He's the one person you trust with everything, so trust him with this. Lean on someone, Cora, and let yourself expect them to be there. You deserve it, and so does he."

~

I hate to admit it, but A.J. has a point. I hadn't let Jake know I needed him to stay, or that I wanted him to, because I thought it was selfless to let him go. And, I was protecting myself against possible future rejection. Walking home from the meeting I stopped in on after I left A.J. and Liam's apartment with my tail between my legs and pride smashed into the sidewalk, I rehash the words of each of the members that were there today, the stories they shared, and then those that I shared.

I always sit in the back to listen and find solace in the words of others, those people like me who can't quite battle their demons and win on their own — the ones who understand weakness and pain and the always present draw of oblivion. But this morning I walked in wearing Liam's borrowed white T-shirt with my black sequined pencil mini and stilettos, and after ten minutes of listening to others, I found myself standing and walking to the front. It came out in a rush, the fact that I'm not sure how to be a person who stands on her own and relies on others. I don't know how to ask for help when I'm so afraid the person I'm asking will look at me and think I'm unworthy. Or that I'll ask for too much and make life impossible for them, like I did for my mother. I admitted that I almost took a drink and then another last night, because the idea of waking up and feeling bad was better than waking up and feeling useless.

Being someone who makes bad choices somehow always looks more appealing than being someone who has no control over her life, but now, in the light, I understand that the darkness is too easy to hide in. Sometimes, we have to feel hurt and out of control, because life isn't just black or white — it's gray and blue and red and every other color, and when we feel them all, we know we've lived.

I can't stop the thought of Jake or how good I felt when I was with him, how safe... and how loved. A.J. wasn't wrong when she said I never let him know how much I needed him — I'm strong, but I'm also an addict who fears falling back into weakness and, in the last year, I've learned to protect myself against that possibility. Now, I'm walking home after a night I can remember with too much clarity, and I understand that sometimes, protecting ourselves from too much is hiding, and it hurts just as much as the emotions we're hiding from. I don't know if I feel better or worse or if I feel anything at all with this revelation, but I do know that before I can deal with what I feel for Jake, I need to deal with what I feel for myself, which means I need to go and see my mother, to sit with her and talk to her, because no matter what my head tells me, I know in my heart that what everyone else is saying is right — I didn't cause the stroke, and I can't change the bad things that have happened in the past, I can only move forward today.

I take the stairs instead of the elevator, my fist version of penance and a damn harsh one in these godforsaken stilettos, and when I walk through the hall door I'm searching my bag for my fucking keys that continue to disappear on the daily. Stopping a few steps from my apartment door, I groan and crouch down to dump my purse out, sifting through the meager contents to discover that my keys are not there.

"Here I was worried that you wouldn't need me when I left," a familiar voice says and I pause in the act of cussing myself out to look up. He's sitting with his back against the door to our apartment, his knees bent and his feet flat on the floor. His head is still resting against the wood, but it's angled toward me and I can't help the shameless perusal I give him, greedily soaking in the black baseball cap that's pulled low to shadow his eyes, that beautiful dark hair flipping out from underneath it. He's wearing a simple white V-neck and jeans that are cuffed over unlaced Nikes. He looks tired, but when he shifts to stand, I get a closer look at his eyes and they're alert as he reaches toward me, taking my hand to bring me to my feet.

He keeps my hand in his as he stares at me and, without

realizing I was holding it, I let out a breath and bring in another, this time filling my nostrils with the glorious scent of Jake Ferrari. He smiles and holds out his free hand until I look down and see the key he's holding.

"How you doing, Blue?"

Chapter Thirty-Five

Jake

Cora excuses herself to go change when we step inside and, because I need the time to pull my shit together and keep from making this about me and her, I nod and turn toward the couch. The minute her bedroom door closes, I close my eyes and scrub my hands over my face. In theory, this was a great plan, romantic even. In reality, it's fucking brutal.

Christ, is it possible to hurt this bad and still be alive?

Must be, since I'm here, in the place that felt more like home than any other I've ever lived, waiting for the girl I'm pretty sure owns me. Jesus, if this is how Romeo felt when he fell in love, I'm not surprised the poor bastard made so many bad decisions when he was trying to keep Juliet. Love really fucks with you.

When Yogi sidles up beside me, I smile down at him and lean down to scratch his ears, slightly mollified when he closes his eyes and arches his back, a deep purr resonating throughout. At least someone missed me.

I hear the door open and then Blue's footsteps as she pads quietly down the hall, so I stand and turn around to watch her walk into the living room, even though my brain is telling me it's a dumbass thing to do. It is, as my abused and aching heart takes another hit when I watch her walk in wearing those yoga pants that stop just below her knee with an oversized tank top the color of summer skies. Her hair is smoothed back from her face and left to spill in a tail past her bare shoulders, and her face clean and free of any makeup and still I can't look away from her, as mesmerized by her beauty now as I was the first day I saw her. The only thing that keeps me from reaching for her are her eyes, haunted, dark, and so unlike the Cora I left sleeping months ago.

Whatever's happening to Blue right now is beyond her and me, bigger than any dream I've ever had or lost. It's her life, what she knows and doesn't, her demons and her fears all rearing up to hit her while she's down. Reminding myself why I came, I take a non-threatening step toward the chair and away from her to sit, hoping she'll take it as the invitation it was meant to be.

She waits for me to sit and then walks around to sit on the couch, curling her legs under her. Yogi looks between us as if to choose, and then jumps onto the couch next to Cora, settling into her side and purring for her fingers like he did for mine not thirty seconds ago, opening his eyes only enough to stare at me as if he knows I'm jealous of him. And I am, the smug bastard.

"I'm sorry they called you," she says without preamble, and I can't help the small smile that curves at my lips. My siren might feel like she's broken, but there's strength left in her yet, and she just showed me the first little bit of it.

"I'm not."

She raises her eyebrows. "You're not what?"

"Sorry they called. But I am sorry that you didn't think you could, or should, that the way we left things made you feel like I didn't want to be here for you anymore."

Something like fear flickers in her eyes before she looks away. I notice that the calm that surrounded her before I left, the ability to be still and process things has somehow been replaced with nervous movements and fidgeting, as if she's lost her center and is searching for it.

"I need some coffee," she says and gives Yogi one last scratch before she stands and heads into the kitchen. I give her eight seconds — the exact amount of time I need to calm the fuck down — before I stand to follow, flipping Yogi the bird as his eyes follow me. I swear if he could laugh at me, he would be. Leaning back against the counter, I watch her walk to the machine in the corner and take a pod out of a jar.

She opens a latch and sets the pod in, pressing it down before hitting some button. Soon, the scent of coffee fills the room and she turns to look at me.

"Jake, it's not that I'm not glad you're here, I am, I just... I don't know, I just can't think right now and it's been a hard few days."

I step forward and stop her before she says anything else, all too aware of why she thinks I'm here and the weight that assumption has put on her already overburdened shoulders.

"Blue, we need to talk because everything I thought I knew about why I walked away isn't so clear anymore. But," I say when that fear settles over her face again, "right now, I'm here for you for a few hours because I wanted to let you know you could lean on me, nothing more, okay? We can talk if you want, or we can sit. We can go for a run, or you can go take a nap while I sit here with you, or we can just sit and not talk. Whatever you need, I just want to be here for you."

She stares at me, studying my face as if to see that I'm being honest. I stay still, my eyes never leaving hers as I let her see that I mean what I say, that I just want to be here for her until I can't any longer. Finally, she breathes out a sigh and nods her acknowledgment and I relax.

"Coffee?" she asks.

"Jesus, yes," I say and she smiles.

When she hands me my cup, doctored with the heap of sugar I usually use, I'm careful to keep my fingers from brushing against hers as I take it. Without a word, we walk to the table and sit, drinking from our mugs in silence for a while. It's not a heavy silence, but there's an energy to it, one that we both recognize, but don't know how to deal with. Because I'm not sure what she wants to share, or if she wants to share anything at all, I'm taking my cue from her and letting the silence hang.

"What if you ask me questions, like we used to?" she says after nearly ten minutes, and I look over from my view of the window to stare at her. She clears her throat. "What if you ask me questions, and I answer them? Whatever questions you want, anything… just ask, and I'll talk, I'll tell you. I want to tell you," she says and I understand what she's doing. She doesn't know how to begin, how to start off what is sure to be a gruesome tale — but she also doesn't want to lock me out, or herself in. Trying again to remember that this is about her and not us, I clear my throat and lean forward, resting my forearms on either side of my cup on the table.

"Are you all right?"

Her eyes flick away from mine and find a spot on the table. "I don't know. I didn't take a drink, didn't go home with anyone, but..."

Her eyes twitch from the spot on the table to me. Devastation coats her face and I squeeze my hands into fists.

"What happened, Blue?"

"My mom had a stroke. I was with her, doing her hair, trying and failing not to be pissed at her for saying she wished my father would just put her in a home and forget about her." Her lips press together and I squeeze my hands tighter to keep from reaching from her. "I finally snapped and told her to stop being selfish, to think of him and me and how much we loved her. And then she had a stroke — brought on by an elevated heart rate and stress, the doctor said."

Bingo. I don't have to ask her the question to know that Cora thinks this is her fault, that she went out looking for a drink and a willing man because she was already so sick of herself she didn't want to think anymore. And yet, she still called her friend, the one that would face down fire with a right hook if she thought she needed to, which is another sign of the sheer strength my siren possesses and forgets about. Hoping to remind her, I ask another question.

"Why'd you call A.J.?"

"Because I knew she would come see me," she answers

honestly. With a sigh, she adds, "Because I'm weak enough to want someone else to save me when I'm not capable of saving myself."

"Wrong," I say and turn her face toward mine with a fingertip under her chin. "If you were weak, you wouldn't be here, Cora; you never would have moved home to face every demon that's ever haunted you, you would have just kept running. You're so fucking strong, Blue, you don't even know it. You want to know why you called A.J.? Because you knew she would come and get you, that she *could*; you knew she wouldn't let you down and you trusted her to help you." If it feels like a knife is slicing into my chest at those words and the fact that she didn't call me, that she had no reason to call me because I'm the one that walked away, I do my best to ignore them.

"It's not weak to admit you need someone, Cora," I tell her and it hits me here and now how true it is. I walked away because I was afraid I would hurt her, or she would hurt me, that neither of us would survive whatever we had because it was so strong, so real, and so fucking scary. Now, shit, now isn't the time to admit that I need her more than I need anything or anyone, because with her I can survive anything.

Swallowing that back, I hold out my hand and wait for her to take it. "You're stronger than you know, Blue, and asking for help only proves that."

She stares at me, her hand in mine, and I wish to Christ I could lean forward and put my lips on hers, pull her into my lap and just hold her, let her know that I'll always be here if only she'll forgive me and let me, that I'll protect her so she never feels the need to give away any part of herself again just to ease the pain. But I don't, because even that offer would have expectations on it, expectations and considerations she isn't ready to deal with, so instead, I hold her hand and wait for her to tell me what she needs.

"I'm sorry they called you," she says again, only this time she continues before I can interrupt. "But I'm not sorry you came, either. Thank you," she says and I understand that she's talking about more than the long drive. Not pressuring her, not asking for more than she has to give, more than she can process right now.

Hoping she understands, too, I scrape my thumb over her knuckles. "Always, Blue. I mean it. I'm not going to disappear again," I say because I can't help it. "So don't be afraid to send a text or leave a message — I'll always call back, and I'll always listen. Okay?"

She nods and I know that it has to be enough for now. Sitting back, I pick up my cold coffee and drain it, swallowing back all of the words I want to say to her. Not the time, I remind myself.

"Any other questions?" she asks and I see how tired she is.

I work to shift gears and ease the tension, to give her a break so she can relax. My grin is almost real when I flash it. "Yeah, did you wear those pants to torture me?"

She responds like I hope, and her smile is light and teasing. "Of course."

~

We keep the rest of the day casual. We do end up going for a run along the water, and even though the sun is blaring and the mid-July weather is near sweltering in the afternoon, I feel more content than I have since I left almost three months ago. Neither of us acknowledges the routine we slip seamlessly back into when we walk home from the water and make small talk. When we walk into the apartment, she heads to the shower and I start dinner, trading off with her when she comes into the kitchen clean and smelling like almonds and flowers and everything else that makes my head swim and my blood hum.

She's wearing a pair of faded jean shorts that are probably new, though they're ripped and short enough that the pockets hang longer than the frayed hem to grace her thighs. Her black and white striped tank top is loose and shapeless, just meeting the waist band of her shorts with wide arm holes, hanging on her in just a way that I glimpse the flesh beneath every now and then, and her skin looks golden and smooth, enticing me to touch, just a brush of my fingertips. I don't, because I'm sure that one touch won't be enough, so instead, I hand her a bottle of water and grab my small bag of clothes.

"Okay if I shower?" I ask and she nods.

Twenty minutes later, I'm wearing a new T-shirt and some gray Volcom shorts that I brought with me, my feet bare like hers while we share a dinner of grilled chicken and pineapple at the table.

We've talked about nothing important since we sat here this morning, and I wonder if we'll keep up the same sort of small talk. She surprises me when she asks a question first.

"Aren't you supposed to be at your game against Boise?"

I pause mid bite and raise my brow at her. "Do you know my schedule, Blue?"

She nods without hesitating, her smile small but honest. "I've been thinking about you, Handsome Jake, and seeing you, even if it's just your name and some statistics I have to have Mia decipher for me, makes me feel closer to you."

Her words wash over me, filling all of those places that have been so empty these past few months. I can't help it; I reach across the table and link out fingers, watching as her narrow, red tipped fingers link through my much larger ones. "I pitched last night, so today wasn't my game. I'm meeting up with the team as they head north to Vancouver tonight."

She nods as if she knew that was our time frame. "Won't your coach be mad that you weren't there today?"

I shake my head. "He understood when I told him I had a family emergency."

I look at her while the words hang between us, and I wait for her to understand and accept them. I can't push, but I have to let her know, to tell her somehow that everything that felt necessary all those months ago doesn't really feel like anything now that I'm without her.

Before either of us can say anything, there's a knock at the door, followed by a shout, and the moment is broken. When she frowns, I offer a smile and let her hand fall.

"I called Mia, figuring you wouldn't have because you knew she was with Ryan." She nods, her eyes wet with emotion, and I go on. "I have to leave, but I knew I wouldn't be able to until you had someone here with you, and I know Mia enough to know she needs to be here for you, Blue, because she loves you. Let them be here for you, Cora," I say quietly, and she takes a deep breath and nods.

Another pound on the door and Nina's voice hollering through has Cora's eyes clearing and a small smile coming to her lips. She stands, and after a second of a debate, she lays her hands on my shoulders and her cheek against mine. "Thank you," she whispers in my ear. "For being here, for calling them, for today. Thank you for all of it."

I turn my head slightly, my nose brushing hers, my eyes at half-mast as I breathe her in. "Always." And I mean it. This girl has my heart and my soul and even though I can't take her now, can't claim her and make her mine without playing on her vulnerability, I know that when my season ends, I'm coming back and I'm not leaving again until I know she's mine forever.

Chapter Thirty-Six

Cora

Contrary to what many people think, sobriety does not mean an addict has conquered their addiction. Sobriety, while being the ultimate goal, is really only a part of recovery. The other part comes from completing the twelve steps and, sometimes, those are harder than saying no to your drug or drink of choice.

The early steps are difficult because as one starts out their recovery, every day is a battle. Waking up, eating breakfast, going to work, even looking in the mirror can be a task, because while you're grateful that you're alive, you're not always grateful that you're sober and, therefore, able to feel. Taking away that substance induced fog is like giving a blind person their sight back only so they can realize the world isn't nearly as beautiful as they hoped it would be.

My first step was easy because it was taken out of my hands. Rafe had no choice but to take me to the hospital when I recklessly chased pills with alcohol, and Mia was no longer content to sit back and let me run my own life, not when it was clear that I could care less which direction I ran it into. So, after admitting to myself that I did in fact have a problem, I began group therapy and admitted to others that I was an alcoholic who found it easier to sink into a bottle and then a person because life was complicated, and often painful. After that came my health craze and my spiritual recognition as I left group and went to AA, and though I've never found comfort in the organized religion like so many of my contemporaries, I did find my understanding of a higher being when I began running. The beach in the morning, the quiet of it as my feet hit the sand, the waves and the endless water as the sun rose overhead — they helped me to recognize that I wasn't in control, not the way I wanted to be, and that life takes its own turns, leaving people to ultimately just live. *How* I lived was the only thing I could control. When I started doing yoga, I learned how to center myself and block out the noise that often surrounded me when I was alone, and focus only on my center, on the stretching and strengthening of my muscles and, eventually, my confidence.

In my first year of sobriety, I learned that life can't be controlled, and the only person in charge of my actions is me. And I learned that being alone doesn't mean being lonely.

Now, over a year in and only days after almost ruining my hard earned eighteen months of sobriety and self-worth, and my finger is hesitating over a name in my contacts because once I press it I've officially re-started step nine, the step I'm not sure how to complete, the one where I make amends with those my addiction hurt. I look at the handwritten list in front of me and wonder if I can really speak to all of the people there and explain to them what I barely understand myself; that I'm sorry, so goddamn sorry that I hurt them, used them, blamed them.

I started with Mia and Nina this morning before their flight left, emotional at the thought of them leaving, grateful for the few days I had with both of them before they began their Ph.D. programs in different states. We sat at the kitchen table and I explained to them what my ninth step was, why it was important to complete it, and then I apologized, not just for lying to them each time they asked if I was okay, but for ignoring that when I hurt myself I was hurting them.

As expected, their reactions were polar opposite. Mia held my hand in her own and showed her quiet love and support while I spoke, and Nina fumed the entire time until I was done, eventually telling me, "Barbie, don't apologize to me. I'm your friend — standing up for you, even when you're being an idiot and refuse to stand up for yourself — is what friends do. You're my friend, which means I'll pull your ass out of bad choices every time, because I love you. Don't forget it again, and don't ever think I need an apology." Then she stood, kissed me smack on the lips and told Mia to get her ass in gear so they weren't late.

It was rather poetic, in a sense, and left me feeling lighter than I had since Jake left. Now, though, I'm taking another step, a more difficult one as I call the one name on my list who has the true right to hate me and blame me for everything.

Taking a deep breath, I press down and bring the phone to my ear, wondering if it will be harder or easier if he doesn't answer.

It only rings twice before he answers, the "Hello?" hesitant enough to tell me that he still has my number programmed into his phone, and he's just as unsure about this phone call as I am.

"Rafe, it's Cora." *You know, the girl who married you and then probably cheated on you because you couldn't spend one hundred percent of your day focusing on her? Remember me?*

I swallow and wonder how the hell people do this, how they *survive* this, when he speaks. "Cora, I'm glad to hear your voice."

My laugh is a little shaky and a lot caustic. "Really? Because I figured you might be happy to never hear from me again after the way I let things happen."

"Cora," he says and his voice is a gentle scold, one I remember him using time and again at the end of our relationship when I walked home in the morning, strung out and hung-over, desperately wishing I could remember what I'd done the night before and lashing out at him when I never did. "How are you?"

"Ha, isn't that a loaded question? I'm here, so that's good." I swallow and go for it. "And I'm sorry, Rafe, for all of it. I'm grateful for what you did," I say and wish for a second I could see his face so he would know how true that statement is. "If it wasn't for you, I wouldn't be here, maybe at all, but definitely not like I am now, sober, and working on being happy."

The line is silent for a second and then I hear a small sigh and in my mind I can see the beautiful boy with the beach-blond hair and brown eyes, the quick smile that charmed me those first months when all I wanted was for someone to love me. "I'm glad, Cora. Are you in San Diego? I... maybe we could meet up, talk. I've actually been wondering about you, but when I went by your apartment a few months after I last saw you, you weren't there and no one knew where to find you. I've been working up the courage to call your cousin and ask her."

I smile at the thought of someone needing to have courage to talk to Mia, the sweet angel of the family. "I'm actually back in Portland now. I'm... working on things, I guess you could say. Making amends is one of them."

Though I can't see him, I imagine him nodding as I hear him agree with me for coming home. "I wish it could have been different for us, Cora," he finally says and I close my eyes, because for an instant I wish it could have, too, and then I think of Jake and understand that whatever I wanted to feel for Rafe was never even close to the things swirling around inside of me for Jake.

"Me, too," I say and mean it. "I want you to know that when we were together, when it was good, it was real for me, as real as I was capable of at that time. It's not an excuse for what I did at the end, but it's the truth."

"For me too," he says, his voice tight with emotion and I know he gets it. Whatever we were is done; I'm different and so is he, but who we were for that brief period of time before I gave in and he got angry, it deserves acknowledgement. "Goodbye, Cora."

"Goodbye, Rafe."

I hang up the phone and stare at it before setting it aside and picking up my list. My fingers brush over the few other names on there, stopping on the last name on the list and the entire reason I moved back home.

Tracing the letters, I pick up my phone and, this time, I don't hesitate before dialing.

"Dad, it's Cora." I clear my throat, realizing that last time I saw him was days ago when I walked out of the hospital and then into a club, too weak to remember that life isn't always ours to control. But I'm here to live another day, I think, and straighten my shoulders. "How is she?" I ask and listen while he relays her progress.

Slow speech, a few slurred words, difficulty in balance and hand dexterity, but, overall, recovering. He doesn't add the words we're both thinking: *from this.* She's recovering from this, but not from the dementia. She'll never recover from that, and this stroke appears to be one of many. The life that my mother was never quite satisfied with, the life that she worked hard to make into everything glamorous and idolized, has now turned on her and made it so that every day is unique, if only because it could be the last she'll have.

"I wanted to come see you and Mom, together, when she's up for some company. I need to see her," I tell him and whether it's the words or my tone, he somehow understands why. When he says nothing, I take a deep breath and understand that he's always going to protect her, and it's time I started to accept that. "I just want to do what I should have a long time ago, and tell her I love her, that I'm sorry I didn't try harder when I was younger, but that I love her. I need to do this, Dad, if you'll let me. Will you call me when you think she's ready to handle me?"

He sighs, not unlike Rafe a moment ago, and then he agrees, ending the conversation with a quiet, "I love you, Cora."

I nod, and before I can think about it, I say, "Me, too," and hang up.

Chapter Thirty-Seven

Jake

I'm in the locker room suiting up for one of our last series of the season against Hillsboro, one of the teams in Oregon, which also happens to be the team in a neighboring town to Portland, where Blue is. We have five games against them and I'm pitching the first. I'm pulling my jersey on, sitting next to Laken, my ever present pain in the ass, roommate, and second baseman, and looking over his shoulder as he texts back and forth with some girl he met two nights ago in a bar in the Tri-city area when we were finishing our five games series there. Sexting isn't even accurate for what these two are doing and since I'm doing my best not to text Cora and ask her if she's coming, I'm vesting myself in Laken's borderline pornographic text conversation. I can't decide if it's more or less painful than just throwing my pride away and sending a text of my own.

When I texted a few days ago to let her know I'd be in Portland, she responded by simply saying she would make it if she could. I had someone leave tickets at will-call for her and her friends in case, and when I let her know that all she texted back was "thanks" and a little smiley face. Though we haven't been as talkative as we were when we were together, we have talked more lately, shared stories, texted more regularly, so her lack of response had my imagination working in overdrive, putting together scenarios of relapse, a new relationship, or just the decision to be done with me. When I called Murph to talk it out, his suggestion was to calm the fuck down, find my balls, and remember that she was going through a lot of shit that required time. Bottom line: when she was ready to talk to me, she would tell me.

I know he's right, but it's still taking all I have not to dial her number and ask her if she's going to let me see her while I'm here, hence, Chris Laken and his distracting, albeit misspelled, conversation.

"Jesus, Chris, *accept* is spelled with an *a*. *Except* implies exclusion or an issue, not an agreement of terms. I know you didn't finish college man, but what about high school?"

He frowns and deletes, retyping at a rapid rate, forcing auto-correct to keep up with him even while it tries to turn words into things like "duck". Yeah, there aren't a lot of ducks being talked about here.

"Hey, Shakespeare, how come you never talk about your girl?"

I glance over at Laken as he slips his phone away and finishes buttoning up his own jersey. We've been here for five hours already, going through our motions, warming up, stretching, getting looked at, and now we're in the final stages before we take the field. We're teammates, so we know each other well, but because we're roommates and friends too, Chris sees more than others.

I clear my throat, zip my pants, taking my time as I stretch out my arms and make sure my jersey isn't too snug anywhere. Really, I'm just buying time and we both know it.

"I guess because I'm not sure I have a right to call her my girl anymore. When I got the call, I had to leave. We hadn't really been together that long so it seemed kind of ridiculous to ask her to be mine when I didn't know the next time I was going to get to see her and what kind of shape I would be in when I did."

He nods like he gets it, and on some level, I know he does. However much he enjoys going out and hooking up, he lives the same kind of day-to-day life that I do. We've reaped the benefits of being athletes all our lives, but no one sees the cost that comes with it either, the dedication to a sport that doesn't give two shits about you as a person, the limited time for anything or anyone else. He's working toward the same dream I am, sledging through the constant bus trips and endless motel rooms like me, despite the fact that reality has told us that the likelihood of us both making it is slim to none.

"I had a girl too," he says after a second and I stop to look at him. "We'd been together since high school and when we got to Kansas all I did was play baseball, and all she did was sit home and wait. Turns out, the waiting is just as hard as the leaving, and eventually she found something better than a kid who couldn't give up the game."

Laken shrugs his shoulders and keeps his tone light, but I can see it costs him a little to say even that much. "We can't change who we are, Chris, no matter how many times we wish to Christ that all we wanted to be was a goddamn car salesman who got to go home every night and live a normal life, where he saw his girl every day while knowing his job would still be there in the morning."

He nods briefly and we both grab our gloves. As we walk out of the tunnel and onto the field, he laughs. "A car salesman? Face it, Shakespeare, in your next life you're going to be a goddamn professor, carrying some big ass briefcase full of papers and wearing tweed jackets and spectacles, making that shit look fly while you quote your damn poetry."

I laugh at the image and then shake it off as I take the mound, picking up the rosin bag of chalk and bouncing it back and forth between my palm and the top of my hand before letting it drop. My cleats kick up dirt and I look over to home plate to make eye contact with Nielson, my catcher, holding out my glove to let him know I'm ready. When he throws me the ball I catch it, leaving it in my glove and running my pitching fingers over my brim for luck, like I've always done. And then I tuck thoughts of Blue and the future to the corner of my mind while I focus on the present.

~

Two hours later, I'm on the mound again, only this time I'm trying to figure a way out of the mess I've created in the last twenty minutes. Coach called time and jogged out, so everyone in the infield did as well, and now they all surround me as we talk in riddles and innuendos and try to decide whether or not I can really take care of the guy at the plate and get us to the next inning, or if I'm done for the night.

It's the top of the fifth and we're ahead four to two. We took an early lead when our centerfielder hit a homerun with the bases loaded, but that was at the top of the second, and since then our bats have produced nothing, while we've had three major errors, two in the third which granted them their two stolen bases and subsequent scored runs. From then to now it's been a battle of high pitch counts and strikeouts or easily fielded grounders that have tempers on both teams soaring. The lights of the field have popped on and as I listen to the guys around me discuss them and us at the same time, I look at the runners on second and third and then to the scoreboard. There are two outs, two on, and their heavy hitter is up — it's not the worst scenario to be in, but it's certainly not the best.

"What do you think, Shakespeare, you want this guy?"

I look at Nielson and then to the batter standing at home plate. His count's at 2-2, and he's crowding me because he fucking can. I want to send him a message, to wing one in there and let him know in no uncertain terms that I'm not afraid of his fat ass, but I can't, because while I'm not afraid of him, I understand that one shift, one graze of the knuckles, or one pitch that just isn't thought out well could lead to full bases or runners batted home. I won't risk that for my ego, no matter how much his stance begs me to.

I glance back at Nielson and then at Coach who hasn't said two words since he stepped out here. "Yeah, I do want this guy."

They all nod and continue to stand there, taking the time we have, giving Coach the time to agree or disagree, me the time to cool off, the batter the time to wait and stew.

"How's the elbow? You were whacking off pretty hard last night, I almost stopped what I was doing to offer you my girl so you didn't get tendonitis."

Laken's comment earns some laughs and I shake my head, appreciating the time he's giving me to get my shit together. When Coach nods, accepting my choice, Nielson does too before slamming the ball into my glove.

"Throw this motherfucker out and, after you do, look to home plate before taking the dugout. There's a bombshell there that's been screaming your name since the second inning. She even called you handsome."

I nod, and though a familiar tingle starts to pulse through me, I knock gloves with the rest of the guys as they head off to their positions and keep my head down for one more second, calling up the calm and the quiet that's always gotten me through. Licking my fingers, I run them over my brim again and take a deep breath. My batter's already at an advantage, because he knows what this conversation was about. He knows they asked if I could finish him, which leads him to believe that it might be a mistake to leave me in here, to let me face the strongest hitter on their team when I've already thrown over ninety pitches tonight. But it's not a mistake, and he's about to learn that.

I start with an inside slider at Nielson's call, and though I think it squeaked by, the ump doesn't give it to me. Now we have a full count and for the next four pitches I decide I'm going to give him what he wants, the fastball. He fouls off all four of them, and his arrogant grin continues to grow, his eyes never leaving mine as he goes through his routine each time of kicking his cleats up, rotating the bat, testing his swing, adjusting his helmet. I wait him out, because I know, in the end, one of us will break. I'll be goddamned if it's going to be me.

I get him on the fifth pitch as he steadies his hips and readies his body for the same pitch I've given him the last four times, stupidly assuming that my ego demands to meet him on his level. Instead, I throw a change up and it drops right in front of him while he blasts away, his bat cutting over it with enough force to knock him off kilter and force him to drop the bat and use it cane-like to steady himself or fall flat on his face. There are cheers from my team and silence from his.

I barely look at him as I jog in, taking the high fives that my teammates give, grinning at Laken as he makes a crude gesture that matches his earlier comment. I stop at the entrance to the dugout and look up and over, and that's when I find her. Four rows up, three seats from the aisle, there's my siren, her hair a little lighter from the last time I saw her, her skin glowing against the white tank top she's wearing. If I also happen to notice that the thin material forms to her breasts quite perfectly, well, it's not a crime.

I stay where I am, staring at her, absorbing the sight of her after what feels like years of being deprived, and then she stills, and ever so slowly she turns away from whoever she was talking to and our eyes meet. The impact of the look punches me and takes my breath a little, and I can tell it's done the same to her, but she doesn't break her stare and neither do I, not until the person next to her taps her shoulder and she smiles, gesturing with her head. When I glance over, any air that I had left leaves me completely as I stare into the face of my father.

Chapter Thirty-Eight

Cora

The first inning is almost over by the time I arrive at Jake's baseball game with his dad, A.J. and Liam in tow. It's now the bottom of the fifth and the game is getting more intense by the minute as Jake faces down batter after batter. Mr. Ferrari — Tony, as he's told me to call him — has barely said a thing since we met him here outside of the stadium, but I notice that each time Jake throws a pitch his breath catches a little and his body stills even more. He's intent on the game, and it makes me wonder if he's missed seeing his son play as much as Jake misses being seen.

Every now and then, Tony mumbles something about a pitch call, saying things like, "Throw what you know," or, "Skimmed the damn plate and we all know it." When Jake escapes the inning after an intense one-on-one that leaves two batters stranded and keeps the score in our favor, Tony visibly relaxes, sipping lightly from the single beer he's been nursing all night.

I didn't know what to expect when I met him today. Three weeks ago, after completing my ninth step and sharing the first intimate conversation with my mother in years, I couldn't help but think of Jake, as my mind has been doing whether I wanted it to or not lately.

He'd pushed me in our relationship, yes, but never in a way that was too much. He'd pushed me to accept him and my ability to feel, just as he had pushed me to trust my feelings rather than run from them, and when I was too afraid to reach out to him he still found a way to get to me. It made me wonder who watched out for him and made sure he got the love he needed.

Our conversation about his father from all those months ago replayed in my mind, and before I could think about it too much, I began tracking down a phone number for his father. After two days and no success, I called Liam to help me which netted me results in under twenty minutes, because apparently he's far more adept at Google search than I am. Whatever.

My phone conversation with Tony was a surprise for both of us, him because I had called, me because when I said my name he knew who I was. It was easier after that, even when I told him why I was calling: Jake's last games were coming up, and I wanted Mr. Ferrari to join me at one of them. There was silence on the other end of the line for a moment and I wondered if he was going to refuse me, but then he did something altogether different and asked me a question.

"Can I ask why you're calling me, Cora?"

His voice was quiet, thoughtful, as if each word he spoke was very deliberate and my heart squeezed a little as I thought of what Jake had told me, that his father had never quite conquered those demons that had driven him to shrink back from life and into his own head. Since I'd already invited him to the game, I also understood that whatever he was, Mr. Ferrari was just as insightful as his son.

"I care for your son very much, Mr. Ferrari, and I know that he might not say it but having you at one of his games would mean the world to Jake."

The line was silent except for his breathing after that, and again my heart constricted, thinking of the battle we go through every day to do what's right rather than just what's easy. I knew Jake's dad wanted to say yes to me, almost as much as he wanted to say no because going to see his son would be going back to a place that had taken everything from him and given very little back in return.

"I'll think about it and let you know. When's the game?"

"Three weeks," I answered.

"I'll call you before then. Cora," he said before I could murmur goodbye and hang up.

"Yes?"

"He's lucky. Jake — he's lucky to have you. Thanks for calling."

He didn't call me again until this morning to let me know that he'd meet me outside of the stadium. I didn't know what to expect, but the minute Tony stepped onto the sidewalk I knew it was him. He wears his hair almost as long as Jake and it's just as dark and thick, with a small sprinkling of gray. Despite the beard and the almost haunted look of his eyes, eyes that are the same liquid brown as Jake's, the resemblance to his son is uncanny. He's tall like Jake, with broad shoulders and long legs, slightly thicker through the chest and waist, the largest difference between him and his son coming in the way Tony carries himself. His shoulders hunch slightly inside of the plaid button down he's tucked into faded Carhartts, and his hands were shoved uncomfortably into his pockets and have stayed that way all game.

Now, I feel him freeze a little beside me as Jake stops before stepping into the dugout, his brown eyes meeting mine before I motion next to me, and then lighting on his father where they widen and stay.

I wonder briefly if I should have meddled, or if the sight of his father will mess with Jake's focus the rest of the game. My answers comes quickly when Jake gives a small smile and a salute, winking at me before heading inside to his team. I let out a small breath and so does Tony.

"I'm going to get a refill," he says and I nod, happy when Liam stands to go with him, saying he could use another as well.

"Risky move you've made here, Snow White," A.J. says as the two men disappear and I nod before sipping from my water.

"I know. I just couldn't not," I tell her and she nods. "Maybe it's because after talking with my own mother I finally understand that parents are no different than we are and sometimes they need to be invited, to hear the words before they give us what we need, or because I've finally just realized how much I love Jake, and I know he needs this, no matter what he said before."

"Well, whatever happens next, you've done a good thing."

I look at her and smile. "You're a good friend, A.J. I'm starting to think you're one of the best, actually."

She grins then, full of girlish mischief and pleasure. "Snow White, I could have told you that a long time ago. Just remember it, especially if you're ever in a place that has you hurting. Understood?"

I nod. "Understood."

~

Jake's team wins, scoring three more runs at the top of the eighth. Jake pitched the sixth and was replaced in the seventh, but not before striking out two more runners. When he walked off with his hand in the air, I added my own cheers to those that were already going, smiling broadly when his dad stood and clapped, yelling his name over and over. It was a good moment, and now we're waiting as the game ends and Jake makes his way over to us, stopping every few feet to say something to his teammates and coaches, pausing twice to sign a foam finger or other item for a young kid.

When he steps up to the bleachers where we're all congregating, a girl behind me goes crazy, holding out her T-shirt and asking him to sign it. I laugh when I see it asks to "drive the Ferrari for a night". You have to give her credit for creativity.

He flashes me a grin, one that tells me he's just as amused and flattered, and then he signs his name with a flourish before handing the pen back. He steps up next to us, holding out his hand to his dad.

"Hey, Old Man, it's good to see you."

Tony takes his hand, dragging him in for a quiet handshake/back slap that seems more intimate than either were ready for. Still, I see Jake hold on for a second and then step back, his eyes quickly scanning his dad. Tony's almost one hundred percent steady, only drinking the two beers all game long, and it makes me happy to see that Jake notices and nods at him in thanks. Tony accepts and then begins to talk about the game, running through the pitches Jake threw each inning and surprising me with his ability to recount every single one. If Jake's surprised, he doesn't show it, just banters back and forth, defending his choices with a smile and shrugging off the friendly questions from his father and Liam.

"I need to get changed but then I have some time. Have you eaten yet?"

Tony shakes his head and then declines, sighting an early flight as an excuse. Jake nods, understanding. He can't change who he is, but he did his best to be here and be sober for his son, and it matters. We say goodbye, and my eyes water when Tony not only hugs me lightly, but releases me and pulls Jake in and holds him for a second before leaning back and clapping a hand on his shoulder.

"Throw 'em hard, Jake."

There's a catch in his voice and Jake nods, waving after him as he walks away. "See you, Old Man."

A.J. and Liam make an excuse to leave, too, and in the span of a few seconds Jake and I have been left alone, staring at one another as the lights of the field glint off the metal bleachers.

"I'm glad you came," he says after a second. "I didn't know if you would when I didn't really hear from you."

"I wanted to surprise you. Your dad…" I trail off and shake my head, putting my hand on his arm when he watches me guardedly, like he doesn't know if what I'm about to say will ruin the moment he just had. "He loves you a lot, Jake. I just thought you should know that."

When he brings me against him, I go willingly, my arms snaking around his waist, gripping the fabric of his jersey, his circling around my shoulders and holding me so close there's barely room to breathe.

"Can you take a few hours and eat?" He nods his head against my neck before pulling back. "I'll wait for you here," I say and then cup his face. "Congratulations on your win, Handsome Jake."

He nods again, his fingers sifting through my hair before he turns to walk back to the dugout. Sitting, I look out at the emptied stands and wait for him to come back.

Chapter Thirty-Nine

Jake

Laken walks out with me, stating that he needs to meet my girl and ask her what her intentions are. Since I know telling him no wouldn't make a difference, I let him come, grinning when he gets a good look at her a few feet away and whistles under his breath.

"Jesus, Shakespeare, maybe there's something to this poetry reading you're doing if you're pulling in a girl like her. Christ, would you look at her? She's got nicer tits than—"

He quickly swallows back whatever he was going to say when my eyes cut hard and direct to his. "Right. Off limits, got it."

Then he's walking up to her, holding out his hand and running his fool mouth about how much he's heard about her. I roll my eyes when she looks at me, eventually pushing Laken out of the way so we can leave. "Okay, Chris, time to go."

"You kids have fun tonight, and be safe, huh?"

Cora laughs and waves as I propel her in the opposite direction, ignoring Laken when he reminds me to use my other hand to give my left arm a break.

"He's a character," Blue says as we reach her car and I laugh, throwing my bag in the back before stretching my legs out in the front seat.

"More like he's an idiot, but a goodhearted one." I turn my head and smile at her as she starts the engine and heads out of the parking lot. "Where are we going?"

She looks at me out of the corner of her eye and smiles. "I figured you were pretty tired since you've been on the road for so long, plus I didn't know how much time you had, so I called in an order at Javier's and thought we could pick it up and head for the apartment. How do tacos on the balcony sound?"

I reach over and grab her hand, linking our fingers. "Perfect."

~

"Thank you, for what you did. I don't know how you found him, but seeing my dad tonight..." I shake my head and sip from the beer Cora handed me when we walked through the door. "It was a trip. A really good one."

She smiles, her hair fluttering around her face as the slight breeze pulls at it. We've been here for just about an hour on the balcony, eating, catching up on things that have been going on. She didn't mention my dad and maybe because of that, I know she understands just how much it meant to see him.

"He reminds me of you. A little sadder, a little more unsure," she adds, "but when you look at him you can see that he's still got strength buried in there, enough to face a few demons and show his kid he loves him."

I nod, staring at her, my heart beating a mile a minute as everything I feel climbs to the surface and urges me to let it out. "I think I know a little bit about that." And then I take a deep breath and plunge ahead, releasing everything that's been building inside of me since that night nine months ago when I looked up and saw her for the first time. "The last time I was here, you had a lot of shit going on and a part of me was hurt and angry because I wasn't the one who could make it better for you. I knew you had to do it alone, but still, I wanted to be the one you ran to and asked for help."

She sighs and brushes her hair back, looking out and over the city that's both given and taken from her, and I watch her, mesmerized as always by what I see. "I'm going to meetings regularly now, and I've finished my twelve steps. When I last saw you… I was scared because I knew I needed to work things out on my own and deep down I knew that if you had been here, if we had still been together, I would have run to you instead of to that club. I would have leaned on you and let you make everything better because when I'm with you it doesn't matter what's wrong, all I feel is how right we are."

There are moments in your life when you finally understand what the writers who came before talked about. I understand the pain and loss and fucking loneliness that so many write about. As I grew from a child to a teen to an adult, I began to understand the physical pleasures that life had to offer, the way that they become addicting because, while you're in the moment, nothing bad touches you. In college, I understood what it meant to have a family, a best friend even. But not until here and now did I ever truly know love.

"What about now?" I ask her. "Do you still need to do it alone, or are you ready for me? Because I'm ready for you, Blue. I never should have walked away like I did and it only took one day apart from you to realize that I'm more than my past, more than my sport. I'm a man, Cora, and I'm yours. You're my heart," I tell her and before I finish she's rising, shifting so that she's in my lap and her forehead is pressed against mine, her eyes close as we breathe together.

"Welcome home," she says and I tilt her head up to take her lips.

Reminiscent of all those nights when we were here just like this, my chest expands until it feels as though I'll burst if I don't say the words. "I love you," I whisper against her lips, then again, as I brush her temple, her eyelids, her cheekbones, down to her lips where I kiss her before standing, keeping her cradled against my chest as I walk us inside and down to our bedroom.

Her eyes are wide and wet when I set her on her feet but, unlike the last time we were together, it's not because this is goodbye; it's because we both know that whatever our lives were before, whatever got us to this moment, it was worth it. This, right here, is our beginning.

"You're so beautiful," I tell her and she laughs, unexpectedly nervous as I cup her face in my hands and swipe at the small tears that have fallen. "I love you," I tell her again, and this time, her smile is brilliant, blinding even as the tears continue to fall.

"I believe you," she says, and then we're all heat and clashing tongues, her eager hands pulling at my shirt as I grip the low neckline of her barely-there tank top and rip. Her shock comes out muffled against my lips, but I don't give her time to protest before I'm filling my hands with her lace clad breasts and backing her toward the bed.

We break our kiss as she shoves my shirt up and over my head and I take that as an invitation to move my lips to her collar bone and down, across her belly to her shorts, which I quickly discard, before moving back up the side of her ribs and back to her breasts, yanking down the cups of her bra until I can take one into my mouth.

I hear her moan, feel her writhe against me, and I snake my hand down until I cup her, working until her pants become screams and my name falls from her lips even as she falls from the cliff I was holding her on. Rolling, I shed my clothes and roll on a condom, moving back to her where I begin to touch her all over, ruthlessly driving her until her whimpers are heady gasps and she's moving beneath me. When I know I can't wait any longer to feel her, I say her name, waiting until her eyes open and focus on mine.

"I love you," I tell her and rock inside, thrusting deep until we both cry out. And then I say it over and over, rolling so she's on top and I'm lost in the glory that is Cora as she rides us both to ecstasy.

An hour later, I've had her again, and though it kills me, I'm already past curfew and so Cora and I rise from bed so she can take me back to where the team's staying. She slips from bed to pull on a shirt and I sit where I am for a moment, needing to see her one last time. When she turns her back, I focus on the thin black scroll that's now etched to the left of her spine, starting near her shoulder blade and stopping just before the curve of her waist.

Without a word, I stand and walk over to her.

Tomorrow is another day. Scarlett and Rhett, the love story we all wanted them to finish.

She doesn't turn around, just stands there while I reach out to touch the words, my fingers tracing them as she once traced mine, the feelings I gave to her on our last night together that she made a permanent part of herself.

"I Googled that quote you left me, then I watched the movie and I realized how perfect these words are, not just for us, but for me. I can't live afraid that tomorrow is going to be the day that something hurts, or that I fail. I can't live fearing the future instead of looking forward to it, and part of living for tomorrow is realizing that some love stories don't have to end, that there's always the possibility of tomorrow if we can't be together today." Now she turns and I let my fingers slide across her skin and rest at her hip even when her shirt falls back down. "I want to live, Handsome Jake and I want to do it knowing that, whatever happens, we have tomorrow together."

They say that the blues are melancholy. To sing the blues, one has to feel them, to know them. I've known the blues of sadness, of anger, of despair; now I know the color blue, the swirling, deep, endless blue that pulled me from the wreckage and loved me. Holding her right here and right now, I know that no matter what lies ahead in my career, the greatest part of my future is staring back at me, giving me the kind of love I could only dream of.

"I love you, Handsome Jake. More than I ever thought possible."

Bringing her close, I hold her against me and know that no matter how many times I have to leave, I'll always come back to her.

She's my port in the storm, my light in the dark, and I'm never letting her go.

Epilogue

Cora

I'm standing with my hand in Jake's, getting ready to knock on the door to my parents' house. We've been invited to dinner and, although I haven't said it aloud, we both know I'm nervous. One glance at him next to me shows me that if he's feeling the same fluttery queasiness that I am, he's got a much better poker face.

"Relax, Blue, it's just dinner. Parents love me, I promise."

"Oh yeah? How many parents have you met?"

His grin is pure and fun and does the trick in easing my nerves slightly. "Got me there. But I figure if I can get Mia and A.J.'s seal of approval, well, parents might be easier."

Since it's true, I lean over and kiss him, lingering a little bit as I soak in his scent and feel amazed that he's next to me. He came home a month ago after his season ended, and we've decided to give this thing a real shot. He's training for next year as he moves up in the Minor League world (whatever and wherever that might be), along with taking some online classes to begin his Master's in English, while tutoring kids at some of the high schools. I'm still working at the salon, but I'm also taking online classes in business, just in case I ever feel like trying my luck with my own shop.

Mia is getting her Ph.D. in Physical Activity, Nutrition, and Wellness at ASU, so Ryan is based there with her until his season starts again in January like Jake. They've been to visit us once, and are planning on coming again in November for Thanksgiving since Mia knows I want to spend as much time as possible with my family.

Before then, though, I'm introducing my parents to Jake, because I love him, and I'm coming to realize just how much I love them, and vice versa. My mom's having good and bad days, but her good days are starting to be really good, and she's even ventured out of the house with Sassy some, surprising me one day by showing up at the salon and asking to have coffee with me on my lunch break. Now, I'm introducing her to my boyfriend, the person who made me realize that life, with all its good and bad, is always worth fighting for.

I try to remember that as I reach up and knock on the door, smoothing my hand down my floral print mini, even while scolding myself to calm the hell down.

Both of my parents answer the door, and before the shock wears off enough for me to say anything, my father's holding out his hand to Jake, bringing us both inside as my mother smiles and steps back. When we're in the foyer, I turn to embrace my mom and introduce Jake when I spot the bedazzled name-tag over her heart. Raising my eyebrow, I look at her and her smile gets a little mischievous as she motions to a table just behind her.

"Our first activity for the night is nametag making — you know, kind of like my cheat sheet so I don't have to keep asking. Feel free to add hobbies and interests as well."

I'm stunned and unsure how to respond, but I don't need to because Jake takes care of it, laughing even as he leans forward and introduces himself, kissing her on the cheek and then following her as she tells him he better make a nametag quickly before her memory goes. She says this all with a small bit of laughter and I find my own laugh bubbling out.

"She's happy — happier at least," my dad says as he comes to stand next to me.

I nod. "It's amazing. I've never seen her like this."

"After you talked with her in the hospital, I think she realized that whatever was happening now, and whatever happened in the past, the most important thing is taking back everything she can, and that means time with her family and it means laughing and being silly, all of those things we forgot to do the first time around."

I watch her with Jake, laughing as she tells him he doesn't have nearly enough sparkles on his tag, and then I link my hand through my father's elbow as he holds it out. "What do you think, kiddo, should we go join them?"

I nod and walk with him, because this time I won't be sitting on the side and waiting for something better. This time, I'm going to live in the here and now, in the light and the love and the laughter that is my family, because I've seen the darkness, and I don't ever want to go back.

Acknowledgements

Thank you, first and foremost, to my husband, Jan, for believing in me and helping me realize just what words were living inside of me. Thank you to my family, for loving me and always reading my work. Thank you to Sara Huggins, for being that friend who supports me unendingly, by way of funny cat pictures and sexy stories, and just hilarious text messages. Pashugs, you're the best.

Thank you to Caroline Smailes from BubbleCow Editing (www.bubblecow.net). Your help, your encouragement, and your beautiful comments made this manuscript better than I knew it could be. Thank you to James at GoOnWrite.com for the beautiful cover that brought Cora to life, and to Candace Robinson at Candace's Book Blog and Book Promotions and all other bloggers who participated in the cover release. Your tweets and support are invaluable.

Lastly, thank you to the people in my life, students, friends, strangers, who have shared their stories with me and trusted me with them. As it says in the beginning, this book is for anyone who's ever struggled to find tomorrow, for anyone who's ever forgotten what love feels like. Here's to you and your strength. Remember to keep living, taking it one day at a time.

xoxo

Kristen

Want to Read it from the beginning? Try Mia and Ryan's Story,

Beyond the Horizon (beyond the horizon 1)

Mia Evans has one goal in life: to be perfect enough that her parents will love her, or at least love each other again.

Three years ago, her brother left her family, choosing a girl over the Evans name. Watching her mother cry and her father shut the rest of them out, Mia made a promise to herself that she would be the one to bring them back together again. Yet, despite her acceptance to Stanford, her perfect academic record, and a flawless resume`, Mia finds her family getting further and further apart.

Enter Ryan Murphy, the boy next door.

Ryan has loved Mia Evans since the day he saw her sitting on her front porch weeping into her knees. Fifteen then, Ryan had been unsure of what to do, so he'd sat at his window and watched over her, and in that time, a piece of him became hers.

Now, three years later, Ryan hasn't told Mia how he feels, but he gets the chance when he's forced to beg her to tutor him and save him from his mother. As their relationship progresses, Ryan realizes that Mia is more than he could have ever dreamed of, and that his feelings go a lot deeper than he ever imagined possible. And still, can they work?

Mia didn't want to want Ryan Murphy. Just the opposite, actually. She agreed to tutor him because that's her job, but she doesn't have to like it, or the fact that she can't seem to stop noticing how gorgeous he is.

Against all of her better judgment, Mia finds herself falling for Ryan, and falling hard. When the time comes for Mia to make the same decision that broke her family three years ago, she's torn: follow her heart, and lose her family, or follow her family and lose the only person whose ever really loved her.

Let's Chat!

www.kristenkehoe.com

https://twitter.com/KKehoeAuthor

https://www.facebook.com/authorkristenkehoe

Keep reading for an excerpt from the first novel in my upcoming The Vert series: Vertical Lines.

Release date

December 2015.

Chapter 1

Jordan

I don't know what made me do it.

Correction: it's hard to narrow down the list of possibilities and decipher just which one was the catalyst for why I pushed my brother's dinner plate into his lap.

Was it because I wanted it, but was unable to have it since I'm a girl and, therefore, not qualified to consume that many calories? Or was it because he chewed, chopped, and talked all at once, with such speed that it was off putting to both watch and hear as he masticated his beef while regaling us with his fraternity endeavors? Or could it have been both of those things added onto years of repressed anger and mother loving hunger?

Sweet bleeding Jesus am I hungry.

I've been at dinner with my parents and my older brother, Mason, for the past hour and a half. In those ninety minutes, I've had water, one bite of bruschetta, and salad—excuse me, *mixed greens* (overpriced restaurant speak for less than salad, we are not a Chili's and there is no bacon in this concoction)—while Mason has consumed a cup of clam chowder, two baskets of bread, the rest of my bruschetta (jerk), sautéed mushrooms, and now, his own dinner. Well, some of it.

Like I said, I don't know if it was the sight of him gulping down calories and flavor, of rolling that *Prime Rib* around in his cheeks while stuffing his face with caramelized baby carrots and garlic mashed potatoes, while I pushed around my mixed green and salmon salad (no dressing) that sent me over the edge, or the fact that when I stopped and really watched him, I saw more than just the difference in our meals.

I saw our childhoods in an onslaught of memories, his full of fun and games and adventures, bugs and dirt and bicycles, while mine was music lessons, art lessons, and horseback riding lessons, cotillions and tea parties.

I saw my present—the here and now where I'm attending a school because Mason wanted to, because Mason had gotten a letter from the Dean expressing his sheer joy in obtaining a student of such a high caliber. (Please, a 3.1 GPA in high school merits the word caliber? Just thank Mr. and Mrs. Richards for their generous donation next time.)

And worse than the past and present that were flashing before my eyes while my brother galumphed and gulped and grossed out everyone in a four table radius, was the sight of the future that slammed into me.

I'm almost nineteen; a freshman in college about to begin my time at a university I did not choose, and though I'm young, my life is already planned. I will graduate in three years (because I've come in with so many credits from high school), attend a respected graduate school to receive my masters and complete my degree in elementary education (but not so respected it will make Mason look bad if he chooses to do post grad work and doesn't get accepted to the institution I do), after which I will get a proper job at a posh school.

In between all of this schooling and job getting, I will meet and marry the man of my dreams who will also be perfect—which means he will be a carbon copy of every man I've ever been allowed to be in contact with: well groomed, on the medical, financial, or justice track (law, not police), and backed by family wealth. Yes, *wealth*. Money is new and ugly, but wealth is hard earned and generational, ensuring security.

In five years, Mr. Boring and I will have children, along with two homes, an apartment in some swanky city where I will travel to twice a year to buy new clothes and have a girl's weekend, a grocery fund, and a Mercedes station wagon. My time will be spent between garden club, Junior League, the arts foundation, and raising my children, and my diet will somehow be carved down to limit even my intake of water. Eventually, smelling food is the closest I will come to ever consuming it.

My stylist will rave about my bony figure and will-power, while keeping me well stocked in staid and expensive suits with matching jewelry and shoes.

This is my life, just like my dinner.

Pre-ordered.

Bland.

Tasteless.

Gaunt.

Everything about my life is small, while the bigmouth behemoth across the table gets all of his own space and food along with most of mine. Well, no more. Today is the day that ends. Today, I'm not filtering or starving or waiting.

Today, I am rebelling… and I'm starting with carbs.

I set my fork down with a clink, ignoring my mother's quick side glance and frown—not because I set my fork down and she's concerned I'm not eating, but because I've dared to make a sound. I ignore her, my eyes on my target as I reach across the table to where the third bread basket sits and snag a piece. I don't know who is more shocked, my mother or Mason, as he has stopped talking for the first time since we sat down what feels like eons ago. Maybe it's because his number one fan is no longer focusing on him, rather, her eyes are trained on me as if I've had a seizure and require medical attention.

I don't know what horrifies her more: the fact that I reached across the table, that I took something from Mason, her beloved little boy who has never been denied anything a day in his life, or that I'm about to consume an empty calorie. Yep, *empty*. As in, has no nutritional value and will go straight to my tummy, or thighs, or hips, or ass, or who the hell cares because it smells so delicious I'd give my left tit just to continue smelling it for the rest of my life.

Feeling brazen, I rip a piece of the bread off and pop it into my mouth. Sourdough, still warm. *Hello, Heaven, I've been waiting to meet you.*

Is there such a thing as a foodgasm? Because I just had one.

"Pass the butter, please."

The minute those words cross the threshold of my lips, my mother's fork hits her plate with a clank (louder than a clink, but you don't see me give her a dirty look) and her breathing becomes ragged. I ignore her as I tear off another piece of crusty sourdough and take an actual bite from it this time. My teeth sink in and I tear the bread apart, my lips folding around the golden apple known as *yeast*.

"Hey, I was gonna eat that."

Unlike my mother's heavy breathing and wide eyes, this statement stops me. I swallow the half bite in my mouth and set down the rest of the bread, eyeing my brother the entire time. There's a sensation coursing through me, different from the pleasure I experienced a moment ago after one bite of food that contained flavor and actual sustenance. This isn't pleasure; it's darker, more foreboding. A sense of déjà vu washes over me as Mason reaches across and snags the bread back from my plate, and somewhere in the recesses of my mind I hear a snap.

Twig, bonds, sanity... who knows what's breaking at this moment, but whatever it is, the feeling I'm experiencing now has a name, and I think it's called liberation.

There is a piece of meat on Mason's fork and another in his gullet, one that his teeth and tongue were working furiously a moment ago. When I watch him shove the rest of *my* bread in there as well, my eyes widen and I understand he's waging his own kind of power struggle, one meant to keep me from usurping his thrown at the table.

What he doesn't know is that while he was playing at war when we were younger, I was being groomed to wage one while wearing pearls and a pink dress. No one, and I mean no one, is more vicious and calculating than society women when their princess is in danger of being overthrown for someone prettier and smarter.

I smile, and I hear my mother exhale slowly. My father hasn't once looked up from his plate, which is now almost completely wiped clean. He learned long ago in their marriage that the minute he set the fork down, the rest would disappear into the well tipped hand of our waiter. Mason turns back to my mother, who's picking up her fork and also turning to him; both pause when I stand.

I grab my small and appropriate Tory Burch handbag that matches my pale, flesh colored dress and cardigan perfectly.

"Excuse me," I say, as if I'm going to the ladies room. One step, two; the minute I'm close to Mason's plate, I reach out and upend it in his lap with a quick flick of the wrist.

Although I would have preferred to stay and watch the entire scene play out, unlike my idiot brother who never saw the move coming—who is even now just staring in shock at his lap where the garlic mashed potatoes and juicy run off from his meat seep into his pants and shirt—I understand that when one makes a move so bold as that, they need to be prepared to make a stealthy retreat. I'm walking out, almost to the door when I hear the first scraping of chair feet and rushing of waiters.

I don't look back, and it is not because I'm afraid. No, right now I'm looking forward and it feels pretty damn good.

Other Titles by Kristen Kehoe

Finding You

Life Interrupted (The Life Series Book 1)

TRIPP (The Life Series Book 2)